THE ELDER CHRONICLES, BOOK 1

SCOTT WIECZOREK

Lycaon Press
Calgary, Alberta
www.lycaonpress.com

Awakening

ISBN: 978-1-77101-127-3

Lycaon Press
www.lycaonpress.com

Acknowledgements:

I would like to extend my sincerest thanks to everyone who has supported me in this great adventure called writing. Your assistance, support, and guidance has been, and always will be, welcome and deeply appreciated. Specifically, I would like to thank my wife and kids for understanding my need to write, to spend hours in front of a computer screen after putting in long days at work, and to allow my creative side to flow. Next, I would like to thank two people who have been instrumental in morphing this rough pile of words into a coherent, cohesive story: C. Carol Halitsky, whose editorial expertise, suggestions, and keen attention to detail make me look polished and put together, and my wife, whose plot and character development suggestions have breathed life into my words. I would also like to thank the crew at Lycaon Press who helped me bring this project to completion. Thank you all!

prologue

At their feet lay the lifeless body of an average young man in his late twenties. No visible evidence of trauma could be seen, but his face froze in a contorted mask of agony. Thin crimson ribbons trailed from his eyes, ears, and nose toward a still cooling and coagulating pool of blood on the floor.

A conversation passed between the two figures so silent a casual observer would have guessed they were not speaking at all. In fact, neither party's lips moved, and a sound never passed between them. The building's central air system rattled above them.

Have you learned anything, yet? The woman asked with no sympathy. Despite the lack of emotional inflection, her "voice," a rudimentary projection of her mind, had always reminded the man of tinkling bells.

No, Mistress, came the man's reluctant reply. *We have not. And, as you can see, we've exhausted the last scientist from his lab.* The man's deep tenor voice had an obvious nervous tremble to it. Giving her news other than what she already knew, or she expected to be in her favor was never good.

The woman's eyebrows arched high. Platinum blonde hair, high cheekbones, and perfect proportions made most men desire her. *So, what you're telling me is none of his colleagues knew what he found?*

I'm afraid so, Mistress. The man, early middle-aged, heavy-set with brown eyes, and thinning white hair, paused. *But we have been unable to locate one of the scientists formerly employed in his lab.* He stared at the lifeless form on the ground. His heart thrummed at the idea of having to tell her the rest of his findings. She would not like hearing this news, and he knew it. *We think he may have been a plant from the Loyalists.*

As most men who feared for their lives, he really didn't like having to give her bad news. If anything could have set her off, mention of the Loyalists would do it. However, it pleased him her only reaction was a slight downturn at the corners of her mouth.

Not good, she responded with no emotion. *If they find the Source before we do, then...* she let her sentence trail off.

But he understood her meaning well enough. All of their plans, thousands of years of work and planning, and their glorious coup, would be undone. They needed to obtain the Source before the others did.

What have we learned from the family?

His pulse pounded in his ears, his breathing quickened. *We have teams watching them,* replied the man. *But so far, they have not obtained any useful information.*

He suspected the scientist had divulged some useful information to at least one member of his family. Basic human nature would not have allowed him to keep something as important as the Source a secret; he would have needed to tell somebody. But their near constant observation of the family over the past few years had not yielded any positive results.

After a pregnant pause, the woman spoke. *Because we haven't gathered information doesn't mean they don't have any. I want you to bring them in. Get the girl first. I want you to squeeze the information out of her any way you can. And if she won't talk, then use her to make the mother talk. We need the code's Source!* The woman paused and pointed to the body on the floor. *And clean up this mess before it starts to stink.*

As she walked from the room she said, *I have waited far too long for everything to come apart now.*

part one

found

chapter 1

She slammed the driver's door shut, knocking rust from the car's undercarriage, and popped the trunk. Inside were all her essential belongings. For Elena Michaels the first day back on campus nearly mimicked what it had been the year before. Standing beside her faded blue Camry, she surveyed her surroundings, glad she'd had the forethought to get her parking sticker early. The campus police were already busy ticketing illegally parked cars. They must have needed something to do to occupy themselves after a long, uneventful summer.

The school's labyrinthine complex of parking lots was packed with hundreds of students moving into their dorms. Some carried boxes and trunks full of clothing, bedding, and personal effects. Others lugged computers, televisions, and audio equipment. An overkill of perfumes and colognes nearly choked the air while the dissonance of shouted greetings, squeals of glee, and honking horns assailed her ears.

One of her favorite things about attending school in New England was the fall foliage, which made its appearance about the time classes began. The never-ending cold weather, though—not so much. She eyed her suitcase, glad she had packed many pairs of sweats and long undergarments in with the jeans and T-shirts making up most of her wardrobe.

Elena scanned the parking lot. Not too far away she recognized one of the resident assistants. Mark, or Eric, or something. It would have been nice to have friends to call on to help her get settled. But most of her close friends had been seniors and had graduated last year. On the upside, she could focus on her studies without having to worry about being antisocial; on the downside, she now had almost no friends on campus.

Mark-or-Eric drove one of the school golf carts used to help move people in. She flagged him down and he pulled up behind her car.

They discussed their respective summers as they loaded her gear into the metal trunk attached to the back of the cart. She had always suspected he may have had a little crush on her, but she would never go for someone like him. He was a self-avowed player, and she preferred someone a little more sensitive and authentic. Something in the distance caught her eye as she turned toward the cart, her television in her hands.

A figure stood in the distance—tall and slender. Her jet black hair blew across her face, obscuring her vision for an instant. As she swept the hair away, her attention drew to a set of eyes in a stunning shade of blue. Their beauty took her breath away. But as fast as the apparition had appeared, she blinked and it was gone.

Shaking her head clear, she loaded the last of her belongings into the cart. When she turned back to Mark-or-Eric he made no attempt to hide his lecherous stare. She glared at him.

Elena didn't think of herself as a pretty girl. She had her attractive times. But on average, she could be passed by in a crowd. Besides, she wasn't the type he went for—tall and fair, blonde and blue-eyed. She had an athletic but feminine build, a light olive complexion, and amber eyes. With the right make-up, she could get some numbers. But on a typical day like today, make-up was less than an afterthought.

"What building you staying in this year?" His voice still cracked a little. Elena knew he'd asked for selfish reasons, not merely because he needed to drive there.

"Daley Hall." Her sour voice carried over the whine of the cart's electric motor. With any luck, her tone would be enough to deter him from further conversation.

"Nice," he replied, missing the hint. "I'm gonna be right next door. I'm staying in Warren this year."

Her address would be committed to the "chicks I'd like to hook-up-with" file he must have kept in the back of his head. It would be a matter of time before she received a drunken visit from this guy. Outwardly, however, Elena nodded to him and said something like *cool,* or *nice* to be polite. Inwardly, she couldn't wait to get to her dorm and away from him. There were too many unwelcomed creepy glances at her chest and legs for her comfort level and at one point, his hand had "accidentally" slipped and brushed the side of her breast for a little longer than necessary.

In her haste to escape his company, Elena neglected to let the cart stop in front of her dorm before jumping out. Her brief stint playing high school field hockey—consisting of a single practice in which she had been given a bloody nose and a mild concussion—had not convinced her she lacked coordination. Not only could her feet not keep up with her body's momentum, but she also neglected to let go of the moving cart. She tumbled hard and rolled into a patch of bushes lining the entryway, landing on all fours.

Her hands and knees stung. Her cheeks burned. "Great," she sighed under her hanging head.

After standing and making a quick self-inspection, she had suffered a few minor scrapes and bruises, and there were no tears in her clothing. At least she had a better start to this year than the last, when she had spilled a slushy all over herself while driving and then later had tripped on her own shoelaces, falling into a car pulling into the adjacent parking spot. The debacle had landed her in the Campus Medical Center for over half a day. Both incidents, however, paled in comparison to when she'd been shoved through a plate glass window in junior high school. It had left her in the hospital for three weeks, and she still had the scars as a reminder.

Mark-or-Eric stayed outside the dorm with all of her belongings while she checked in, collected her keys, and began to take her stuff up to her room. She really didn't want him to have her room number and tried to dispel the notion he'd raid her luggage for souvenirs. When she finished moving her things, she could hear him snicker as he drove away to find another girl to impose himself upon. At least, with any luck, her spill would knock her off his radar for the year.

Her roommates had not yet arrived and she executed the unwritten law of first come, first served by staking her claim on the single top bunk and stashing some of her belongings in the furniture situated beneath.

Hoping the college bookstore was open, she made her way across campus to get her books for the semester.

The bookstore sat in the basement of the college's student center—a popular place for all of the commuter students to either hang out or grab a quick bite to eat. Having been through this rigmarole several times before, she selected her books without soliciting help from the bookstore staff.

At the register, she closed her eyes, handed over her credit card, and grudgingly signed her soul away on the dotted line. Picking up the bags of books from the counter, one slipped and spilled its contents on the floor, to her side. She bent down to retrieve the books.

Spots of bright white light exploded across her vision. Her head swam and throbbed with fury. Had she shifted her gaze before bending over, she would have noticed a display had been placed in front of the counter, the one her head had crashed into.

Dropping to one knee with her head in her hands, she tried to collect her thoughts for a few seconds. It somehow did not surprise her nobody came over to help her out. In fact, a rather heavy-set girl behind her in line tried to shove her aside and squeeze her massive bulk in front of the register. Exasperated, Elena wanted to go back to her room, put sheets on her bed, and take a nap. Noon, and she had already had one hell of a day. Unfortunately, there was to be no rest for the weary.

Back at her dorm room, she found herself having to make her best effort to appear sociable. Her new roommates, Skye and Brittney, had arrived. They were what, for all intents and purposes, could have been a set of skinny, pretty, bright-blonde-haired and blue-eyed twins. It seemed impossible such identical girls could have been born of genetically unrelated parents.

After exchanging awkward greetings and being minimally social, the three girls spent about an hour moving Skye's six large suitcases, desktop computer, and two traveling trunks up to the dorm.

"You certainly come with a lot of baggage," Elena mentioned while they were schlepping Skye's belongings. But neither of her new roommates understood the joke.

"Anybody hungry?" Elena asked after they stowed the luggage up in the room. "It's almost two o'clock, and I know I could go for something."

"Sure," both girls replied in unison.

Great. Stereo. Elena smiled and led the way out of the dorm and over to the dining hall, staying close enough to seem social, but far enough to avoid being dragged into any shallow conversation.

The dining hall sat to the east of Forestall Hall—a mansion named for the wealthy oil and railroad magnate who had owned it in the early twentieth century. The mansion occupied the crest of a small hill, and the 1950s-era concrete-block dining hall sat below it along a shallow slope. Inside, Elena headed straight for her old standbys, and loaded a tray with a cheeseburger, cheese fries, and a slice of pizza. Making her way down the line, she added a large soda, and headed into the dining room to find her new roomies. It didn't take her long to find them since they were seated front and center, surrounded by several tables full of the school's average hot guys.

As she approached the table, Skye and Brittney, both of whom had chosen to graze on miniscule salads, gawked at the food on Elena's tray.

"You're not seriously going to eat that?" Brittney asked.

Elena smiled, choosing to ignore the snotty look and the judgmental tone in her roommate's question. She needed to make the best of her new living arrangements. After all, she had no other choice.

"Yeah. Comfort food," Elena replied with a painted-on smile. Placing her tray on the table, she sat down.

"Do you always eat like this?" Skye started in on her this time.

Skye had impeccable and deliberate timing. She had asked her question after Elena took a big bite. Elena choked down the pizza, and chased it with some soda. "Pretty much," she replied. "I have a really fast metabolism. I can eat practically anything and not gain an ounce. I could never really live life like a rabbit—grazing on bland salads all the time." *Well done!* She congratulated herself.

After a second she added, "I don't even go to the gym." This was true to a degree, but she did try to go for morning jogs before her classes, which would be way before either of these princesses managed to rise from their beauty sleep.

"You're lucky. I gain weight even if I smell a hamburger. It sucks!" At least Skye attempted to be cordial.

"Yeah, it does suck," Elena said as she savored another large bite of her pizza.

Elena zoned out while Brittney and Skye continued with idle banter about guys they had hooked up with over the summer, about their summer jobs, and about half a dozen other mindless topics. Elena listened with less than half an ear. The girls held her interest as much as watching a lawn grow, which in itself could be riveting, if you're into it.

Sinking her teeth into her burger, Elena scanned the dining hall. The room's decor could best be described as some stiff, corporate designer's idea of hip. Vacant blue-topped tables and numerous empty chrome chairs nailed home the obvious, many of the students still hadn't returned to campus. Most students would wait until either the night before classes began, or the first day of class to actually move back to the dorms. There were a couple of tables situated here and there where an early bookworm or two had started to get the jump on the semester's reading.

As her eyes came back toward her own table, movement caught her attention out of the corner of her eye. In the back corner, a book titled *The Book of Enoch* had lowered enough for a pair of eyes to glance over its top. Her heart stopped in her chest. A lump formed in her throat. Her palms were sweating. It seemed impossible eyes such a deep, rich, dark sapphire blue could exist. They were beautiful. They sought her out, not looking at her, but into her—into her heart—into her soul. Those same eyes belonged to this morning's apparition.

After the third mention of her name and a crouton bouncing off her forehead, her two new roommates grabbed her attention. Elena shook her head, and turned back toward the girls; her ears burning with embarrassment. *What the hell was that about?* She chided herself. A quick scan of the room failed to find those eyes again. They were gone. Whipping her head toward the exit, she caught a glimpse of the back heel of someone hurrying out of the dining hall.

"Is there something wrong? You were in La-la-land," Brittney taunted.

"No. Nothing's wrong. I'm fine," she lied. "What did I miss?"

"Well, I asked you a bunch of questions," Brittney retorted with a huff, "and you zoned right out."

Elena responded with a sheepish grin. "Sorry. I sometimes drift off. What did you ask?"

"Nope. Sorry, but I do not repeat myself." Elena could hear a very distinct emphasis on the words do not. Brittney stuffed a forkful of her salad into her mouth and turned her head away.

Elena made a mental note to mark room-switch day on her calendar.

"What little Miss Cranky here asked," Skye intervened, "is whether or not you have a boyfriend either here or off campus." Skye shot Brittney a smirky little glance.

Sapphire-blue eyes flashed through her mind. "I—Uh, no," Elena replied. "I don't have anyone back at home—or on campus." *The Book of Enoch.* "Unfortunately, I don't get much time to go out. I have a major in microbiology and minor in anthropology, and spend most of my time in labs or at the library."

"Oh my God!" Skye exclaimed. "Are you crazy? Why do you want to torture yourself?" Skye and Brittany's interest were piqued, both girls turned to her.

"Well," Elena replied, "I was hoping to get into a good grad school. I want to be a genetic researcher."

"What a dork!" This time, Brittney had decided to put in her two cents. Both she and Skye laughed at Elena's expense.

"Yeah," she responded, unfazed. "I guess I am a bit of a dork."

Most of the time Elena didn't regret she didn't have time in her busy life for a boyfriend. But from time to time, there were pangs of longing. She'd often wondered what it would be like to curl up into a pair of strong arms. Or to stay up all night talking about anything. She had dated a guy once in high school for a few weeks, but it ended badly. As a result, Elena traded any wondering about romance for a preoccupation with her studies. However, in response to her roommate, she continued, "I find the whole field of genetics fascinating. It's almost like studying history through the lens of evolution. Did you realize geneticists have been able to track the migrations of various racial groups into the Americas through studying the human genome? Besides, I want to make sure I have a good job when I get out of college."

The blank expressions on their faces made it clear the girls didn't understand what she'd said. Turning to each other, some kind of strange code must have passed between them because all at once they both broke out in hysterical laughter. They laughed so hard Brittney snorted and nearly choked on a bite of her salad.

"What's so funny?" Elena's face grew warm with aggravation.

Skye regained composure first, while Brittney continued snorting away. "Honey, what are you talking about a good job?" The grimace on Skye's face made it clear the girl believed she had three heads. "Didn't your mama ever teach you the point of college for girls is to find wealthy husbands?"

Her head began to ache. How could two "educated" girls be so locked into such outdated stereotypes? Her blood boiled. With a false smile, she pulled her cell phone from her pants pocket.

"Excuse me," she said, collecting her tray. "I have to get over to the bookstore to check on one of my books. I think they close early today." Her voice was flat, measured, and controlled—as it had to be to hide the Everest-sized mountain of outrage welling inside her. Rising to leave, her eyes wandered to the seat where those stunning blue orbs had been. Something inside her wished to see them again.

chapter 2

Several weeks into the semester, room switch day had come and gone. Elena's personal list of *do's and don'ts* helped her deal with her two roommates, and things with them had normalized. Classes were in full swing, and her reading list of extra books and articles nearly touched the ceiling of her dorm room. There were plenty of excuses to either avoid or minimize contact with what she referred to as the less-pretty Barbie-sisters she lived with. Brittney lived within an hour of the campus and tended to go home on the weekends. Skye, however, stuck around. Nevertheless, after about the first week of classes, both girls stopped paying much, if any, attention to Elena.

This morning found Elena bored in her Western Civilization II class. As the squat tweed-clad professor rambled on, his chalk screeched across a dry spot on the blackboard, causing half of the class to wince at the sound. The man paid no notice and kept rambling.

To Elena's right a student slept with his head on his desk. She had seen him once or twice on campus—kind of cute, with dark hair and brown eyes, but the puddle of drool on his desktop left something to be desired. To her left, were rows of other glossy-eyed students.

No luck. Her casual searching of the faces of all the male students on campus was with the faint hope she could identify the owner of those alluring eyes from nearly a month ago. After all, there were not *so many* students on this campus she couldn't find him. Based on the odds alone, she should have run across him at some time over the past weeks.

Class ended about ten minutes late and the unfortunate delay left her hard pressed to rush through the spitting rain to her next class, and the sad reality of another boring lecture. As the lecture ended, a loud growling noise startled her. Her stomach back flipped—she needed some lunch. The computer lab would have to wait until her thrashing hunger demons were appeased.

The walk from the science building took her across the South Lawns. The morning's hard rain had left the paths and steps damp and slippery—a condition worsened by the blanket of wet leaves autumn's chill had deposited on them. After managing to survive the treacherous conditions of the paths, fate's cruel sense of humor let the wet concrete steps leading to the dining hall entrance put a hiccup into her lunch plans. Wet leaves on the top step caused her right foot to slide forward as her body lurched backward.

Her momentum carried her straight down the short flight. A shock of pain shot up her back as her rear-end smacked the concrete. Numbness traveled from her right elbow to the tips of her fingers. Air rushed from her deflating lungs as her back struck the ground. Her head thumped against the solid path, causing bright explosions of white light in front of her eyes.

With any luck, none of the other students were paying enough attention to see her fall. Closing her eyes, she took a deep breath and tried to take a mental inventory of her body to figure out if she'd broken anything.

After what seemed like several seconds, her eyes opened to be welcomed by the gray pall of clouds overhead. Something resisted her attempt to sit up, though, pushing her body back to the ground. Craning her neck up, it became clear what held her down. She gasped. "Beautiful." A whisper, but the word had escaped her lips.

In front of her were those haunting eyes, the ones invading her dreams. Bit by bit the rest of his features came into view. He couldn't have been more than twenty or so years old. Yet, gazing into his sapphire eyes, he possessed a wisdom and serenity beyond his years. The effect of his warm expression was instantaneous: calm and captivating. It dispelled any sense of embarrassment over her clumsy descent to the bottom of the steps. Dark wavy hair cascaded down and framed the finer chiseled features of his face—like the faces from DaVinci or Botticelli paintings. He had an aquiline nose, high, strong cheekbones, and a very slight cleft in his chin. Something about him felt out of place, but still comforting and safe. He had a familiar old soul.

"Are you okay?" To her surprise he had a gentle, but commanding voice.

The sound of it left her dumfounded and speechless. Unintelligible words escaped her lips as she stared, mesmerized by his eyes.

"Are you okay?" he repeated. Words wouldn't form.

After a short pause, he addressed her again. "Can you talk?" Beneath the mask of concern on his face, his warmth never wavered.

"I—uh. Yeah. I think I fell," she stammered. *What am I saying? Of course I fell. Why the hell else would I be lying flat on my back like this?*

Embarrassed, she tried to sit up again. "I'm fine—I think." He reached down and assisted her to an upright position.

She made a failed attempt to give him a coy smile.

His smile never wavered. "It would appear you slipped on some wet leaves." His hand gestured to a wet leaf-littered spot on the concrete above and behind her. Then with a slight wink he returned to his inquiry, "Do you think anything is broken?"

Elena turned enough to see the step. As she did, she noticed no other students had come over to help. "I—uh—no," she replied. "There's nothing broken. Thank you."

He pulled her to her feet and with a feather-light touch placed a hand at the small of her back to steady her. Electricity passed from his hand to her skin. Or was it a stinging pain?

"Ouch!" she yelped. Despite his gentle touch, her lower back hurt.

"You should go to the health center and get yourself checked out," he told her with honest concern. "To make sure nothing is seriously hurt. You took a pretty good spill."

"Yeah..." she replied, unable to focus on anything but his eyes.

"I could take you there," he offered. When she failed to respond, he added, "If you don't mind."

His question finally sank in, but so did the intensity of the pain radiating from her lower back. Her lips felt numb. As she turned to address him, dizziness washed over her. Her mouth froze open. She needed to see the nurse as this was obviously a hallucination. Such a beautiful man would never offer to take her to the campus health center. Before she could say another word, however, her world disappeared in a cloud of blackness.

Her eyes opened to the intense pain of the overhead light. What happened? Where was she? As her vision cleared and her eyes acclimated to the light, it became apparent she no longer lay on the concrete outside, but instead stared upward at a checkerboard of stained cardboard ceiling tiles.

She turned her head to explore her new surroundings. "Hold on a second, honey," an unfamiliar, but pleasant woman's voice said. "I need to check you out before you move around."

Elena saw another bright light, this time silhouetting a finger. "Can you follow my finger with your eyes?" the woman asked. Elena obeyed.

"Can you tell me your name?" The woman asked.

"Yeah, it's Elena."

"Your full name, dear?"

"Elena Michaels, I am a student on campus. What happened? Where am I?"

"You're in the Health Center. You collapsed and one of your friends called the campus police. They brought you here." Elena's sight began to gain more clarity. The nurse seemed pretty young—probably in her early thirties, a bit frumpy with auburn hair and bright green eyes. She appeared haggard from exhaustion.

"One of my friends?" Elena's head swam. What was the last thing she remembered? And why did her head hurt so much? "Wait...I slipped outside the dining hall, and some guy helped me up." Elena bolted upright. "Is he here? Where did he go?"

"I think it's safe to say you're all right," the nurse responded scratching some notes onto a clipboard. Switching off the penlight, the nurse handed Elena a cup with two pills inside. "Take these. It's ibuprofen—for the headache. If you begin to feel nausea, or the headache persists, please either come back or go to the hospital. You don't have any indications of a concussion, but let's be safe. They can be tricky sometimes."

Elena downed the pills and nodded. "What about the guy? The one who brought me here? Is he still here?"

The nurse frowned. "The officers who brought you here were alone. There was nobody with them. They said one of your classmates called them. I don't know anything about any young man. Sorry, dear." The nurse left the exam room.

"Damn," Elena said.

Several weeks later October was coming to a close, and midterm exams had arrived. Her mystery man had not been seen since her fall, and it made no sense he had appeared out of the blue to help her and then disappeared again into thin air. Poof! On such a small campus, it seemed a mathematical improbability she had not seen him since she fell.

Tonight found Elena sitting alone in one of the campus library's upstairs reading rooms. This particular one, her absolute favorite, had wainscot walls painted in a cool apple green accented with warm tan, and a coffered ceiling in alternating patterns of white and off-white. In a strange, girlish fantasy way, sitting in here made her feel like an heiress to some great family fortune.

Her parents had not been exactly poor. They had done well for themselves: put away a little money for her college education, helped her buy her car, those kind of things. But they were not wealthy by any extent of the imagination.

Her father had been a research scientist for a genetic research company, her mother an accomplished homemaker. But all of it changed before her freshman year.

The phone call came while Elena was still in school—a conference call from the owner of the research firm, its CEO, and the Vice President for Human Resources. They had bad news. One of the research assistants had found Elena's father on the cot in his office. He'd been found dead.

The autopsy concluded he had died of an aneurism likely brought on by the excessive strain of working long hours, a high caffeine intake, untreated high blood pressure, and poor diet. Aside from the meager savings her parents had managed to put aside and a small life insurance policy, his death left them with no other means of income. As a result her mother, who had never once held a job outside the home, needed to get a career. And fast.

Lucky for Elena, she had managed to win a full scholarship to school. The money her parents had saved for college supported them until her mother could get a job. Her father's company had given them a 500-dollar "gift" for the family's loss, but it served to defray the funeral costs. Fortunately, the company hired Elena's mother as an administrative assistant for one of the executives and told Elena she should call them for a job when she graduated. It was a good thing she wanted to get into the same field as her father.

Sitting in the reading room, Elena hung her head over her microbiology text, reviewing for her upcoming exam.

"Hi." The somewhat familiar disembodied voice startled her. The text in which she'd been engrossed slipped from her hands and clapped shut.

She peered up, scowling, but her heart stopped as recognition sank in. Her mysterious stranger. She stared right into his sapphire eyes. Her mouth fell open. Words escaped her.

"I'm sorry. Am I disturbing you?"

He began to turn his head with one thumb pointed over his shoulder when she finally blurted out, "No!" She paused. "I mean—no, you're not disturbing me." She couldn't hide the sheepish grin on her face. "Please, sit down."

Oh God! He was here, talking to her. What to do? *Okay, calm down. Play it cool.*

"I was wondering how you were doing. You had such a terrible fall the other day." In such close quarters, she could hear a bit of an accent, except she couldn't place it. Perhaps Eastern European? Slavic?

She studied his face for a few moments. "Well, what I would like to know is: what happened to you?" Her voice betrayed a note of anger. "I fall down on the steps, you come and help me up, and next I wake up *alone* in the health center to learn I was unconscious for *several hours*." When her question stood unanswered, she repeated her initial question, "What happened to you?"

"Sorry. But I waited as long as I could. Didn't you get the note I left you? The nurse said she would give it to you once you woke up." He sighed in exasperation and mumbled something under his breath. "I had to get going and couldn't stay. I mean, I felt really bad leaving. I even put my phone number on the note so you could call me and let me know you were okay." He paused. "When you never called, I figured I must have done something to upset you. And then I happened to come by and see you sitting here. So I figured I would take the opportunity to see how you were doing." Something in the tone of his voice suggested he told the truth.

She paused, nodding. "Okay. Well, it explains a lot."

He continued, "Now, I would like to start this off the right way. Let me introduce myself." He paused, stood beside his chair, and bowed low. "Hello. My name is Alexavier Edmund. It is a pleasure to make your acquaintance. And you are…"

"Elena."

"And do you have a last name, Elena?"

"Elena Michaels," she said.

"It is nice to meet you, Elena. May I?" He gestured toward the seat he sat in and raised his eyebrows.

She nodded.

He sat back down. "So how are you feeling after such a nasty fall?"

"Much better, thanks." Despite her best efforts, she couldn't help but let her anger dissipate in his presence.

"I'm sorry I didn't visit you at the health center. But as I said, I couldn't wait. I had an exam. And I almost missed it, as a matter of fact."

"It's okay," she replied, doubting herself. After a few seconds, she made her decision. For some reason she couldn't stay angry with him.

They each sat on opposite sides of the table assessing the other, unsure what to say. Given the secluded nature of the reading room, and the hour of night, they were alone.

"Alexavier. What an interesting name. Do you prefer Alex, Alec, or do you go by Alexavier?"

"My personal favorite is Alec," he replied. "But I often leave it up to the other person to decide rather than impose my own preference."

"Okay, Alec it is."

Alec gave her a broad, warm smile. "Your name is actually quite interesting."

Elena cocked her head and shot him an inquiring expression. "What do you mean?"

"The meaning of the name Elena ranges from torch to bright, but most commonly means light, while Michaels could be interpreted to mean one who is close to God. So, depending on the interpretation, your name could mean you are the light of God."

She smiled. "Interesting. How come you know so much about names?"

"I'm pursuing a double degree in history and philosophy. I took several courses on genealogy and it hooked me. I've read more than the average share of books on the topic."

"History and philosophy? Hmm. Certainly explains a lot," she said. "I saw you on the first day of the semester. You were sitting at a back table in the dining hall. You had this book in your hands called the book of something or other."

"Yes, the *Book of Enoch*. It is an old Hebrew text. It very much influenced the New Testament. It talks about the heavens, angels, and all sorts of interesting ideas found in Hebrew and Christian belief." He paused for a moment. "There are many names used today derived from the names of angels."

"Really? I may have to borrow it some time." *Why did I say that? I don't even belong to a church.* She wouldn't really be interested in reading the book, ever. Her old standbys fell into two general categories: textbooks or science fiction novels.

"With those two degrees, what kind of career do you want once you graduate?"

"I'm not really sure," he responded. "I think maybe something to do with church history or theology maybe. I'll probably go on for my PhD in theology."

She laughed. "I'm the complete opposite."

"Oh really? How so?"

"I'm a microbiology major with a minor in anthropology. I want to be a genetic researcher," she replied with pride. "I want to chart the human genome, figure out how the people of the world came to be the way they are, learn about how we as a species evolved."

His eyebrows arched high. "How ambitious." After a moment, he added, "Why genetics? Why not become a doctor or something? Is there some particular draw to genetic research?"

His voice had a strange tone, but she attributed it to him being a theologian-in-training. In her experience, the "evolution" discussion didn't usually sit well with the devout. "I've always had an interest in science. I guess I'm my father's daughter. He was the division head of a genetic research firm."

He smirked. "Did he ever find anything interesting?"

She shrugged. "He was working on some huge project right before he passed away. He swore it would shake the foundations of science. Unfortunately, he was sworn to secrecy, and he never discussed it with me or mom."

"I'm sorry to hear about your father. I'm sure he would be proud of you following in his footsteps."

The sincerity behind his words made her well up. It had been a long time since she had talked to anyone about her father or his passing. And she didn't understand why she'd tell this near stranger about it now. He seemed to be safe, trustworthy. Though she didn't know him outside of the few chance encounters on campus, he also seemed very familiar to her. For the next two hours, until the library began to close, they continued to talk, each trying to learn as much as they could about the other.

Soft footsteps echoed from the hallway outside of the reading room. A head, belonging to one of the library staff, poked into the room. "You gotta wrap it up folks. Library is closing in ten minutes." The staff member emphasized the words "ten minutes."

Elena glanced at her watch. Could it be midnight already? And she had not finished reviewing her notes for tomorrow's test. *Damn*, she admonished herself. Next on her list of worries—

walking across campus alone at this hour of night. This had to be her least favorite thing. She sighed.

"Would you like me to escort you back to your building?" Alec asked.

Relief washed over her. Plus, now she'd have the added benefit of learning more about him. They talked the entire way back about anything and nothing all at once. By the time they reached her dorm, it seemed as though they were old friends.

"This is me," she said gesturing to her dorm building. "Thanks for walking over here with me." As she peered down and studied her shoes in disbelief, she played the bashful girl.

"My pleasure," he replied with a slight bow. "My dorm is on the other side of the quad." He nodded toward Davis Hall across the way.

A light breeze gently tossed her hair about in the dim light of the quad. The late night air carried a faint mist, which partly obscured the other residential buildings from sight. Her body shivered, forgetting she held her jacket.

It would have been a perfectly romantic moment had the air not carried the faint trace of a fetid odor. It reminded her of road kill; the smell of something dead.

An odd shuffling sound drifted from over Alec's shoulder. A rather burly, dark-haired student shambled toward them with his eyes fixed on Alec.

Before she could react, the student engaged them. Without a sound, he balled both of his fists together, raised them above his head, and swung them down onto Alec's back.

Alec fell to the ground. The attacker spat what appeared to be dirt down at Alec and muttered some unintelligible guttural word. Elena froze with shock as one of the student's hands shot forward with unimaginable speed and grasped her by the throat. Adrenaline coursed through her veins as he compressed her esophagus. Her heart pounded. Her senses were on overdrive. Something akin to the stench of rotten meat emanated from him.

Tears welled in her eyes at the foolishness of being out on the campus so late at night. Alec still lay in a heap on the ground. There was nobody to save her. And even as she could feel the student's cold, rough hand squeezing her throat tighter, the idea this stranger attacked Alec and now choked her was baffling. She gawked in disbelief.

Her attacker stood a few inches shorter than her and wore a blood-stained varsity football jacket embroidered with the name Byron. The sight of his face, though, jolted her out of her paralysis.

Blackish bruises and dried blood covered his face. Two of his teeth were visible through a hole in what used to be his right cheek. His top and bottom right eyelids were marked by a series of nasty gouges, and his milky left eye contained no pupil.

She tried to scream. But the crushing power of his hand prevented air from escaping her lips. Acting on sheer reflex, her right knee swung up with all of her might and drove up into his groin. The force or placement of her blow had no visible effect on her attacker. She could swear his face instead contorted into a wicked sneer.

It had to be a figment of her imagination. Right?

Her knee lashed out again and again. Bursts of light danced across her eyes. His unrelenting grip blocked the passage of air into her lungs. Her chest burned. As darkness began to overcome her, a blinding flash of white light exploded through her closed eyelids. The last thing she remembered feeling was the sensation of wind whipping through her hair and the hardness of the ground disappearing from beneath her feet. It made her think of floating in space.

chapter 4

Whether the pounding in her head or the burning in her throat, something caused Elena to jolt from the inky blackness of sleep. She whipped around, very much alert, trying to ascertain her whereabouts. Her throat ached to the point she had to force a cough.

In her mind, the attacker still choked her. She could still feel the force of his powerful hand. But her brain deceived her. She began adjusting to her new surroundings, though despite her eyes being wide open, she could not make out so much as a hint of light in the complete darkness of the room. She coughed again. The lack of any discernible echo suggested the room had to be small.

Her hand reached out to explore. Below her, she could feel the firm softness of a mattress—above her head, a headboard. Her feet touched no footboard. As she made more observations, it became apparent the mattress edges were close-by. By her estimation, she lay on one of the college's long twin beds. She prayed she had not wound up in the medical center again.

Her eyes acclimated to the enveloping darkness thanks to a small bit of light filtering into the room from somewhere. Through the gloom were the dark shapes of a dresser, a desk, and a wooden slat-back chair. The institutional furniture and cramped surroundings confirmed she was in a campus dorm room.

Sitting upright, she swung her legs over the side of the bed. However, a second before sliding off the mattress, her motion halted, held by a firm but soft hand with a familiar voice.

"I wouldn't if I were you," the voice cautioned. "You are sitting on the top bunk about to make a grave and painful mistake."

The tension washed from her body—Alec.

"Where am I? What am I doing here?"

"You are in my dorm room. I brought you here." He sounded cool and calm.

"It really happened?"

Silence.

"What happened to the guy who was choking me?"

"Cover your eyes for a minute," he said. "I am going to turn the light on. It's still the middle of the night."

Even through her shielded eyes, the bright-white light stung. Air hissed through her clenched teeth.

"I fell pretty hard when the guy attacked me," Alec explained. "But I managed to get back up. The next thing I knew, I saw him with his hands at your throat. I don't know how, but I managed to pull the maniac off of you. I think somebody must have seen what happened and called the police because they showed up pretty quickly and had their hands full trying to subdue the guy. While the police were busy, I helped you up. However, I think he managed to run off because I saw several of the police officers tearing off after something."

"Why am I here and not at the police station, or in the health center?"

Her eyes grew accustomed to the light. He sat on his desk across the room with his feet resting on the seat of his desk chair with a surprised expression on his face when she asked the question.

"You mean you don't remember?" he asked in shock. "I mean, I guess it makes sense if you don't. You went through one hell of a traumatic event. But..."

"Remember what?" she asked, becoming perturbed by the apparent black hole in her memory. Yet something tugged at the back of her mind.

Alec sighed. "You were adamant you did not want to go with the police. And since they were swarming the outside of your dorm, you asked me to bring you back to my room." He shrugged. "So I did."

Elena sat in silence for a few moments trying to comprehend the meaning of his words.

"Since you obviously don't remember much of what happened," he added, "I need to say you don't have to worry. You slept up there; I slept on the floor. Nothing happened." He held up three fingers on his right hand. "Scout's honor."

The mutilated face of her attacker came into mind. With a sharp gasp, she muttered, "He seemed like he was dead."

Alec shook his head, turning to face her. "What?"

"I said, it seemed like the guy was dead or something. He had all of these cuts and scratches on his face. And I could see his teeth through a hole in his cheek. By the smell of him, I could swear he was a walking corpse or something."

"Really?" Alec scoffed. "Zombies on a college campus? Now there's a scandal." He chuckled. "I think the more likely explanation is maybe he was deranged from a bad concussion or something, or some kind of steroid freak. All I can say is he was strong. He actually lifted you off the ground with his one hand. He was probably roid-raging and got scratched up on his way back to the dorms from the gym."

"Maybe," Elena conceded. But she couldn't help the strong feeling of doubt in the back of her mind. The guy looked dead. Something else struck her.

"I remember the sensation of flying," she blurted.

Alec gazed deep into her eyes. "You were being strangled by a deranged madman," he replied. "Oxygen wasn't getting to your brain. He was holding you at least six inches off the ground. Of course you felt like you were flying. You were probably high as a kite from the oxygen deprivation before you passed out."

After a moment's pause, he continued, "Speaking of deprivation, you should probably get some sleep. You have a lab tomorrow, right? In spite of what happened, you still need to get good grades. Get some rest."

As an afterthought he added, "You are more than welcome to sleep here. My roommate goes home quite frequently, so there should be no problems. Or, if you prefer, I could escort you back to your dorm."

"No," she replied while shaking her head. "I don't want to go back to my dorm. The maniac could still be out there."

She took Alec's advice and stretched back out in the bunk bed. Laying her head on his pillows, it surprised her how clean and fresh they smelled. As her eyelids drooped, the conversation replayed in her mind. Despite the assertion of her attacker being some hopped-up steroid-junkie, she decided to check into the guy. Perhaps an early trip to the library would give her some useful information.

Below her, Alec moved about tidying-up the already spotless room. He must have some secret store of energy keeping him moving despite the late hour. Somehow, even with the sound of his rustling about, she managed to drift into the world of dream.

The place always made her feel uneasy for some reason. Clad with perforated steel panels, the ceiling reminded her of a sieve; the walls were painted in a strange grayish-white color, which oddly absorbed and reflected the overhead fluorescent light. The floor above all, she remembered, disturbed her. The poured concrete surface, painted with a textured multi-color paint, had a central floor drain. However tacky the decoration, it could not hide the floor's multitude of blood stains.

A shiver ran down her spine.

Her father had brought her here as part of bring your daughter to work day. She'd always had a strong fascination with what he did. Her interest likely stemmed more from curiosity about why his job could keep him away from her and her mother. She had never really had any kind of interest in bioresearch or genetics.

"What do you think, honey?" her father asked. The sound of his voice washed over her. Even in her dreams it occurred to her she missed his voice. In fact, she hadn't even realized how much until now. She fought hard to push back the upwelling emotions. In her rational mind, she knew this was a dream. But in her heart, she welcomed the chance to see him again.

"It's okay, I guess," she replied. "What is all of this stuff?"

He turned to her, and smiled. She always loved his smile. It made her feel warm, loved, at home. "Do you want the geeky explanation," he asked, "or the simple one?"

She peered back up at him and returned the smile.

"Okay," he responded. He ushered her into the center of room with a gentle but firm hand against her back. "This is the genetics research lab," he explained. "This is where I conduct my experiments." He paused. "Would you like to see how a DNA test is done?"

"Sure." She tried hard not to sound so excited.

"Okay," he said. His warm smile helped to quell her uneasiness. Putting his hand on her shoulder, he squeezed it in the way dads always did. The simple gesture did the trick, making her feel a little more relaxed. "I think the best way to do this," he told her, "is to take a sample from you."

Any sense of calm she'd had disappeared. Her eyes filled with panic, and she cringed away from him a little. Her throat let out a soft mewl.

He understood her unease. "Hold on," he told her. "All we are going to do is something called a finger-stick test." He picked up a small device from the counter top. It reminded her of a strange pen. "This will pinch a little bit." In a few seconds, the pen stuck her finger, and a small drop of blood welled up on her fingertip. He dropped the blood onto a microscope slide and slipped the slide into a small machine.

chapter 5

Despite her mind-numbing grogginess upon waking the next morning, she was in a very good mood. She scanned her surroundings, pleased to find herself still in Alec's dorm room. It wasn't a dream. However, this meant some weirdo really had attacked her last night. Elena decided for the time being to ignore this unpleasant part of the story.

She stretched her arms over her head and struck the wall. It stood a lot closer than she had realized. The arrangement of Alec's bunk bed almost mirrored her own.

As she brought her arms down, her eyes caught sight of something, which made her jump. In an instant, any sense of safety and comfort disappeared. Her watch served as a cruel reminder her microbiology lab would start in about twelve minutes.

"Oh no!" Her legs swung over the side of the bed.

"Caref—" began Alec. His words died in a flurry of expletives from Elena's mouth. Her arms moved with purpose as she gathered her things and snatched a pen off his desk before bolting for the door. Alec glided into her path.

"Wait, don't go. You can make up the lab." His offer was tempting.

Soaking in his features, his words crept into her mind. What did he say? Skip a lab? He didn't skip his exam after she'd fallen. Her knees buckled a little drinking in the intricate patterns in his eyes. Perhaps she could reschedule.

No! She had to get to the lab. It was thirty percent of her grade, an automatic point deduction for a reschedule. She couldn't make it up.

A slight feint to the left slipped her past him. But he stopped her again.

"Please?" he asked, batting his eyes at her.

She responded with a stare.

Sighing, he stepped to one side. "Okay," he said. "If you won't indulge me with your presence, then how about you meet up with me after the lab? I'll wait for you at the student center."

She melted, unable to resist his smile. Alec did not have any classes in the morning and could meet her anytime. Without hesitation, she kissed him on the cheek before running out the door. Alec never had the opportunity to ask if he could escort her to class.

Mornings like this made her appreciate she kept up with her morning jogs. It made the fact she needed to run all the way across campus a little more bearable. Emerging from the tunnel connecting the dorm side of the campus to the academic side of the campus, she froze in her tracks. Blocking her dead in the center of her path stood somebody who resembled Alec. Her breath caught in her chest. No, it was Alec. But how did he make it here before her?

The expression on his face was unsettling. Her skin crawled.

"You can't go to your lab. You're in terrible danger." Was this some kind of sick joke?

A million questions ran through her brain. "What do you mean, danger? Wait, how did you get here before me?" She wanted to pinch herself and make sure this was not some kind of twisted dream.

He reached out his hand to her. "You have to come with me. I can protect you."

His tone scared her. She watched as his eyes grew wide with shock. She didn't think it possible, but his voice took on a tone of even greater urgency.

"Now!" he exclaimed, wagging his hand at her. "It's not safe for you here." He began walking toward her.

"No!" She pushed past him. "Alec, I have a lab. I have to get to my la—"

She again froze. In the distance, two identical men were walking toward them. Both men were average height with long white-blonde hair swept back behind their ears. The white cable-knit sweaters and dress slacks the men wore could not hide their muscular bulk. Most noticeable of all, Elena could see both men were fixated upon her as they broadened their pace and picked up speed.

Alec followed her gaze. "It's too late," he muttered. "Crap!"

Elena heard a strange buzzing sound. It reminded her of standing in the middle of a cocktail party with hundreds of conversations prattling on around her. Her body tingled with the same electric sensation she had felt when Alec helped her up after she'd slipped outside the dining hall. Her jaw dropped and she stared, unable to move, as the two men approached.

"Elena," he pleaded, "we've got to get you out of here. Those are the men who killed your father. And now, they're coming for you." The words struck a deep chord. She turned her gaze from the approaching men back to Alec and stared into his eyes. Reflected in them were both fear and truth.

"What do you mean they killed my father?" she asked.

The two men were but a couple hundred yards away now. They'd closed the distance without any visible effort. "There is no time to explain," Alec said as he grabbed her by the wrist and ran, dragging her behind him.

Elena stumbled for the first few steps, but soon exploded into a full sprint.

"We have to leave. Fast! Where is your car?"

Back through the tunnel, Elena led the way as she and Alec ran across the quad and between the dorms to the parking lot. On her way to her car, she fumbled in her pockets for her keys. Once beside it, she nearly dropped them several times in her haste but finally managed to unlock it. They both slipped inside as the two men appeared at the edge of the parking lot. She slipped in the key and tried the ignition. Her gut sank at the sound of a spinning starter motor.

Not... Now! Dammit!

"C'mon...C'mon... C'mon!!!" she screamed at her dashboard.

The men were closing fast.

The car roared to life.

"Yes!"

She jammed the shift lever to reverse and mashed her foot to the floor, whipping her Camry around out of the parking spot, surprised she had managed to pull off the maneuver without crashing into another car.

She slammed the transmission into drive and sped through the maze of parking spaces.

"Who the hell are..."

Her question was cut short by the plinking sound of two bullets punching holes into the thin sheet metal of her car. Another bullet pierced her rear window, shattering it. Alec flinched at the last shot and his hand grabbed his left side.

She turned to him and the car began to slow.

"Drive!" he shouted at her, "Go! Go! Go!" She thrust the accelerator to the floor again and the car lurched forward.

She over steered around several short turns, but never once let her foot up off the accelerator. The tortured engine screamed. The stop light separating the parking lot and the main road through campus raced toward her. It was red. Gritting her teeth, she sped into the intersection and whipped the car hard to the left, heading toward the interstate. The car took purchase on the pavement and bolted down the road. Elena let out a huge sigh of relief, grateful for the lack of morning traffic.

"You need a doctor," she told him. "I need to get you to a hospital. We need the police." The words were coming out fast.

He seemed far too calm for a gunshot victim. "I'm fine," he said. "Don't worry about me. You need to get as far away from here as fast as you can." Then, he added, "And whatever you do, do not call the police."

In a few quick turns she headed south on the interstate, not quite sure where to go. But she knew where she wanted to go. And it was south of school. Far south.

"You need a doctor," she said again, panic still in her voice.

Alec shook his head. Lifting his closed right fist toward her face, he turned his hand palm upward, and opened his fingers. Within it were the shattered remains of a bullet.

"Like I said," he told her, "don't worry about me." The smile had returned to his face.

Her jaw dropped open. She eased up a little on the accelerator.

"Don't slow down yet," he cautioned her. "We're nowhere out of the woods. They are still coming after us." In her rearview mirror there were no cars visible anywhere. Despite being a state highway, it was never heavily trafficked. The men might be coming after them. But she knew she had a great head start, and given the usually empty nature of the road, any pursuers would be easy to spot.

"Can you answer some questions for me?" she asked him with more calm than she believed she'd be able to muster in the present circumstances. She turned her eyes from the road to address him. He slowly nodded in agreement.

"Good," she replied. "First: who are those people?" Her voice flat, and cold.

"The two chasing us are very bad," he responded. "They are wicked henchmen who have no respect for human life and specialize in killing. They are the ones responsible for killing your father."

"My father died of an aneurism at his lab," she retorted.

"No," Alec replied. "Your father was murdered. Damage to his brain caused the aneurism and his death. The two following us caused the damage to his brain."

Elena's head swam. *How could he know all of this?* "Why would somebody kill my father?" she asked. "He was a genetic researcher. I mean, how can you be sure he was murdered?"

Alec explained, "Because of the implications of his research. And to answer your next question, based on what happened to your father, it is my job to protect you."

The needle on the Toyota's speedometer crept down toward sixty. Unaware of the declining speed, Alec continued, "The people chasing us will stop at nothing to capture you."

It amazed her at how calm he seemed to be talking about a couple of cold-blooded murderers wanting to kill her. In a way, it almost made sense. After all, they weren't after him; they wanted her dead. Why should he be scared and get riled about them wanting to kill her? She decided to move on before becoming too agitated at his nonchalance.

Her eyes finally crept down to the speedometer. "Crap," she exclaimed. She pressed her foot to the floor and the car leapt forward again with a whine of the transmission.

Alec glanced at the speedometer. Elena could see his face take on a vacant expression. "Dammit," he said in a hushed voice. "It's too late."

He hadn't even finished mouthing the words when a dark shadow overwhelmed the speeding car. Elena could see something fly over the car and land on the road in the distance right in their path. A heavy thud echoed through the interior of the car as the roof dented downward.

"Pull over," Alec said to her. "It's no use running. They've got us." Alec's voice lacked emotion, and Elena had trouble hearing him. The ringing in her head had returned with force, its din nearly deafening her. Despite the noise, there were some occasional words amongst the din. But the words she heard were in addition to those spoken by Alec and did not belong to his voice.

She pulled over onto the shoulder. As they slowed, the shadow, which landed in the road ahead glided toward them. The creature standing before her almost caused her to steer into the ditch.

As a person in the scientific disciplines, Elena did not think of herself as irrational. However, the being standing in front of her car defied any rationality. She recognized him as one of the men who had been chasing them. He wore no shirt, but still had the dress pants he had been in. The cold, fierce expression on his face made her cringe. However, the sight that shocked her most, taking her breath away, was the fourteen-foot-wide span of opalescent feathered wings spreading outward from the man's back.

He drew back his fist and smashed it into the hood of her car. The sheet metal nearly tore from the impact.

She heard a strong voice command her, "Elena Michaels. Get out of the car. Now!"

The man's lips never moved.

Alec leaned in to her and whispered, "Stay in the car. No matter what happens. Do not go to them willingly." Without allowing her a chance to respond, Alec opened the door and stepped out of the car onto the shoulder.

Amidst the noise in her head, Elena could hear an unfamiliar voice speaking. *Youngling*...silence...*the girl*...more silence...*you must!* She could hear Alec's voice respond. *Leave the girl alone!*

And then it began. The movements were fast and she lost track of the action. One second Alec stood beside the car, staring down the winged being; in the next, they were both gone.

Pushing her face against the windshield, she gazed up into the sky. A patchwork of shadows danced across the roadway and hood of the car. However, her view was quickly blocked as the hood of her car crunched and a pale face pressed itself up against the outside of the glass. Startled, she shoved herself backward into the seat.

Wild white-blonde hair framed the pale face against the glass. *Hello Elena. I was wondering if we might be able to talk.* The face behind the windshield cocked sideways, an unspoken question in its eyes. It cocked again, back the other direction. *You do hear me, don't you*?

Without thinking, Elena nodded in response to the unspoken question.

Good. The face smiled in a failed attempt at seeming warm and inviting. Instead, the smile screamed danger to her. *I would like to speak with you out here. Out in the nice, fresh air.* As the voice spoke in her head, the atmosphere in the car became stale. Her lungs struggled to catch breath.

It really is nice and crisp out here. She could see the beast kneeling on her hood breathing deep as her lungs struggled even more.

Her hand sought the door handle.

Elena! No! Whatever happens, do not leave the car! Alec's voice invaded her head. Was he shouting at her?

She reached for the steering column and turned the key in the ignition. A slight sense of relief washed over her as the car started on its first try. She turned on the radio and cranked up the music.

The face staring at her through the windshield grimaced. *Do you think the music... You call this noise music? Odd... Do you really think it can block me out?* Then the creature's maniacal laughter filled her head.

Elena turned the radio up as high as it would go. She forced herself to focus on the music and sang along at the top of her lungs.

The laughter grew more intense. The sound of his mental voice numbed her head. Outside, in the distance, something fell to the ground. The faint impact of a solid mass striking the pavement preceded a hollow metallic thud on the roof of her car.

Outside the window, her tormenter had disappeared. Against her better judgment, she leaned forward to peer out again. What met her eyes made her jump back in her seat, throwing her hands over her face. Her scream drowned out the blasting car stereo.

A body hurtled toward the earth at amazing speed. Her heart sank and her stomach twisted in fear as she recognized the coat wrapped around the falling form belonged to Alec.

Chills ran down her spine. The trajectory of the falling mass made it clear she would soon be crushed as it fell through her windshield to land on top of her. An instant before impact, though, the falling body slid sideways and landed in the road inches from the car. The creature who had guided Alec's body down through the sky leap off a split second before it struck the pavement with a hard thud. She screamed.

Her voice halted with a gasp. She must be going insane, because she recognized the figure standing before her car as a smirking Alec. Though what shocked her more was a powerful pair of pure, snow-white feathered wings stretching wide from Alec's back. She blinked. The wings were gone.

Wait! How could this be? She had seen wings there. They were there! Elena shook her head in disbelief. Perhaps it had been a phantom memory of the wings she had seen on the other being.

He walked with purpose to the car and tried the handle of the locked car door. Elena fumbled with the power door locks and managed to let him in. "We have to get out of here," he said. "They're not going to stay down for long. These are a tougher bunch than I figured they would send." He spoke with urgency. Sitting in the seat beside her, he closed the car door, and put on his seat belt.

She stared at his shirtless form dumbfounded. He had an amazing physique, like something from the cover of a cheap harlequin romance. Never would she have guessed such a solid and toned body could hide beneath his shirt. She lacked the will to shift her attention back to driving.

And yet a question burned in her mind. She needed answers. "What the hell is going on?"

"Drive," he told her, "and I will explain." He spoke in a calm, even tone. After a quick glimpse out the car window added, "Elena, we have to hurry."

She sat numbed for a few more moments. Alec reached over and grasped her right hand. His touch felt soft, warm, and electric. Her skin tingled. She couldn't understand why, but the feel of his skin on hers somehow calmed her. She turned to gaze into his alluring blue eyes. "Elena, I understand this is a lot for you to take in. Your whole world has been turned upside down. But you have to trust me!" He clasped her hand to lend her support. "We have to leave. And we have to leave now!" Almost to illustrate his point, the being in front of her car began to move around.

Elena blinked and snapped back into focus. *He...it's not dead!* It would be pretty pissed when it recovered. She stomped on the accelerator, nearly hitting the body in front of her car, maneuvered off the shoulder, and continued speeding down the highway, thankful for an empty road.

Chapter 6

For the next three hours, they drove south and west on the highway at about eighty miles per hour in complete silence. They had crossed state lines into Massachusetts two hours ago and were about to enter New York State. The roads were more heavily trafficked, but everything moved well and they were able to maintain their speeds, especially on the multilane highways. Elena could not take the oppressive void of silence any longer.

"So, you said you would explain," she prompted. Glancing up from the road, she turned off the highway onto a back road. Alec's eyes never turned away from the side window. To Elena, he seemed hypnotized by the passing scenery. Yet, she could almost swear she had heard him mumble something under his breath once or twice.

"So?" she sniped at him. This time, she turned from the wheel and stared at the back of his head.

"You really should pay attention to the road when driving this fast," he responded in a flat, emotionless voice. He sounded tired. "You never can tell when a deer might jump in front of the car." He turned back to face her.

"I am sure," he continued, "it's an understatement to say you have a long list of questions." His voice had a sense of comical amusement to it. "And I can't say I blame you. After all, for someone like you, this has to be quite bizarre."

"Yeah, there's an understatement." Her voice had a slight tremble.

"So shoot," he responded. "Ask me anything. Oh, and you can slow down now. We should be relatively safe for the time being. They gave up the chase about an hour ago." He chuckled to himself, and then said, "It's harder to fly with broken wings. Unfortunately, by now they have your whole life history." She could hear a little hint of frustration in his voice.

As the speedometer eased back from eighty, she blurted, "Okay. Who the hell are you?" *Perhaps*, she considered after the words escaped her lips, *I could have asked him a little nicer*.

"Don't worry about being nice," he replied to her. She started at his words. Had she said it out loud? After a brief moment of reflection, she concluded she hadn't.

"What?" she asked, "Can you read my mind or something?" She couldn't keep the anger from her voice.

"Yes," he replied. "I can hear your thoughts when you think out loud." Before she could interject with another question, he continued, "In answer to your question: I am here to protect you. As you can tell, I am not human. Would you care to venture a guess as to what I am?"

"Given the immense set of wings I saw sticking from your back," she began, "and believe me when I say I don't believe I am about to say this, but I would have to guess you are something like an angel."

With a smirk he replied, "You saw those, huh? I tried to tuck them in before you could see."

She could not believe his nonchalance about the encounter, but it also seemed a little forced, like he wanted the whole thing to appear laughable.

"The simplest explanation is I belong to a very old race of beings," he explained. "Our kind predates the emergence of what you understand as modern humans. I myself was born more than three thousand years ago." He paused.

Elena asked. "So, who are you?"

Alec seemed to consider this for a moment, then turned and asked, "Long story, or short?"

"I don't want a story; I want the truth."

"Fair enough," he replied. "Long it is—" He sat in silent contemplation for a few seconds. He glanced up and called her attention back to the road. "You're going to miss your turn."

Elena snapped her head forward in time to see he'd been correct. She almost drove right past the same small street she had driven onto hundreds of times since receiving her license.

"How did you know where I was going?" she asked.

He ignored her question and spoke with extreme caution. "Elena," he told her, "our meeting was not by chance. I have been watching over you for a long time. I am here to protect you."

"Protect me?" she asked. "From what?"

"Yes, protect you," he replied. "What from? Well, how about those two creatures I fought back there and the ghoul I fought the other night? All of which were sent for you. Elena, I am your protector, your guardian."

"What do they want with me?" she asked him. Her voice sounded helpless, despite her best efforts at bravado.

"Because," he told her, "you're special." Elena detected an unintentional slip of emotion in his voice.

"What do you mean I'm special? You're not making any sense." The helplessness gave way to frustration.

"I cannot tell you about it now. This is not the right time or place. Let's say it concerns your father's research. Until now, my associates and I have kept you hidden. But now you are vulnerable. They'll have every detail of your life. And, as you can see, you are in grave danger."

"So you said our kind. What is your kind? Who are you?" Elena asked.

"My race has been called by many names. The name we most commonly accept amongst ourselves comes from Ancient Greek. We are called *Daimones*."

He watched her for a moment. "Humans generally react poorly to a name sounding so close to the demons of ancient legend and modern myth. But the translation of the word is divine beings. At one time we lived together in peace with humans and acted as their advisors and protectors. From this relationship we became the angels of legend. However, later Christian chroniclers painted an image of the name and of our kind much more sinister. What humans see as angels and demons are one and the same; and I am one of them."

Elena couldn't make sense of anything he said. As a scientist, and for all practical purposes an agnostic, she had never entertained a belief in the existence of such mythical beings. Yet how could she refute the evidence sitting right next to her? Talking to her! She'd seen his wings with her own eyes.

An approaching car drew her attention back to her driving. Staring out the windshield, she drove a little faster through the familiar streets. She knew them like the back of her hand. They were the streets back home.

With greater confidence in her driving, she collected herself. "Alec, if you are one of them, then why are you trying to protect me?"

"Because, I was assigned to watch over you."

"But why? You mentioned something to do with my father's research. I don't understand," she confessed.

"This really isn't the time to discuss it. We'll talk about it later." Alec stared out the window, signifying an end to the conversation. Elena made a final turn.

"We're here," she announced.

She pulled the car to a stop in the driveway, slammed it into park, removed the keys from the ignition, and leapt out the car door with Alec a few steps behind her.

The tan-painted ranch where she and her mother lived sat on a sloped lot bordered by trees at the back. The house had a garage located beneath it at the basement level, and the yard stepped downward from its highest corner in the front to the driveway in a series of tiers. A set of stone steps flanked by beds of colorful but fading impatiens wound its way upward to the front doorway. The driveway held Elena's car alone, meaning her mother was at work.

Nevertheless, Elena ran up the steps and barring the formality of turning the key in the lock, nearly burst through the front door into the foyer. "Mom?" she called out. She knew she would not be answered. Being noontime, her mother would be at the office. She wanted desperately to see her.

She scanned the familiar living room with its kitschy colonial furnishings. Despite the standard mess of daily living, everything appeared normal. Elena rushed through all the rooms to satisfy herself of her mother's absence, and then returned to the living room, where Alec stood waiting. He appeared concerned, staring at the floor. Elena followed his gaze to a patch of carpet on the floor, unable to see anything there to catch his attention.

"We should go visit your mother at her job." Without any further explanation, he strode from the room.

She grabbed his arm as he walked out. "Hey!" she called to him. "What's going on? What's wrong with my mother?"

Alec shook his head. "I don't know. But if they found you at school, then they could have found her, too."

She let his arm go and followed him back to the car. Elena's mother worked in a small industrial park about a half hour away. Elena knew the route well. As Executive Assistant to the company's president, her mother had managed to get her a part time job in the secretarial pool over the past few summers. A troubled expression adorned Alec's face for the entire drive.

When they arrived, Elena stopped at the guard kiosk. After exchanging some casual greetings with the guard, she gave him Alec's name and the man raised the gate, waving her through. It took but a moment to find an available parking spot, and they made their way inside.

The massive concrete office building stood about two-stories in height away in the far reaches of a small industrial complex. An aluminum plaque near the door bearing the company's name and logo betrayed its tenants' identity.

Elena pushed the button on the door buzzer, waiting for the doorman to answer. "Come on in, Ms. Michaels. I'll tell your mother you are on your way." In a few short minutes, Elena stepped up to a massive oak desk in a large, empty reception area outside an executive office. Behind the immense piece of furniture, she could see the smiling face of her mother. Katarin Michaels was a slight woman with more salt than pepper in her hair. Her naturally olive skin had evidently not seen a sunny day in some time, and the few creases time had bestowed around her smile and eyes gave her distinction rather than betrayed her age. However, her smile soon faded, replaced by an ashen pallor as she saw Alec's face.

"Elena," she said with a cautious tone, "what are you doing here? Don't you have exams?"

"Mom," Elena urged, "we need to talk."

"Fine, we can talk," Katarin said, "But why is *he* here?" Katarin had a hard, accusatory tone. Elena stepped back a pace. She couldn't understand why her mother could be so cold to him.

Alec finally spoke up, "Hello, Katarin, it's nice to see you again." He spoke to her in the way old friends or acquaintances did.

Elena's jaw hit the floor in shock. She turned to Alec. The lack of an expression on his face spoke volumes to Elena. "Mom," she asked, afraid of the answer, "have you two met before?"

Elena's mother paused, staring from Alec to Elena and responded, "I am not sure how to answer."

"What do you mean," Elena replied, her voice growing louder, "you're not sure how to answer? The question is quite simple. How do you two know each other?"

Alec fidgeted, looking around. "Katarin," he said with urgency, "we should leave."

Several people walked in and out of nearby offices. Most, Elena knew, were workers returning from their lunch breaks. But Alec's apparent nervousness did not let up.

To Elena he whispered, "This is not the time or place for this conversation."

"I am getting a little tired of the evasiveness," she snapped. Several of the office's inhabitants had poked their heads out of nearby cubicles.

"Fine," Katarin conceded, "I'll meet you in the parking lot in about five minutes." She then set to work, tapping away at her keyboard. Elena knew from her mother's demeanor the conversation had merely begun.

Elena made a beeline for the exit with Alec in tow. In the empty parking lot they should be able to discuss whatever they needed to. However, nobody spoke a word until her mother came out the front doorway. "Here we go." Elena sighed under her breath as her mother approached, thinking about how she'd lost her temper back in the office. She couldn't read the expression on her face, but knew her mother did not appear happy.

"Elena," Katarin called to her daughter, "let's get in my car." Katarin unlocked the car doors.

"Mom," Elena began to protest, but after receiving a glare from her mother stopped. "Tell me what the hell the big secret is—" she whined.

"Elena," Katarin said over the roof of her car, "get in my car. Now!"

"Mom, I..." she began, but stopped after turning to Alec. He nodded toward her mother's car. He never said a word, but she knew what he wanted her to do. Reluctantly, she climbed into the passenger seat.

Before Elena could close her door, Katarin addressed Alec, "You follow us back home with Elena's car." Alec nodded. Elena handed him the keys. Katarin turned the ignition, and had the car thrown into gear, speeding out of the parking lot before Elena's door had even closed.

"Mom, what the hell?" Elena exclaimed, "Why are you driving so fast? What is going on?" It shocked her that her mother would speed or behave so recklessly. She'd always been the most safety-conscious person Elena knew.

"We need to make sure you're safe," Katarin said, glancing at the rearview mirror to make sure Alec followed behind.

"Mom," Elena blurted, "will you please tell me what the hell is going on here? Seriously!"

The car skidded out onto the main road and accelerated. Alec followed close behind. Katarin did not say another word to her daughter until all three of them were inside the house.

Seated at the kitchen table, Katarin tried to settle herself a little before beginning. But she couldn't hide the fact her hands were shaking. "Sweetie," she said taking her hands into her own, "don't be angry with me." She squeezed Elena's hands. "I never wanted you to find out about this, especially not this way." Katarin glared at Alec and then studied the girl's hands.

Elena opened her mouth to interject, but stopped dead in her tracks as her mother spoke right over her.

"God," she swore in frustration, "I can't even say it."

There was an agonizing pause. Elena could see her mother welling up and wanted to do something to comfort her. She let go of her mother's hands to put them on her shoulder, to pull her close. Elena slid closer to her.

"Elena, you're not my daughter," Katarin blurted. "You were adopted."

Elena froze. Katarin buried her tearful face in her hands as sobs racked her body.

Adopted? Elena wondered. *How could I be adopted?* It had never once occurred to her she might have been adopted. While growing up, they had often compared her appearance to both of her parents' old photographs, and she did resemble them both. In fact, her parents had often noted some of the more stunning family traits and characteristics belonging to both her mother's and father's sides.

"How could I be adopted?"

Her mother picked her head up out of her hands for a brief second. "Sweetie," Katarin said between sobs, "it's not even the worst part of it."

Her face tingled with pins and needles. *How could there be more?* she asked herself. *My life's already a sham, and now there's more?*

Katarin paused as another couple of sobs escaped. "Your father... He analyzed your DNA," she told her daughter, taking her hands again and squeezing them. Putting both hands on Elena's shoulders, she stared her square in the eye. "Elena, honey... You're not... You're not human."

Elena's face felt warm. She couldn't breathe. *Not human?* She couldn't comprehend what her mother said. Her mother who was not really her mother. The room started spinning around her. *If I'm not human, then what am I?*

"I need to lay down."

Elena opened her eyes. They adjusted to the orange glow of the setting sun as it pierced her blinds and filtered into her room. She must have dozed off. Her last memory consisted of entering her room so she could lie down and absorb everything she'd learned so far.

The clanking of pots and pans down the hallway and the miasma of delicious aromas wafting under her closed bedroom door—garlic, olive oil, onions, and browned beef conspired to make her stomach growl. She couldn't identify the dish being cooked, but didn't really care either. It smelled too good.

After a few moments of self-encouragement, her legs swung over the side of the bed. She crossed the room, flipped on the light, and began rummaging through her closet, finding a clean, comfortable change of clothes. Freshly attired, she walked down the hall and into the kitchen. Her stomach growled.

Her mother stood at the kitchen stove, tapping a long-handled wooden spoon against the rim of a large pot. Elena knew by the cans of stewed tomatoes and tomato paste sitting on the counter her mother prepared her homemade spaghetti sauce.

Katarin turned around, and greeted Elena with a big smile. "Hello dear," she said. "I was getting worried about you."

Katarin mixed the last of her ingredients together into the pot, gave it a quick stir, covered it, and sat down at the kitchen table. As her mother sat, Elena realized they were not alone in the kitchen. Her heart raced as she studied the man sitting at the table drinking coffee as if he were in a street-side cafe.

She set aside the growing crush she had for Alec. "Mom," she began. "What's going on?"

"Why don't you have something to eat first?" Katarin asked. "You have had a long..."

"Mom!" Elena exclaimed. "You hit me with a double-whammy and expect me to sit down and have a meal?" She wanted to scream at her until her voice gave out. She wanted to kick something. Her rational nature, though, prevented such behavior. She had never been one for outbursts. Instead, she stood table-side shaking, failing in her attempt to calm her nerves.

"Mom," she said in a quaking voice, "I want some answers."

Elena sat down in one of the kitchen chairs, and placed her head in her hands. "I feel like this is some kind of sick, demented dream." She fell into tears.

"No. It's not a dream," Katarin replied. "I'm so sorry." Her red eyes were swollen and moist.

"After your father and I got married," she explained, "we were having trouble conceiving. I had miscarried several times, and we were on the verge of giving up. I couldn't bear the idea of not having a baby in my life.

"One of my friends from the old neighborhood suggested an adoption agency. I mean, your father and I had toyed with the idea for a while, but never really took it seriously. We wanted our own baby. Our own flesh and blood. But after I miscarried for my fifth time, we decided to contact the agency. I couldn't handle another disappointment.

"My friend had a brother who worked at the place and got us an appointment," Katarin continued. "The initial process was stressful and slow, but once all the paperwork was finished, it all happened so quickly. We got a call within a few days and before we knew it, we were taking you home. You were ours. They hadn't yet named you, but when I saw you, it was like you were glowing. Your name came to me right then and there: Elena...light.

"We always loved you like you were our very own. Because, to us, you are." Katarin's eyes were welling up again.

Elena reached out and melted into her mother's outstretched arms. Despite how much she wished it could all go away, she knew a kiss or a hug could not fix it. She had to come to terms with her adoption, with her parents not being her own flesh and blood. And yet, she found it hard to tear herself from her mother's warm arms.

Conflicting emotions washed over her: betrayal, anger, fear, and greatest of all, confusion. Her parents had been lying to her since she could remember. But yet, feeling her mother's warm embrace, seeing her cry, understanding how much she hurt, she couldn't bear it. Elena didn't know what to think anymore. She felt numb, like she'd lost her father all over again. Except now she'd lost both parents.

All these ideas passed in the blink of an eye, while she soaked in the love from her mother's hug. She'd already lost her father. She couldn't really bear losing her mother as well. Elena knew she wouldn't be able to go through such a loss again so soon. Her heart ached.

After what seemed an eternity, Elena came to a decision. Her mother was her mother, no matter what her biology suggested. She cared for her when she was sick, bandaged her boo-boos, helped her with her homework, and sat up long nights with her when she had nightmares. Did it really matter their blood—their genes—didn't match? Did it change the relationship they'd had with one another?

"It's okay, Mom," she said with a sniff. She leaned back out of the hug and threw her arms around her mother in consolation. "No matter what," Elena said, "you will always be my mom. Nothing can ever change the fact."

After they broke their embrace, Elena turned to Alec, then back to her mother. "Now," she said in a voice laced with a heavy dose of skepticism, "what's this nonsense about me not being human?"

Hands shaking, Katarin paused. "Sweetie, before your father died, he tested your DNA. His tests discovered your DNA is not human."

"Wait," Elena exclaimed, "if I'm not human, then what the hell am I?" *As if finding out I'm adopted isn't enough? What the hell is their problem? How could it even be possible?* It wasn't like she had wings or anything.

Alec spoke up. "You are one of us," he responded. "A Daimon. The last Daimon."

"I don't believe you," Elena said to Alec with a joking lilt to her voice. "There is no way I am one of you."

She shook her head at the ridiculousness of his suggestion. Even despite what she herself had seen, believing in the existence of these Daimon creatures defied reason. Now he expected her to believe she could be one of them?

She turned to her mother. "Mom? You're joking, right?"

Katarin shook her head studying the table.

Elena's stomach sank. Elena sighed in exasperation and stared off into space. After a few minutes of tense silence she finally spoke. "How did this happen?" she asked. "How can I be a Daimon?"

Alec smiled at her, taking her hand in his. They were warm and comforting. She wanted to be angry with him. He'd betrayed her by not being forthright. She'd let herself be betrayed by this beautiful stranger. But even as she fumed inside, she could not resist his smile or his sapphire eyes.

"Elena, you've been a part of my life a fraction longer than your parents. I delivered you to the adoption agency. We received you when you were a day old and were told you were a very important Daimon child. We were entrusted with the responsibility to keep you as far away from our enemies, those people who are chasing you, as possible. So, we did the one thing we figured would keep you safest. You see, the Opposition has little regard for human life. They consider humans to be little better than swine. The most logical solution, as far as we were concerned, was to place you with a human family.

"So," Alec continued, "we contacted an adoption agency and offered to give them a sizeable donation if they helped us expedite the process. They were very helpful, and even provided us several of their best files to review. When we saw your parents' information, we felt they would be a perfect match."

"After making sure you were safe in their family," he said, "we stayed involved in their lives to make sure you remained hidden from the Opposition. A handful of us had been entrusted with the secret of your existence, so we made sure not to involve any other Daimones in our mission. We alone were the ones who knew what and where you were. To all others you seemed to be a normal human child. And it's how we wanted to keep it."

"Wait a second, here," Katarin interjected, anger spilling from her lips. "Are you telling me you Daimones have been meddling in our lives since we adopted Elena?"

"There have been three of us, and we all took active roles in your lives," he replied. To Elena, he said, "Many of us worked alongside your father in his laboratory."

Katarin interrupted again, "Really? Who were they?"

"Drs. Kotwas and Romanova," Alec replied, and Katarin raised her eyebrows in amazement. "Both of your father's supervisors were played by my parents. I took a more recent role as one of his research assistants. In fact," he said as his eyes slid to Katarin, "it's how I first met your mother and why she recognized me. We knew each other through your father's work."

"Anyways," he said trying to restore his derailed explanation, "while working alongside him I tried as hard as I could to dissuade your father from testing your DNA. But, try as I did, he was determined to figure out if there were any latent medical issues he should be concerned about with you. You were adopted and he knew nothing of your medical history. He persisted and his concern for you spurred the most important discovery of his career. He found evidence of our DNA."

Elena finally broke in, shaking as she spoke. "Wait a minute. You knew my father found my DNA. You knew I was different and you did nothing to protect him? You let him get killed?"

"Your father's research uncovered evidence of our DNA. He told his discovery to a handful of people," he replied. "I was not one of them. If he had told me about it, I would have done anything to save him. Your father was a good man and a great friend. But, unfortunately, he didn't say anything. There was nothing I could do. His death was as much a shock to me as it was to you and your mother."

"But if he discovered Daimones existed, why did they kill him?"

"It's really quite simple," Alec responded. "Daimones have been in hiding for thousands of years. Long ago, many of the world's early cultures welcomed our kind, and in turn, many of our kind enjoyed helping humans. However, not all of our kind shared a desire to live in peace with humans. Some believed humans were an inferior race who should be forced into servitude. Because of these conflicting views, our kind is embroiled in a heated war lasting several millennia. If knowledge of the existence of Daimones, or the war, were to be publicized..."

"Then the whole race would be in danger and their efforts at enslaving humanity would be lost," Elena finished the idea.

Alec nodded.

She glared at him, memories of the day her father died flooding back to her. A lump formed in her throat, and her eyes stung with emerging tears. But she'd had enough crying for today and wanted to move past it all. What Alec had told her made sense. She didn't like it, but it made perfect sense.

She and her mom both knew he'd been working on a huge project having to do with some new and interesting genetic code he'd discovered. Elena had overheard him telling her mother about it one night. He'd told her it would shake the foundations of conventional science. She didn't understand what he'd meant by it, but knew he'd been so busy with the project she never saw him anymore. Working almost nonstop, he used to sleep at work on a cot the company provided him. Toward the end, he'd been gone an entire week.

"You must believe me," Alec implored. "Your father was a good friend to me. I would have done anything to protect him and your family. And I will do anything I can to keep you safe now. It has been and will always be my sworn duty to protect you." Pride filled his voice as he spoke, but she also heard something more there also.

Elena nodded. She believed him and understood he did what he could to keep them safe. She couldn't blame him for her father's death. The Opposition were to blame. They were the deserving targets of her anger.

Alec paused for a few moments before continuing, "As I am sure you can guess, the Opposition is very well connected with a wide web of informants. Once your father began to spread his discovery to some of his older colleagues, it must have gotten back to an Opposition agent because not long after he started to broadcast his discovery I found him dead in his lab."

Elena's jaw dropped to the floor. "Wait a minute! You found him?"

Alec nodded, staring at his folded hands resting on the kitchen table. "I contacted your mother a few weeks afterwards and discussed his death with her."

Katarin cut in. "I remember," she said. "You said you wanted to discuss some things with me. Then you told me you were the one who first arrived at the lab. You were so certain something devious was going on and kept asking me questions about his research."

"And it's a good thing I did," Alec said. "I learned from your mother he had shared his discovery with her. She knew you were not human. And so I was able to be more open with her about who we are. I was also able to enlist her aid in trying to keep you safe and hidden."

"Luckily," he continued, "your mother is the last human, aside from your father, to know it was your DNA he studied. On the day I found him, I was able to search his office more thoroughly. He had not left any information indicating the source of the blood sample. But my search revealed the sample itself was missing."

"I was fairly confident the Opposition had taken it," Alec told them. "But I also knew it would take the Opposition quite a while to discover who the sample's source was. As a precaution, I followed you to school in order to watch over and protect you. For the past two years you never once saw me on campus. I don't understand why it was this year," he said, fidgeting, "you finally noticed me."

Elena blushed, thinking of his stunning eyes.

Inside she wondered, *had he really been on campus the past few years?* Those eyes, how could she have missed them? They were so beautiful!

"I, uh..." Elena stammered. "I'm not quite sure. I think it had something to do with the book you were reading," she lied. "I think it piqued my curiosity and drew me in."

She could feel herself blush harder; she had to change the subject, fast. "So, why me? Why not one of his colleagues?"

"According to my informants, many of his colleagues have already been exhausted. You are next on their list to question to find out anything about your father's research. But..." He let the sentence trail off. When he spoke again, his voice had taken on a much more ominous tone. "But when they learn what you are, they will certainly try to kill you. They will try to kill you because you should not exist. You are a new Daimon in a world where none should exist. And you are on the verge of awakening."

"Awakening? What do you mean?"

"It is the term we use to describe the development of a newborn's abilities," Alec explained. "The abilities awaken within the newborn. During this time, there is no telling what the newborn will be capable of. They can be very dangerous."

"Okay, but what I don't understand is who is this Opposition?"

Alec leaned against his chair back for a few moments.

"Who is the Opposition?" he repeated her question. He placed his forefinger against his lips. Another short pause, and then he began to explain. "There is a reason classical literature and art have portrayed images of angels and demons locked in mortal combat. It is because two groups of Daimones have been at war with each other for most of human history. If you remember when we spoke during the ride here from your school, I told you we were once viewed as humanity's advisors and guardians."

Elena nodded.

"Well," he continued, "then you will remember some of our kind want to enslave humans. There is a very strong faction among us who believe since we are stronger and immortal, we should be treated as gods. They want to enslave humanity. We view them as the Opposition to everything we have worked so hard to build. They are the opposition to freedom, to choice, to humanity."

"The wars began," he said, "in the Mediterranean. And they became the stuff of legends, spreading over Greece, Turkey, Israel, Syria, and all the way through the Middle East to Iran. Most of humanity's greatest epic tales, in fact, have stemmed from these battles. In time the legends of nearly all human history grew from these wars."

"The fabled siege of Troy," Alec explained, "was, in fact, part of this war. One Daimon lord sought to destroy his nearest adversary and concocted a story about his human wife being kidnapped by a rival state. The humans rallied behind him and together they sought to destroy the other Daimon lord and his domain. The sad truth was he had no human wife."

"The wars of Roman conquest, the Crusades, even the modern world wars were battles between Daimon lords—between those loyal to protecting our bonds with humanity and the Opposition. Of course, humans have become the unfortunate pawns in this great war of ours. They are often tricked into believing the blood they shed would be of great benefit to them. But it never is. Humans merely suffer the consequences. Daimon lords rarely ever perish in battle."

"So how many Daimones exist?" Elena asked. "I mean, how many are there?"

"An interesting question," Alec replied. "And, in fact, it is a very poignant one. As I mentioned, the Daimones live a very long time. For all intents and purposes, we are immortal. We do not age. We are not affected by common earthly illnesses. As you saw earlier from the gunshots, our bodies are very tough, and we heal very quickly when we are injured. However, it is not impossible to kill a Daimon. A well-placed missile or bomb could easily kill and incinerate one of our kind.

"There are not many of us remaining in this world," he continued. "Right now, I would guess not many more than two hundred of us, and our numbers dwindle more each day. You see, we cannot reproduce."

Alec stopped speaking, his face frozen in a mask of fear. Elena had seen this reaction before, there was something wrong. Elena and Katarin turned from Alec to each other, then back to Alec again. As she opened her mouth to ask what had happened, the buzzing cocktail-party din she'd earlier heard filled her ears. She and Alec exchanged glances and she instantly knew this did not bode well.

Alec spoke at last. "Sorry," he said with a distinct note of concern, "but we need to stop right there." Rising from his chair, he held his hand out to Elena. "We have to leave," he told her. "Now."

Elena didn't question or protest. She knew it, too. Their time had run out, the Opposition had found them. They needed to run again.

Alec turned to Katarin as Elena stood from her chair. "Katarin," he said, "you have to go into hiding. Somewhere nobody would ever think to find you. Don't tell your job. Don't tell anyone. Disappear."

Turning back to Elena, Alec said, "Elena, you need to come with me." Another bout of the din invaded her mind, much louder this time.

"We need to get you as far from here as possible," he said. "We need to keep you safe."

Elena began to protest. She couldn't leave her mother by herself; not with some society of ancient immortal beasts chasing after her. Alec had anticipated her objection and told her, "Don't worry. They want you. I'll be able to get in touch with her. She'll be all right."

Alec walked over to the counter beneath the telephone. There were several pens and a notepad kept there for taking messages. He tore off a sheet of paper, wrote down a name and address, and then handed it to Katarin. "Go here," he told her pointing to the paper. "Contact this person. He'll be able to keep you safe."

He turned back to Elena, placed his hands on her shoulders, and looked her square in the eye. "Don't worry, Elena," he told her. "She'll be in good hands. You have to trust me."

Elena nodded. She trusted Alec but couldn't help worrying about her mother. Even after everything she'd been through tonight, she still loved and cared for the woman who had been the center of her world for so much of her life.

My God! Elena wondered, *Who am I? Why is this happening?* She wanted to cry.

Alec grabbed her hand. The same hands, which had earlier been soft and comforting, were now hard and strong. "They will be here soon." To Katarin he said, "You have to go."

Elena turned to her mother. Both women had tears welling in their eyes. "Mom," she said suppressing a sob, "promise me you will stay safe."

"I promise," Katarin said. "Now hurry!"

Elena's Camry sped through the darkness of night, its speedometer pinned as far as it would go. Alec's control over the hurtling mass of steel and plastic amazed her. She tried to watch the world speed by, but found it impossible to focus her eyes fast enough to discern patterns in the inky blur.

"Is my mother really going to be okay?" Elena asked. It had been over an hour since they had parted ways, and she'd refrained from asking the question out of concern it would distract Alec too much. But her concern for her mother trumped her concern for Alec's control of the speeding car.

"Yes," he replied matter-of-factly, "your mother will be fine." Elena heard a light buzzing again and froze. Alec turned his head.

A gasp escaped from Elena's lips. "Keep your eyes on the road," she exclaimed. "God! Are you trying to kill us or something?"

He chuckled under his breath. After a few seconds, he turned his focus back to the road ahead of them.

Nearly another half hour passed before Elena could no longer stand the silence in the car. Her head started throbbing. Conversation should at least get her mind off the oncoming headache. "Where are we going?" she asked

"I can't tell you."

"Oh?" she asked. "Why?"

"Because," he replied, "I'm not sure if your thoughts are being..."

Alec's mouth moved, but she couldn't hear the words as a thousand white-hot needles of pain tore into her head.

She rubbed her forehead fiercely. "Ouch!" she groaned. "Oh God, what the hell is this?"

Alec's smile faded. "What's wrong?" he asked with no humor. Did she hear concern in his voice, too? No. It sounded like fear.

"I'm not sure," she told him. "I think it's a headache, but..."

"Crap," Alec mumbled as he pressed the accelerator even harder to the floor. Elena never imagined it would be possible for her car to go any faster, but somehow Alec had managed to squeeze a few more horses from the already screaming engine. "They're coming," he said. "I can hear their din. We need to find somewhere to hide out. And quick." The Camry hurtled down the empty highway.

She is near, Elena heard a voice say with unusual clarity, *and he is with her.* The speaker had an unfamiliar voice. She couldn't explain why, but the sound of it scared her. Her body began to tremble.

Do not worry about him, a second voice said. *We can deal with the youngling easily.*

Do not underestimate the youngling, replied the first voice. *He understands far more than you think.*

"Alec," she asked, turning to face him, "who is the youngling?" Elena's simple act of speaking banished the voices from her mind.

"Where did you hear it mentioned?" he asked. A slight crack in Alec's voice signaled his obvious concern.

"I heard them say it," she replied. "Two voices, talking in my head. They said they could deal with the youngling easily."

He turned and stared her in the face again. The emotion painted in his eyes scared her. "What do you mean you heard them say it?" he asked.

Elena never figured Alec would be so easy to scare.

"Two voices were talking," she responded. "They were louder than all of the others I've been hearing since this morning. The others had been more like being at a cocktail party. Lots of voices, but you can't really make out what any one is saying. But these two were different. They were clear—almost like they were seated right here in the car with us. I heard them talking to each other in my head." After a pause she added, "Why do you ask?"

"Because," he told her, "I didn't hear a thing. I haven't heard them since I sped up." He turned his attention away from the road again and studied her face. "You shouldn't be able to hear them if they aren't projecting their thoughts to you purposely. We can control our thoughts and project them into other people's minds. But they ordinarily shouldn't be heard."

"Well, I heard them," she replied crossing her arms across her chest, "and it's what they said." She couldn't believe he was going to debate this with her. She paused and then decided to change the subject, "So now, who is the youngling?"

Alec sighed, turning his attention back to the road before him. "It's me," he said. "I am the youngling."

"Wait," Elena replied, "aren't you like more than three thousand years old? Why do they call you the youngling?"

"Because I am, or rather was, the youngest of my kind," he told her. "Until you came along."

The words struck her like a weighted boxing glove. "What do you mean you were the youngest?" she asked.

"Like I said," he replied. "I was the last born of my kind. I was born more than three thousand years ago in a place called Mycenae. A few months after my birth, a terrible plague decimated our numbers across the world. There are almost no records of this epidemic ever happening, but mainly because it didn't affect humans as severely as it did our kind. You see, it mutated some of our kind into strange aberrations and made the remainder of us sterile. Neither our females nor our males could produce any more offspring. For the past few thousand years, our numbers have dwindled through a host of causes. And as this war continues to rage on, more of us die each day."

"This is why they all want me?" she asked. "For my DNA?"

"Close," he responded, "but there's more. You see, you are the first of Daimon blood born in many millennia. As far as anyone can tell, you are not sterile like the rest of us. In terms of your potential for the future of our race, you alone could produce a whole new generation of Daimones."

She was stunned into silence. Was this the reason he protected her? To be bred? To spawn a litter of Daimon puppies?

She narrowed her eyes and studied Alec. "Why are you helping me?" she asked.

"No," he told her. "I am trying to help you because I swore to protect you. And..."

The silence between them stretched on, but Alec never finished his idea. Alone with her thoughts, she realized she no longer heard the voices in her head. She tried not to think about the words Alec left unspoken, but they kept creeping into her mind. When they did, she tried to banish them by staring at the trees whipping by at alarming speed in the darkness.

"I think we have lost the ones following us," he said to her after a short while of silence.

Elena did not respond to his comment.

"Can you please explain to me what you meant by hearing their thoughts, again?" he asked.

Again, she did not respond.

"It baffles me," he said, "you could hear them. You should not have any of your abilities for another few decades. And besides, Daimones have always been able to shield their minds from others. Have you ever heard any of mine?"

"Well, yeah," she said. "You have spoken to me in my mind, remember?"

"Right," he replied. "But what I am asking about is whether or not you have ever heard my thoughts beyond what we've spoken. Can you hear what I am thinking now?"

She tried to pick his brain but failed to hear anything. "No," she replied. "I can't."

Alec sighed in relief. She almost didn't want to think about what he didn't want her to know.

Alec pulled off the highway onto a main road. Several quick turns later, they were on a remote back road. "I am not certain this is the most prudent course of action," he told her, "but we need to lay low for a while."

Nearly an hour and several other back roads later, the car pulled up in front of a small log cabin. Elena didn't recognize where they were, but it seemed like they had been driving down rough dirt roads for hours. She worried the shocks on her poor car would either give up, or mire down in some impassable terrain.

"Where are we?" Elena asked.

"We are with someone safe," Alec replied. "We should be able to hide out here for a while."

"Are you sure you can trust them?"

"I am positive," he responded with a wink. "After all, she is my mother."

Alec climbed out of the car and walked toward the front door. Elena surveyed the place from the virtual safety of her car's passenger seat.

The dense woods were dark as pitch. If it were not for the fact the headlights of the car painted the dwelling with light, it too would have been pitch black. The cabin had a basic form with a door centered on its front gable–wall, flanked on either side by small awning windows. From the appearance of the place, it had at best one bedroom and one main room. Her hopes for working heat, indoor plumbing, and a hot shower were fading.

"Is she sleeping?" Elena asked.

"No," Alec replied with a slight grin, "she is not asleep. Our kind requires very little sleep." Alec headed toward the cabin. "Come," he called to Elena, "she is waiting."

Elena slipped out of the car and walked toward the place on shaky legs.

Bring her in, a new male voice said in her head. *I can feel her presence. The Power within her is awakening. She is crucial to our plans, to our survival. I need to meet with her.* The strong, clear voice comforted her, though the sheer strength of it made her head hurt.

Elena stopped dead in her tracks halfway to the door. The hackles on her neck stood at attention. "Alec," she said, "why did you bring me here?"

He paused. He furrowed his brow and asked, "Why do you ask?"

"Because," Elena replied, "I heard what he said to you."

Alec stared at her with a mask of bewilderment. "What are you talking about," he asked.

His tone suggested honesty. But how could he not hear the voice? He brought her here. Her ire began to percolate.

"What do you mean?" she asked him. The anger building inside seeped through despite her best efforts to conceal it. "I heard what he said. What did he mean?"

Alec's jaw hung open. "Elena," he said in a low voice, "I truly have no idea what you are talking about. What do you mean? Who?"

"I distinctly heard a man tell you to bring me to him," Elena countered. She crossed her arms. "Seriously," she demanded, "tell me what's happening before I take another step forward."

The man spoke to me, dear, said a clear, sweet female voice in her mind. *Those words were not meant for Alec*. Elena could see a woman standing in the open doorway of the small cabin. *You already have very powerful talents,* the woman continued. *Not many of our eldest are capable of snooping on others' minds, let alone a newborn.* There was a pause. *Your talents aren't perfect, though. It's odd you were incapable of hearing my response to him.*

Elena glanced at Alec and then back at the small woman standing in the front doorway.

The elfin woman stood barely five feet tall. Remarkably young, she possessed rare effortless beauty with short-cropped reddish-brown hair and almond-shaped chestnut-colored eyes. She had an intensity in her, however, suggesting immense power.

"Come in, Elena," the woman said. "My name is Ori. You will be safe here from the ones who are hunting you. I have many sets of eyes and ears in the forest who will notify me before anyone can even come close to this place."

Elena turned to Alec with a puzzled expression. In a hushed voice, she said, "I thought you told me there were no more females among the Daimones."

"No, Elena," he replied. "I mentioned nearly the entire Daimon race had been rendered sterile by a terrible disease. Ori, too, is incapable of producing offspring. There are females, but none can produce any more offspring."

Elena nodded, turning back to Ori. She gave the woman as warm a smile as she could muster given her feelings of unease about the encounter. After a short pause, Elena continued on her way toward the front door.

"Hello Elena," Ori said. "It has been a long time since we last saw you. We have been expecting you."

"What do you mean, *we*?" Elena asked.

Ori laughed. It was a sound full of jubilance and mirth. "I mean the few of us who knew of your existence. We have been waiting a long time to see how you would develop. You have to understand it has been more than three thousand years since a Daimon was born. We have been very excited to see what abilities you would have." She turned to Alec, "So, does she have wings? Can she fly?"

Alec shook his head. "Not yet," he responded. "It seems her abilities begin to awaken. It may take some time before we see what she can really do."

As they were speaking, Elena stepped into the cabin. Her hopes of a shower were dashed on the wide-plank floor. The whole cabin consisted of a single room heated by an old wood-burning cook stove. There were sparse small pieces of furniture scattered about, including rough wooden chairs, a small kitchen table, and a patchy area rug. She sighed.

"What's the matter?" Ori asked. "Is there something wrong?" She had a warm, soothing voice.

Elena's cheeks burned in embarrassment. "No, there's nothing wrong, I was—"

Ori chuckled. "Let me guess," she said. "You were expecting something a little more comfortable than this? Some creature comforts, like running hot water, a shower, a microwave, refrigeration."

Elena blushed and nodded.

A wide grin overcame Ori's face. "Follow me, dear." Ori walked over to the far end of the room and lifted a corner of the area rug there. Underneath, a wooden trap door had been cut into the floor. Ori lifted it and then stepped down through the opening onto a ladder.

Halfway down, Ori stopped and glanced up. "Okay, the trap door is a little cliché," she smiled, "but it works." She continued down.

Elena climbed down the dark shaft into an even darker cellar cut into the local bedrock. It took several minutes for her eyes to adjust to the lack of illumination. A narrow board-and-batten door had been inset into one of the walls.

"Please excuse the darkness down here," Ori said. "Our eyes are much stronger than human eyes are." Ori opened the door and stepped inside.

The brightness of the space beyond made Elena's eyes sting at the change in light from the cellar. She gasped as the room came into focus. It seemed like the foyer to a royal palace. The immense open-plan space occupied about the same space as her house back home. The walls were dressed in some kind of reflective white metallic cover magnifying the light from the fluorescent fixtures on the ceiling. Plush carpet covered the floor. Decorative white concrete columns splayed outward where they met the ceiling, forming an interconnected series of ribbed vaults.

Familiar works of art by Monet, Van Gogh, and Renoir adorned the walls. As she stepped farther into the room, she could see the art was actually not so familiar. These paintings were similar to but not the same as many of the more popular works she had seen.

In response to Elena's fascination with the artwork, Ori spoke. "Those are all one-of-a kind originals. I had them all commissioned personally. They are my pride and joy." She had a sweet smile. "I love art."

Elena kept surveying the room. The furnishings were modern in style and comprised several zones. A conversation pit consisted of a blocky white couch and chairs surrounding a black coffee table, while farther down the room, a similar setup at a smaller scale focused around a plasma-screen television hanging from the wall. This must have been a media center. Two doors were situated on the wall to her right, with another located on the far wall across the room.

"Follow me," Ori said to Elena. "I will show you where you can take a shower." She gestured for Elena to follow. The doorway on the far side of the room led to the beginning of a long corridor. As they headed to the right, she noted how similar the walls were to the room they had left—stark white and covered with rare pieces of original artwork. Three doors were located along the right wall of the hallway.

Ori gestured toward the first door. "You can have this first room here to the right. It has its own bathroom, and there should be a fully stocked linen closet. I may have some clothing available for you."

Elena stepped into the room and plopped herself down on the bed. She didn't even stop to survey her surroundings. After a few minutes, she made her way over to the first door she could find and happened upon the bathroom. A small closet door did in fact have a full store of white linens behind it. She pulled some out, grabbed a bottle of shampoo and conditioner from the shelf, and started the shower. She waited a few minutes for the steam to build in the shower before disrobing and stepping into the warm cascade.

Stepping out of the tub and onto the tile floor, she found a small pile of clothes left for her including a pair of jeans, a white T-shirt, and some clean underwear. A note on top said, "Leave your dirty clothes and towels in the bathroom. They will be cleaned later. O—"

The fresh change of clothes smelled nice and felt great. It made her feel much more human. She chuckled at the irony. She was feeling *more human,* and could be no further from the truth.

She looked at the bed and it called to her. Crawling from the footboard up to the pillows, she tucked herself under the covers. Gone from her mind was any danger or urgency. Tomorrow they would be on the run again. But in the meantime, she welcomed sleep's warm embrace.

part two

the search for the elder

Chapter 9

Elena woke and rubbed the crust of sleep from her eyes. The sound of soft footsteps coming down the hallway startled her. Her heart hammered in her chest. *Have they found us?* she wondered, moving herself to the edge of the bed. The memory of the two men from Alec's roadside fight sprang to mind. *No, they couldn't have found us here.* Her breathing quickened. The steps stopped in front of her door. She slid back toward the headboard and swung her legs over the side of the bed. Her body tensed, ready to spring for cover at the first hint of trouble.

The handle turned. As the door opened, soft light leaked into the room. She leaned herself forward, letting her feet touch the cold hard floor.

"Hello?" Elena called out toward the doorway, her voice trembling.

"Hello," called a soothing and familiar voice. "Good morning, sleepyhead. Did you sleep well?" Elena could feel the tension in her body slipping away. Her heart still beat fast, but now for other reasons. Even in the dim light from the hallway outside, she had never been happier to see his gorgeous face appear before her. He greeted her as if they were best buds.

"Yeah," she responded to him, her mumbled voice still heavy and garbled from slumber. "How long have I been asleep?"

"Almost a whole day," Alec replied. "We were starting to get worried about you. It's actually not morning. It's about three o'clock in the afternoon."

Elena's eyebrows snapped up in surprise. "Oh. Wow!" she exclaimed. "I can't believe how tired I still am."

"I could imagine," Alec responded. "The stress of the past two days' events alone would be enough to wear on you. Then add to it the fact you are beginning to awaken..." He let his sentence trail off.

Standing, a rumble escaped her stomach. She blushed and crossed her arms over her belly. "Sorry," she said. "I guess I'm a little bit hungry, too."

Alec's face lit up with a smile. "I figured as much," he said. "What would you like to eat?"

She smiled. "I guess. I mean, I don't want to impose on Ori or anything."

"It's no imposition," Alec replied. "Ori has plenty of food available. She owns a pretty expansive farm. She has all the eggs, milk, beef, and cereal grains anyone could ever want." He gave her a wink and said, "Not to mention, she is a fantastic cook. She can whip something up for you in no time."

Elena considered this a few moments. Her growling stomach refused to quiet down, but she didn't want to wear out her host's hospitality. "I guess tell her to surprise me."

"Okay," he said with a laugh. "Are you sure?" he asked.

No. She nodded to him without saying anything further.

Alec pointed to the far corner of the room. "Ori also laid out some more clothes for you and washed the clothes you came here in," he said. "They're all on a chair over there." Alec turned to leave the room. "I'll leave you so you can have some privacy to get yourself together," he said over his shoulder.

"Okay, thanks!" Elena exclaimed. As his foot crossed the threshold to the hallway, she called out, "Oh, one more thing. How do I turn on the light?" Alec reached his hand inside the doorway and flipped a switch next to the door.

Elena scanned the room and took a few minutes to absorb it all again. She decided to wake herself up with another hot shower. After slipping on the fresh clothes, she answered a knock at her door. Alec waited in the hall, and together they headed back to the dining room.

Ori had prepared two soft-boiled eggs, toast made from fresh-baked bread, bacon, and cantaloupe. It all tasted wonderful. A large coffee pot sat on the table, the taste of which she savored like nectar from the gods. Alec had already eaten, but didn't seem to mind sitting and watching her enjoy the fruits of Ori's labor.

She hadn't had a chance to see the dining room the night before. The dining room table itself seemed to go on forever. Decorated much like the rest of Ori's place, it must have been large enough to seat two dozen people without bumping elbows. The chairs were white metal with molded glass seats. Despite the hard materials, the seats were quite comfortable.

The plates were platinum trimmed with gold. Not the sort of thing for use in a microwave. She turned to Alec. She had been so focused on eating. Not a word had been spoken between them.

"Alec," Elena asked, "why does Ori have a farm?"

"Why don't you ask her?" he replied with a grin.

"But she's not here," Elena responded noting she had not seen Ori at all since she awoke. "Where is she?"

He tapped his finger to his head and said, "Ask her yourself."

Elena projected: *Ori, are you there?*

No answer.

Elena tried again, this time while focusing on a mental image of Ori as she had seen her last night. *Ori, are you there?*

Yes, dear, came the clear mental response. *I am.*

Elena smiled, delighted to learn she could control her thoughts by focusing and directing them to a particular person.

Why do you have a farm? Elena asked. *I mean, you have been walking this earth for thousands of years...*

More years than you can imagine, interrupted Ori.

Wow! She couldn't even imagine such longevity. To have walked the earth so long ago the limit of human civilization had focused itself in a handful of established cities. *Why don't you live in a mansion somewhere, or on your own island? Why a farm?*

Because I like farming, came Ori's reply. *I own all of the land in this area for more than five miles in every direction. I own mountains, forests, and streams, and provide a place for all of my friends to live without having to fear they will be killed by a hunter.*

What friends? Elena asked with mixed fear and excitement. *You mean more Daimones? They are hunted?*

Elena could hear Ori chuckle in her head. *No, dear,* Ori replied, *I mean my forest friends. You see, I have a special gift somewhat like yours. Like you can hear the minds of our kind at will, I can hear the minds of all manner of animals and fish. I can communicate with them. They can also hear me. Because of my abilities, I am called the Angel of the Forests in human myths, Orifiel.*

Elena found it bizarre to be sitting in Ori's immense dining room holding a conversation with her. And yet, no word had been truly spoken. She marveled at this ability she had developed and the amazing speed with which a conversation could be carried. Words didn't travel at the speed of sound, but at the speed of thought.

As she reflected on the implications of such speedy communication, another voice, not Alec's, entered her mind. It sounded like the other voice she had heard last night. The powerful male voice. *Orifiel,* the voice commanded, *you must bring the girl to me. She and I have much to discuss.*

To Ori, Elena asked: *Who was speaking?*

The Elder.

Who is the Elder? Elena continued.

He is the first of our kind. He is our progenitor.

Why does he want to see me?

Because you represent the salvation of our kind.

Elena felt numb. *What do you mean? How could I represent salvation?*

Ori paused. *I have already said too much,* she said at last. *Perhaps, this is something for the Elder to explain. And he most assuredly has other things to discuss with you as well.*

What kind of things? Elena pushed.

The Elder alone may answer the question.

Why doesn't he talk to me, then?

Because, Orifiel responded, *he is not familiar with you or your mind. It is difficult for us to detect or contact people we have never met. But as you noticed, some may overhear a conversation not intended for them.*

Elena's faced burned with embarrassment.

She heard Ori's voice again, but this time much weaker. *Elder,* she said, *Alec will bring the girl to you.*

After a pause, she added, *Alec, you must bring Elena to the old city.*

Alec replied. *If it is the Elder's wish, Mother, then of course I will. But then we must get going soon and keep the element of surprise on our side.*

Ori replied, *Yes, I agree you must keep moving. I have sensed their presence nearby. My friends have warned me three unfamiliar Daimones are inbound to my farm. They are coming for her. Somehow they have managed to find her.*

I am not sure it was a difficult task for them, Mother, Alec replied. *They probably figured out yours was the safest and closest place for me to bring her. It was a matter of time.* Alec paused, and then added, *I am glad she had the chance to rest. Perhaps it has helped move along her awakening.*

Yes, perhaps, Ori responded. Her voice took on a lighter, teasing tone. *I see your attachment to her has grown much stronger, son.*

Alec replied with silence.

Ori continued. *Let us hope her powers develop fast and strong for all our sakes.* She paused a moment. *Alec,* she finally added, *you must find the Elder and bring her to him before they get to her. If they find her, they may bring her to their Mistress.* With a tone Elena would have expected of a commanding officer, Ori then ordered Alec, *Go to Paris and seek out our ally there. He should be able to find the Elder. You cannot fail in this task.*

Yes, Mother, Alec replied. *I understand.*

Alec turned to face Elena. His cheeks reddened a little as his eyes fell upon her. Was he blushing? Alec took her hand in his. "We need to take a trip."

Elena smirked. "I heard."

Alec stammered. "W—wait a minute, what do you mean you heard?" His voice had a hint of embarrassment.

Elena nodded.

Deciding not to embarrass him further, she changed the topic by asking, "When do we leave?"

"As soon as possible."

Alec's muffled mental voice once again sounded in her mind. *Mother,* he said, *please take care. These Daimones are ruthless.*

It would appear their Mistress is getting desperate in her bid for power.

Ori replied, *Alec. Don't worry about her. I have nothing to fear from the Opposition or its leader. I have lived many millennia and can handle any pups they send for me. Now go. And take care of Elena.* Then, as an afterthought, Elena heard the woman say, *She is truly precious cargo.*

I will. Alec replied. *I love you.*

I love you too, son. And you too, Elena.

Elena answered, *Thank you, Ori. I will always be grateful for your kindnesses.*

The two left the dining room to prepare for their journey. Within a short time, they had put together bags with clothes. In the kitchen, Elena packed food. Alec opened a flour canister on the counter and pulled out a thick wad of cash.

Alec smiled at the wide-eyed expression on Elena's face. "We're going to need this," he told her.

"How much is there?" The words had come out before she could stop them.

Alec glanced at the wad and thumbed through it. "A lot." He stuffed the cash into his pocket. "When you have lived as long as we have, you tend to accumulate a little bit of savings," he said to her. "Don't worry about asking about it. It's a natural reaction." He paused. "We will need a new identity for you if we are going to get to Europe undetected."

Within half an hour, they were driving back down the same country road they drove in on. They'd taken one of Ori's new trucks. Weaving through the back roads, a cloud of dust stretched behind them.

"Where are we?" Elena asked.

"The farm is an hour outside of Buffalo," Alec replied. He pondered for a moment before adding, "A contact of mine in Buffalo can get us some new identities. From there we are going to take a plane. We need to stay under the radar."

They drove on for about forty more minutes. The truck turned onto Walden Avenue, then onto one of the smaller backstreets, Koons Avenue. They stopped in front of a small house.

Alec stepped out of the truck, came around its front, and opened Elena's door. "Now let me do the talking," he told her. "This man does business with all sorts of shady characters all the time. We cannot afford to let slip where it is we will be going because I am sure our counterparts have dealings with him as well." Almost at a whisper, he added, "You see, he has a specialized skill."

Elena hadn't expected Alec to be acquainted with the seedier side of things. Given his youthful appearance, she still considered him a college student rather than a three-thousand-year-old man. To hear him speak so comfortably about buying fake ID's seemed out of character, even surreal. In response to his direction, she nodded. Together they walked up the property's brick walkway. The neighborhood had some time ago given up quaint for urban blight. Lots where houses once stood were barren holes between rundown homes. The neighborhood seemed, for the most part, as if it had been abandoned in some silent apocalypse. She clung to Alec's arm without thinking, and could feel his muscles tense beneath his shirt. Again, her skin tingled with electricity where it touched his.

She studied the house as they approached. It had two stories, and a porch spread across the front façade. The little paint still clinging to the home appeared scratched and peeling. One of the upper floor windows seemed as if it had been cracked by a stray bullet, and the visible parts of the roof were either covered in moss or missing large sections of shingles.

The yard held piles of empty beer cans, and it seemed the local stray animal population left a litter box where a lawn had once been. The bare soil supported not so much as a single weed.

As they approached the front door, Elena whispered to Alec with a slight chuckle, "So, I guess business is good?"

"Don't be fooled," Alec replied. "This man is actually a top-notch attorney with a very large bank account. This place is for show and to attract his seedier clientele."

Alec rapped on the front door. As he did, it rattled like it would fall right off the hinges. Not because of his strength but because of the rot falling from the doorframe.

She heard shuffling behind the door, followed by a series of clicks and scrapes suggesting a large number of locks opening on the other side. After the last click, pregnant silence hung in the air before the door wracked inward on its swollen frame. The rusty hinges creaked as if cued for a horror theme park.

The interior appeared as shabby as the exterior. The doorway contained a short, pudgy man wearing a grease-stained T-shirt and torn jeans. His potbelly poured over the waistband, and she could see he hadn't had a haircut or a shave in several years. Nor had he taken a shower in at least a week, given his matted greasy black hair. Averting her eyes, kind of embarrassed for him, she could see his bare feet were hairy, dirty, and marked by patches of black and purple. It was an understatement to call him slovenly. She could not believe what Alec had told her earlier about him being wealthy or sharp. She would use neither of those words to describe the miscreant standing before her. He didn't have the refinement of an attorney, let alone a wealthy one.

"Jameson. It has been a long time." Alec shook the man's hand. "How are the wife and kids doing?"

Jameson chuckled. "Mr. Henderson. It's good to see you again. My, uh—wife and kids are fine. Of course, they are living with another man on my former Caribbean island. But I can't complain. I still have my business."

Alec paused. "Wait. Adrienne has your island?"

Jameson nodded. "Yes. She took the kids, and my former associate moved in with them." His laugh sounded like the chitter of a chipmunk. "I guess it's what I get for going into business with a criminal."

"I'm sorry to hear it. But you are here at your office. Are you accepting clients?"

"I am sort of, um, semiretired. But for the sake of an old friend..." Jameson stood aside and welcomed them in through the doorway.

The furnishings within the dusky room were sparse, but Elena could definitely make out some basic decorations. There were paintings scattered about the walls, hanging at skewed angles, and a large brass mirror hung on the wall immediately opposite the door. A couple of stiff-back chairs were positioned around a scratched coffee table missing one leg.

"So," Jameson said, "what is it I can get for you this time? Papers, I presume? Are you and your—companion—going somewhere exotic?" Jameson winked at Elena.

"My companion and I will be traveling extensively throughout the U.S. But we may wish to head south to some warmer climates when the temperatures start to fall. We could both use a vacation in the sun." The words dripped silver from his tongue.

"Okay," the man responded. "Travel documents should not be too hard. It will take me about an hour or so. I'll need to take your photos and then if you would like to come back..."

Alec interrupted, "No! We will stay and wait. If it's okay with you. I have always been fascinated watching you at work. It's not every day you get to observe one of the world's greatest forgers."

Jameson's smile reminded her of a gecko's face. She almost expected him to start licking his eyelid.

"Very well, then, my friend."

Something in his voice sounded strange. She didn't trust this man as far as she could throw him. But she did trust Alec. And if his experience with this "Jameson" proved he could be trusted, then she would go along with it. "Let me see what I have in the house to give you two for drinks," Jameson said as he disappeared through a doorway. Alec and Elena sat in relative silence in what proved to be the most uncomfortable chairs she'd ever been in, barely even noticing each other. Elena kept staring around the room, trying to make sense of this place while Alec seemed to be lost in space.

She is here. She had heard the mental voice before but could not place it. She wracked her brain and then gasped as she realized its source. It belonged to one of the men who had been chasing them from the college, the one who tried to make her leave her car. *Our contact will keep them detained until we can arrive,* the voice continued. *He suspects they will be leaving for South America from Buffalo-Niagara International. We should have her in our grasp within a few minutes.*

"Alec," she blurted with obvious panic. "We have to leave." Elena's words pierced the silence in the room. She hadn't realized she'd spoken so loud. "They found us."

"Are you sure?" he asked, "How do you—"

"I heard them," she interrupted. Her hands and voice were shaking as she stood from her seat and grabbed at him. "Jameson must have talked to someone." She tried to whisper, but couldn't quite control the volume of her voice.

Alec held his hand up to stop her from speaking and motioned her to sit. His eyes said she should trust him. Jameson stepped into the room as her body settled onto the chair.

"So, then," he said, "you would like to watch the work of a master?" Jameson gave them an awkward grin. Elena could see a bead of sweat making its way down his forehead.

Alec stood and squared himself up with the man. "Jameson," he asked with a wry smile, "what have you done?"

The man's hand trembled. Additional beads of sweat formed on his head. "My friend, I assure you—"

Alec's eyes narrowed and he crossed his arms in front of him. *"Are you really* my friend, Jameson?"

Jameson hung his head and dropped his hands to his sides. Quick as a flash, they came back up with a 45 automatic pistol, which he pointed at Elena.

"You understand the power these people have," he said. "They can give me my life back. My wealth. My family. I am sorry, Mr. Henderson, but I am, alas, human."

Alec moved with startling speed. In the blink of an eye, he had crossed the room to Jameson, ripped the pistol from his hands, and had him on the floor unconscious. "Let's go," Alec said to Elena, holding out his hand.

Elena's heart tried to pound its way out of her chest. Stunned, she couldn't move as her mind absorbed the fact she had been mere moments from dying.

Alec stepped over and squared up to her. "Elena, we have to get going. They will be here any second. We need to get far away from here."

The numbness cleared from her brain as he released her. She knew he was right. After all, hadn't she been the one to tip him off? She stumbled forward. The far-off buzz of a mental conversation infiltrated her mind and she pumped her legs faster. In the truck a few moments later, they were speeding off down the road. Alec pushed the truck to its limit. The engine protested, but he held the accelerator to the floor. He swerved from back street to main street and then to back street again until he managed to get onto the highway. Within fifteen minutes, he had found his way to the nearby town of Lewiston and a marina nestled along the Niagara River.

They left the truck on the street outside the marina and walked along the docks until Alec spotted his target. "This one," he said as he jumped into a thirty-two-foot cigarette boat. He stopped to help Elena on board and then set to work hot-wiring the ignition. The fans took a few seconds to vent the gas fumes from the engine compartment, and then he tweaked the ignition and started the engines. The roar of the exhaust, though muffled by the water, still roared like a terrible beast. The vibration of the powerful engines working their mounts to the stops made Elena's feet numb.

Alec turned to Elena, "Can you get the lines?"

"The what?" she asked, searching.

He pointed to the ropes stretched between the boat and the docks. "There are several ropes holding us to the slip. Could you please cast them off?"

Elena crawled up to the bow. It took a few stressed moments to understand how the ropes were tied to the moorings, but she undid them and dropped the lines into the water. She quickly moved to the stern and removed those lines as well. As soon as the last line hit the water, Alec goosed the throttle and backed the boat into the river.

"So much for a no wake zone," he commented. He nudged the throttle forward and came about driving the boat north.

"Where are we going?" Elena asked.

"Canada," Alec replied.

"Canada?" Elena exclaimed. "Why are we going to Canada? Won't we need to go through customs to cross the border?"

"We are going to cross the border on the water, and ditch the boat somewhere near Toronto. We're not going through the border checkpoints." He threw the throttle forward, and the craft's bow leapt up out of the water. "One way or the other," he said, "we are going to see the Elder!" Alec yelled over the roar of the boat's screaming twin motors.

"Do you think they followed us?" Elena yelled to him to compensate for the engine noise.

"It's hard to tell," he replied with a shrug. Then he added, "Why don't you try and listen to their minds?"

Elena focused on the voice she had last heard. The "sound" came in faint at first, but after a few minutes of steady concentration, she could hear it better.

She has escaped, Mistress, the voice said. *She and her protector have fled from the criminal's house. The criminal mentioned they were heading for either Mexico or South America.*

Elena could not hear the second voice in the conversation respond to the first but surmised this may have been the leader of what Alec had referred to as the Opposition.

Yes, Mistress, the voice said again. *I will make sure we keep an eye on the airport and on the Canadian border. Our police contacts will make themselves useful.* Elena could hear a wicked tone to the voice. *It is, after all, what they are paid for.*

The voice became much less clear. The distance between her and its originator was growing too great too fast. Alec had driven the boat into Lake Ontario and opened the throttle up to its stops. The sleek, slim hull surged, forcing the bow even higher into the air and skimmed across the water. The world flew past on fast forward while the engines roared with fury. The noise was deafening, and cupping her hands over her ears to muffle the sound served to accentuate the deep bass of the exhaust. The vibration of the motors made her teeth chatter.

"They are watching for us at the Canadian border and the airport!" Elena screamed to Alec over the sound of the motors, not wanting her mental voice to be overheard. "The voice I heard also mentioned they have corrupt police feeding them information about us. I couldn't hear who he spoke with, but he kept referring to her as *Mistress*." She paused, "Make any sense?"

She couldn't see Alec's face but heard his voice float back toward her. "Are you sure he called her Mistress?"

"Positive," she asserted. "Why? Is it important?"

"Very," Alec replied. "He was speaking directly with Her. The leader of the Opposition. She is very powerful, well connected, and extremely cunning. I was afraid she was involved at some level, but for her to be almost directly involved..." Alec paused for a moment. "This is not good."

Elena didn't entirely understand what he meant. "Why?" she asked.

"Because," he explained, "it suggests she feels threatened. And if she feels threatened, she may go to extreme measures to counter the threat."

"Oh," Elena said, crossing her arms. She gazed out on the great expanse of Lake Ontario. "Great," she muttered under her breath.

After a few minutes of silence, Alec asked, "You said he mentioned she has the police involved?"

"Yes," Elena replied. "And they would be watching the Canadian border for us. I think they may have our identities somehow."

"I am sure of it," Alec responded. "The police will likely have your face on file from your driver's license photo." After a moment he added, "If they are actively hunting us, then various police agencies may be screening crowds."

After about twenty minutes screaming across the water, Elena could see the Canadian shoreline fast approaching. She could also hear the voice begin speaking in her head again. *Mistress. So far, there has been no contact with either the girl or the youngling at the airport. However, our law enforcement contacts have informed me there has been a boat stolen from a marina in Lewiston. They figured it was suspicious and wanted us to be aware. They also mentioned a pickup truck fitting the description of the one the criminal told us about was found nearby the marina. I think they may be making their way up Lake Ontario by boat.*

"No!" Elena shouted. "They found the truck and know we have a boat."

Alec never said a word but pushed the engines harder. Despite the startling speed at which they were traveling, she wished they could go a little faster.

Elena started scanning the skies, half-expecting a Daimones to swoop down and snatch her from the boat. Nothing was visible across the bow, to the starboard, or port sides. But off the stern, she could see a distant shape in the sky.

"Alec!" she yelled to him. "How fast can Daimones fly?"

Almost in response, Alec shoved the throttle harder again. The tachometer on the dashboard indicated the engines were being overworked, their needles pinned in the red zone.

"Fast," he replied.

Alec took his belt off his pants and wrapped it around the steering wheel and a nearby handhold. He set the boat on a trajectory for a small island and tightened the belt. "We are leaving," he said turning to Elena and letting go of the wheel. Alec tore his shirt off, wrapped his arms around Elena, and leaped into the air. For a brief instant, she wished for more time to admire him. As her feet lifted from the deck of the boat, Elena's heart stopped for a long second before it began pounding fast again with the exhilaration of flight. She couldn't ever remember being held so close to anyone before. The feeling of his solid, muscular body against her made her tingle with excitement while her pulse raced faster.

Alec beat his powerful wings a few feet above the water, maintaining a parallel course with the boat. The speed with which they flew shocked her. However, the boat approached the small tree-covered island. She could see no houses or anything on the island, but it seemed all of the trees were covered with a wide assortment of birds.

The boat struck the island's rocky beach and leapt into the air. The whining of the exposed rotor beating the air drowned out the motor's roar. It crashed into a group of trees sending timber, fiberglass, and birds flying about. At the same time, Alec banked hard to the right and flew even faster. He set Elena down on a small point of land covered in scrub pines with small sandy dunes.

They are in Canada, the voice said in her mind. *I have them pinned down at Lemoine Point, near Kingston, Ontario.*

Elena could see the approaching shape as it came closer, definitely a Daimon. She recognized him in an instant—the same one who had tried to lure her from her car the other day.

"Hello, youngling," the Daimon said within earshot. "I am very disappointed in you. You have brought great harm to my loved ones." The Daimon motioned to the birds flying overhead. "You did it intentionally, didn't you?" He paused. "Never mind, I will forgive your transgression and take it as a poor attempt at a distraction. You intended to disrupt my path. But of course your attempts were futile." The Daimon turned to Elena. "I trust you will give us the girl."

"Anpiel, it was no distraction," Alec told the man. "It was a warning. Like I brought harm to your precious birds, I will also bring great harm to you. I implore you leave us now and forget what your mistress has bidden. Your mission will not succeed." Alec paused, stared their winged pursuer in the eyes, and added, "The girl is not going with you."

"You are wrong," Anpiel taunted. "She is coming with us."

Elena peered over Anpiel's back, several more dark shapes approached.

Alec rushed at Anpiel and grasped him around the neck. Alec's wings wrapped around them both and together they fell to the ground, grappling. Anpiel's wings spread open and he pushed away from Alec. The two Daimones separated, and Anpiel lifted off into the sky with Alec in immediate pursuit.

As they flew off, helplessness washed over her. A quick glance up in the sky confirmed the other dark shapes, at least two other Daimones, were nearly upon her location. As she watched, one of the shapes diverted its course to join the fray between Alec and Anpiel while the other continued flying straight at her.

"Oh no," Elena mumbled under her breath. She focused on the shape and reached out with her mind.

Stay away from me, she screamed at it. When the voice replied to her, it carried no words, only sinister laughter. She ran.

She could hear Alec's voice in her head. *Hide, Elena,* he told her. *Hide. I will be there as soon as I can.*

Her legs pumped hard as she ran through the scrubby pine forest. She followed a small deer path winding itself through the woods and then ducked off into the denser underbrush. Small branches and thorns ripped at her arms, legs, and face, she ignored the pain and kept pushing onward.

A shadow passed over her, dark and ominous.

Elena came to a dead halt. Another step forward and she would have crashed into the massive form landing before her. Blinking her unbelieving eyes did not alter the image of his four-foot broad, nearly seven-foot tall form. His wingspan stretched almost ten feet to either side of his massive body.

You can hear me, little one, the Daimon's deep thundering voice said. *Do not even attempt to resist. You are coming with me.*

A single word popped into her mind, and unfortunately it also entered her mental voice: *huge.*

She could hear the large form begin laughing again. A wide, toothy, disarming smile grew across its face. The handsome Daimon had auburn hair and mint green eyes. His every muscle seemed as though it had been chiseled in marble.

I am larger than most others, it said to her. *I am also much older. I have been on this world more than nine-thousand years. Some have called me Israfil, and some have called me Michael. I was a warrior at Jericho, and I am awaited on Judgment Day to sound the end of this human world.* The massive Daimon smirked.

My name does not truly matter, he said as he raised his immense hands and studied them. *At Jericho, my horn rallied us to tear down the walls brick by brick. I have killed thousands of humans and Daimones alike. My mistress wants you alive, but do not have such hopes for your companion. To him, I am the final Judgment Day. His executioner.*

Elena's anger flared in response to the taunting. She feared for Alec's safety. *You bastard!* she screamed at him. *You leave him alone. I'm the one you want, not him.*

She wanted to hurt this creature who threatened Alec. She scanned the skies to find any sign of Alec, but found disappointment instead. Movement caught the corner of her eye in the form of Israfil stalking toward her.

Stop! She shouted in her head. *Stop right there! Or, I'll hurt you.* He laughed at her again. When he didn't stop, she shouted at him again. *I mean it!*

You cannot hurt me, you insignificant human.

Elena took several steps back. *No,* she replied. *But Alec can. He can hurt you!*

The child cannot hurt me, either. Besides, he is not here now. He swept his hand through the air to illustrate his point. Anger filled his voice. *Now, either come with me willingly, or I will take you by force.*

Then take me by force, Elena replied in defiance. She narrowed her eyes and added, *Do your best.*

Elena braced herself and watched the Daimon's eyes. He strode toward her, his chest puffed up.

You make me sick, you puny girl, he said, a couple feet from her now. *You cannot stop me.*

Elena took a few steps back, but Israfil's long legs closed the gap. Her heart beat so fast, it would explode.

The massive creature raised his large hands towards her with a slow, deliberate movement. He intended to cause fear and she knew it, he was savoring every moment of her torment. The wicked sneer on his beautiful face confirmed her suspicion.

Elena turned as fast as her body would allow and ran with all of her might. She heard a faint chuckle. The giddy sound disturbed her. The man's massive form landed in front of her.

I tire of this game. He stretched out his massive hands. *Now come with me.*

The creature's huge arms moved so fast she never had a chance to comprehend what happened. One moment he stood before her, the next his arms wrapped around her, crushing her against his hard body.

Numbness filled her mind. She needed to flee, to escape his grasp. The cloying warm stench of his body made her retch. She couldn't breathe.

She pushed and writhed with all of her strength, but couldn't budge against his massive strength.

The man wrapped his arms tighter around her.

Elena remembered being stuck in her Toyota, the Daimon kneeling on her hood, and how the air had been so stifling. Perhaps it was a trick—some kind of mental ability they had to impress physical sensation on each other. The time for hoping something would work had passed. She had nothing to lose in giving it a try she wasn't about to lose anyway.

Concentrating on his mind, she imagined the most intense pain she could—the pain of being cut by a million shards of glass, a pain she'd experienced when accidentally shoved through a sliding glass door back in Junior High School. The memory filled her to the point she could almost feel the pain again. With a great surge of her will, she forced it on him—sending it into his mind, forcing it to fill his mind and spread throughout his body.

"Let go of me, damn it!" She mentally pushed the memory again, feeling the intense sensation like icy shards piercing her brain. She screamed out in pain.

Israfil let out a tremendous bellow as he threw Elena from his grasp. She hit the ground hard, flat on her back, the wind knocked out of her. The hollow, resonance of Israfil's yell had such power it alone could have brought down the walls of Jericho. Her mind told her to get up, to flee. But her body fought for air, incapable of movement.

"You little bitch! You will certainly pay." The creature's once-beautiful face became a mask of fury.

Finally able to pull shallow gasps of air into her burning lungs, Elena scrambled away from the advancing beast.

He moved faster than a striking viper. In an instant he straddled her prone body with his hands at her throat. Her mind froze, unable to comprehend her predicament. His powerful hands compressed her vocal cords, choking off the few sweet breaths she had drawn into her lungs. His massive weight squeezed her chest, smothering her, preventing her from expanding her chest.

The burning in her airways turned to a raging inferno. Bursts of light swallowed up her vision. Her attempt to scream never had a chance.

Something changed inside of her. The mixed feelings of helplessness, desperation, and terror melted away, replaced instead by determination and anger. She conjured the memory again, except this time making it far worse. With all the mental strength she could muster, she thrust the sensation into the beasts' mind and amplified it, filling his mind with excruciating pain.

Israfil let go of her throat and clutched his head, leaping back and away from Elena, releasing a deafening roar of agony. Elena jumped up and sprinted away with all her might, trying hard to keep focusing on his pain.

She headed for the shoreline, but lost sight of the massive Daimon. Scanning the skies, not so much as a bird flying above could be seen and she feared the worst for Alec. The idea he could not handle himself against the other two Daimones had never crossed her mind. Her face felt warm. *What if he didn't survive? What do I do then?* She searched the sky in a panic. Where was he?

She heard a light crunch in the pine needles behind her. Her heart sank. She had stopped focusing on Israfil.

I did not enjoy that, Israfil scolded her. The fury on his face explained it all. Despite his rage, she knew she had hurt him. *My mistress told me you had to come back alive. She did not say you had to come back unharmed.*

He moved fast. But as she reacted, his body could not compete with the speed of her mind. She refocused on the pain and projected it into his mind like an explosion.

Israfil stopped mid-stride and crumpled to the ground.

She heard another light crunch behind her and whipped around to see Alec standing there with shock on his face.

"I was about to help you out," he said in a stunned voice. "How did you incapacitate him?"

"It isn't easy," Elena replied weakened from the mental effort. "And I can't hold it much longer. We need to get out of here. What happened to the other two?"

"They won't be bothering us anymore. Ever," Alec said. Elena hadn't noticed until now parts of his upper body and his pants were smeared with blood.

"You killed them?"

Alec nodded. "Let's go."

"Okay, where to?" she asked. "And what do we do about him?"

Alec pointed inland to the east. "Head that way. I will take care of him."

Elena paused. Alec nodded in the direction again. She started walking down the path and Alec rejoined her a few moments later.

"We don't have to worry about him anymore, either."

"You killed him?" Elena asked.

"Yes. He was still dazed by whatever it was you did to him, so it didn't take much." A brief silence passed between them as she watched him seemingly drift away in thought.

"Elena," he said, "I think for the first time in my long life, I am truly amazed."

Elena opened her mouth, unsure how to respond. Before she could say anything, however, Alec turned away.

"We need to go," he said. "They'll send reinforcements, we need to move fast." He scanned the trees. "This way," he said as he walked away. "Let's put as much distance between us and this place as we can. They'll be all over this area soon, and in greater numbers."

chapter 10

Elena contemplated about the laundry list of felonies she had been racking up over the past few days. Forget the mundane misdemeanors, like speeding and blowing through stop signs. Within the last few hours alone, she had crossed international borders illegally, had been an accomplice to killing several superhuman beings, and as of moments ago, she could chalk up a count of grand theft auto to the tally. It was a good day.

The SUV Alec stole from the park at Lemoine Point hurtled down Bath Road, weaving around traffic before turning off onto a crossroad.

"Okay," Alec said, breaking the oppressive silence, "I think I have a plan. We are going to catch a flight from Ottawa International. We need to get a hold of some new identities."

Despite her best efforts, Elena chuckled. The chuckle rolled on to a bout of full-blown laughter. She couldn't understand why she thought this funny, especially considering the dire gravity of the predicament in which she now found herself. But she did.

"Why are you laughing?" Alec asked her, puzzled.

"Because..." she said while trying to catch her breath, "our last attempt at obtaining ID's went *so* well. Let's do it again." She threw her hands up in the air.

Alec ignored her sarcasm. She could tell by his expression she'd either insulted or embarrassed him. They spent a long while in silence as they drove up Route 416 into the outskirts of Ottawa from the south. Alec turned off the main highway and wound his way through the various suburbs. He came to a stop in a recently built neighborhood of cookie-cutter, Queen Anne revival-style houses with tidy brick facades and vinyl siding. The lawns were all well kept, and the landscaping meticulous. *Perhaps,* Elena wondered as she took it all in, *the fake ID business did better here.*

Alec stepped out of the truck. He leaned in and told Elena before closing the door, "We need to walk a couple blocks up this way. I hope you don't mind." More than two blocks up and one over, Alec approached the front door of one of the houses with Elena a few steps behind. His two sharp raps were answered in short order. The man who came to the door also appeared a sharp contrast to the degenerate from New York, being tall, thin, and fit. He wore a pair of khaki pants with a powder-blue button-down shirt, had a neat goatee and a welcoming smile.

"Your Grace," the man said with a touch of reverence, "it has been a long time." Alec shook hands, his eyebrows arched high. The man's face brightened, "Ah, where are my manners? Come in, come in." He ushered them both into the foyer.

"Luc, old friend, we are urgently in need of papers, and your utmost discretion."

"Of course, Your Grace," replied Luc. Elena shot Alec a quizzical glance.

"We will need to move about incognito. The papers must pass muster in any country. We also need to have them within the hour."

"Of course, Your Grace. They'll be ready soon." Again, Elena glanced at Alec.

"Thank you," Alec responded. "Once we have our new papers, we will no longer be 'Graces,' understood?" Alec spoke with a firm, but courteous tone.

"Yes, Mr. Appleton?" Luc replied.

"Thank you, Luc," Alec said nodding. "Much better. Where shall we wait?"

Luc escorted them to a very comfortable study with well-stocked bookshelves. They settled into two deep leather chairs. After offering them cold beverages, which they were more than happy to take, Luc disappeared from the room, closing the door behind him. Time flew while they waited for Luc to finish his work. Alec sat in his chair, studying his beverage, and Elena roamed the study, examining the books on the shelves. Luc returned a short while later with a handful of documents.

"These should be able to pass scrutiny in nearly any country," Luc told them as he climbed in behind his desk and sorted through the papers. "I have given you both Canadian identities, complete with driver's licenses, passports, and birth certificates. Mr. Clark Appleton, you are from right here in Ottawa; and Ms. Melinda Richter, you are from Newfoundland."

"Thank you, Luc," Alec said as he slipped something into the man's hand. "As always, your help is greatly appreciated. You will be well compensated."

"Of course, Your Gr—Mr. Appleton," Luc replied.

"Thank you," Alec told him. "I am sure you won't mind if I double your usual fee?"

"Of course not." Luc smiled and guided them back to the foyer.

Outside, Elena turned in the direction of their pilfered truck, but Alec grabbed her hand to stop her. Her skin tingled at his touch, electricity coursed through her entire body. She gasped at the suddenness of the action.

"Wrong way." His voice was smooth as silk.

"What a-about the..." she stammered.

Alec turned and raised his finger to her lips. She shivered at his touch. So soft, gentle, and sensual—like he was trying to seduce a lover. She wanted to press her body against him, to feel him close to her. He pressed in against her, his lips inches from her ear. She could feel his warm breathe on her neck.

"We need to leave the truck. By now it will be reported stolen. We'll need to procure other transportation." He spoke in a hushed tone. His lips brushed her ear, sending an electric current down her neck. She wanted to taste his kiss. She wanted him more than she'd wanted anyone before.

She drew in a sharp breath and held it, trying to regain composure. But her heart beat so fast. In a forced hushed tone she asked, "W—why are we walking?"

"We don't want to leave a trail of breadcrumbs leading them to us, do we?"

Elena nodded. "Are we going to fly out from here?" she asked him.

He chuckled.

"I mean, Ottawa has an international airport, right?" she corrected.

"No," he replied as he pulled away from her. "We are not. If they find the truck, then they will search the airport. We need to make sure we are not followed. The location of the Elder cannot ever be divulged to the Opposition." He stopped and soaked her in. She turned and faced him. "And," he said, "we need to keep you safe from them as well."

Alec pulled a cell phone from his pocket and dialed some numbers. Elena could not overhear his hushed conversation, but he hung up and slipped the phone back into his pants pocket.

"Sorry," he told her, "but we need some money. And I needed to make sure Luc got his compensation."

"What does a pair of fake ID's go for nowadays?"

"For his trouble," Alec replied, "I've decided to give Luc about twenty thousand dollars." Alec raised his eyebrows. "Do you agree?" he asked.

"Well, I guess a fee so high is nothing, Your Grace," she responded with a smirk.

Alec smiled. She could see in his smile reflections of some fond memories.

"Unfortunately," he said, "I am not a real duke anymore. I was, once upon a time. But I had to abandon my post to keep up a human pretense. Upon my 'death' I liquidated the entire estate and transferred it to my 'heirs' in perpetuity. My 'heirs' are a long line of false identities I have used for many generations to control my accounts. It's partly where some of my fortune comes from." He smirked. "I use the false title from time to time as a way to explain my accounts."

"So," she asked, with no regard for propriety, "how rich are you?"

Alec laughed.

Good, at least I didn't offend him.

"I like to think I have enough," he told her. "We will be picking up some walking-around money at my bank. If I am not mistaken, there is a branch at the mall up the road." He stared off in the distance and she wondered what ran through his mind. "I would say we have about a two-mile hike ahead of us. Are you ready?"

"Okay," she replied with a playful grin. "So what do you say we jog? I've been sitting on my butt too much with all this driving. A little exercise would be good."

"We're not exactly dressed for jogging," he said. "It will be suspicious."

"Wait," she countered. "With all of the pull you keep telling me the Opposition has, you're telling me you are afraid of the police being suspicious of joggers? We're going to be on their radar anyway. Why bother keeping a low profile?"

"Because," he replied in a tone meant to remind her to be serious, "having a low profile will hopefully increase our chances of not getting caught. If the police get suspicious, they may tip the Opposition off. We may have eliminated a few of their members, but they have plenty more in reserve." He paused. "We'll try to blend in and take our time. As someone who has lived as long as I have, I can say with certainty time is on our side."

They walked for the next half hour in silence. Elena hated seeming foolish in front of Alec. But instead of brooding about it, she enjoyed the walk and the scenery. From the modern suburbs of Tanglewood, they crossed over to the commercial development along Merivale Road.

They entered a modest-sized mall and found Alec's bank. However, once Alec entered the bank, the process took quite a while. He didn't come out until an hour had passed. For a wire transfer this size, he explained, there are innumerable forms to fill out. "I got some money for our trip transferred from one of my untraceable accounts. We don't need the Opposition following us through our purchases."

"Well," she asked, "how much did you take out?"

Alec smiled at her. "I have about two-hundred thousand in various currencies. We have some shopping to do. And, we need a new car, don't we?"

Elena coughed. *Two hundred thousand? Who walks around with so much cash?* But then, there were not likely to be any humans who could challenge Alec and wrestle the money away from him. And the people chasing them weren't interested in his cash.

She raised her face, locked eyes, and said, "Then I have one question."

"Which is?"

"Can we at least take a cab to the car dealer?"

"No," he said. "We can catch the bus outside the mall. But how about we go clothes shopping first?"

To be on the safe side, Elena mentally scanned the area for any Daimon voices, feeling relieved when she heard none. "Sure," she told him. "Clothes shopping sounds great."

They spent about two hours shopping for enough clothes for a week or so—pairs of jeans, layers of shirts, and fresh underwear and socks. Despite the danger they were in, Elena enjoyed one of the largest shopping sprees she'd been on in years, if not ever. Outside the mall, they hopped on the bus and headed over to a car dealership. After about an hour of haggling, they drove off the lot in a used 1980s Mercedes Benz diesel.

"So, Elena, do you like hiking?" Alec asked under a raised eyebrow as they pulled onto the main road.

"Yeah," she replied. "Why?"

"Because it is going to be our cover. We'll be a couple on a backpacking trip." Within minutes, they arrived at a sporting goods shop to equip themselves.

Back in the car with their new vacation gear in the trunk, Alec popped open the glove compartment and removed a small electronic unit with a wide screen. "The great thing about this car," he explained, "is I was able to negotiate with the dealer to throw in a GPS unit. It should make it easier to plot our way to Winnipeg." He turned the unit on, tapped the screen to input a destination, and attached it to the windshield with a suction-cup mount.

"Wait, won't they be able to track us with the GPS?" Elena asked.

"No," he replied. "It's a generic plug-in unit. They're not typically registered and not really traceable. They would also have to be able to link our new identities to us in order to figure out who purchased the car. The paperwork for the sale and registration won't make it into the system for a few days." Alec grinned. "By the time they figure out whose car it is, we will have been long gone from Canada."

The sun had settled beneath the horizon by the time he pulled onto the Trans-Canada Highway and opened the throttle. Despite its advanced age, the car accelerated. They must have been traveling at least eighty miles per hour.

They sat in silence while Alec drove. Elena relaxed her guard enough to enjoy the passing scenery. But after a while, the monotony of dense forest hypnotized her into sleep. When Elena woke up, her legs were stiff, and she had a cramp in her lower back. Wiping the crust of sleep from her eyes, a sign on the side of the highway piqued her curiosity. Turning to Alec, she asked, "So, why are we going to Winnipeg? Don't we have to go to Europe."

"We do," Alec replied. "It will be harder to track our position if we stay on land as much as possible. And the more distance we put between ourselves and Ottawa, the less likely it is there will be a Daimon welcoming party ready for us at the airport."

He continued, "We need to fly to Europe, but I want to make sure we can do it in relative peace and without alerting the Opposition. Whatever the inconvenience or delay in our current mission, we cannot afford to be careless enough to lead the Opposition to the Elder."

"Why? What would the Opposition want with this Elder?" Elena asked.

"Since the Elder is our progenitor, our alpha and omega, he represents the ways things are and always have been. He represents our mission of cooperation, understanding, and protection of humans. To kill him would be a major symbolic blow to those of us who wish to maintain this mission. It would show the Opposition as more powerful, able to destroy our creator, capable of toppling what, for lack of a better term, is our equivalent of a god."

Alec's comparison caught her off guard, though she could not understand why. She often described her religious beliefs as agnostic, if not atheistic. For legends of Angels and Demons to be right made little sense to her. Despite having been to church as a child with her grandmother, a devout Roman Catholic, she would never call herself a *believer*. But now a question burned inside her, one to which she needed answers.

"Alec, I'm not sure how to ask this. So I'm going to go ahead and ask it." She couldn't figure out why she'd be so nervous to ask him. So she blurted, "Is it real?"

Alec brow furrowed. "Is what real?"

How could she follow it up?

After a moment she answered, "You mentioned when we were leaving school something about Christian chroniclers, you discuss the Elder in very religious terms, you introduced yourself to me as a theology student, and you—you are something right out of the Old Testament itself! Is it real?"

"I still don't understand your question."

"Is he real? God? Is there a heaven? Or, a hell?"

Alec stiffened. "Elena, I am really not sure how to answer these questions. Things are not as simple as you think."

"What do you mean?" she asked, annoyed at him for trying to dodge the issue.

"Daimones don't have religion," he explained. "To us, the idea of an all powerful, omnipotent being is embodied in the Elder. But the difference is he is a tangible being. Human religion, on the other hand, is all about belief: the belief in a hereafter, the belief there is some prime mover driving everything in existence, the belief in all of creation as intelligently designed by some supreme architect, and faith in the supreme architect's plan. This is not our way of seeing the world. In essence, humans would say we are atheists. There is no afterlife, no supreme architect, or great driver steering the course of existence. There is no faith except in our own selves. There was only ever and always will be the Elder."

Elena nodded. "So then, he is kind of like your God."

Alec shook his head. "No," he said. "It's not so simple. It would be like saying a child's father was her God. From the child's perspective, it would seem a rational assertion. The father is larger and stronger, he seems to have answers to nearly any and all questions, and the father is the child's creator as the child is his offspring. But the reality of the situation is they are both sentient living beings who are equally prone to the same mistakes and behaviors but yet still share the same limitless potential as the other. During maturity, it eventually becomes evident to the child she and the father are equals."

"Okay, so he's not a god. But you refer to him as the alpha and the omega—a term Christianity uses to describe God."

Alec nodded. "Yes. You're right, I did use a Christian term to describe him and to illustrate another facet of his importance to us. You see, he was the first of our kind. He has been on this earth since time forgotten and will probably be here once we have all perished. Therefore, he is also the end. I was trying to explain his importance in a way you might understand without getting into a lengthy discussion."

"Yeah, it didn't work out so well for you, did it?" she teased.

Alec laughed. "No, I guess not."

Elena still had questions, though. After a few moments she asked, "But, if he is so revered by the Daimones, then why is there all the secrecy about where he is?"

Alec smiled at her. "Because the Opposition wants him destroyed. His destruction is their goal because he stands in the way of their attempts to enslave both the Daimon and human races."

This seemed to make sense to Elena, but something else didn't feel right. "Okay, but don't all Daimones know where he is?"

"No," he replied. "After the Opposition's uprising, all Daimones were banished from our ancestral home, where the Elder lives. Legends and tales tell of its location, but in a very general sense. And then there are the stories of him being moved to a new location. His actual location is known by a select few of our kind, his sworn protectors. They alone possess the location of his resting place."

"Wait a minute. Did you say resting place? Is he dead, or something?"

Alec shook his head. "No, he is not dead. Don't you remember what I told you about our kind? We do not die of natural causes, but such longevity does have its own price to pay. None of us know his true age, but his eldest offspring are well over a hundred millennia old. Time wears on a body, be it human or Daimon."

"Wow," Elena remarked. "Do you think the Elder lived when both Neanderthals and modern humans cohabitated?"

"More than likely," Alec replied.

Elena turned back to the side window, where she watched the darkness of sunset creep westward across the land. In her mind danced images of humans and Neanderthals, the emergence of human cultural traditions, and the answers to thousands of questions about human biological and cultural evolution.

After a short pause, she turned back to Alec again. "So how long are we going to be on the road to Winnipeg?"

Alec checked the speedometer. "At this speed, probably another twenty hours, give or take. Of course," he said with a wink, "we could get where we're going a lot quicker if you could fly!"

Elena's eyes rolled in exasperation. "Great! I'm super psyched!" she exclaimed. "Twenty more hours of riding in a car."

Elena glared at him then turned her attention back to the world whipping past her window. Despite having a new identity and her own personal guardian angel while heading off on an international flight, a shiver ran up her spine. She couldn't shake the feeling this trip wouldn't be as easy as it sounded. Pushing her uneasiness aside, Elena decided to focus on something much more palatable. She spent her time wondering what it would be like when this adventure ended and she could have Alec all to herself. Would he want her like she wanted him?

chapter 11

"Folks, this is your captain," came the voice over the airplane intercom. They had made it to the airport in Winnipeg without incident. There they abandoned the car and boarded their flight to London.

"It is nearly 7:30 am, local time," the captain continued, "and we are currently circling above Heathrow Airport. We will be landing in about fifteen minutes. Please make your final preparations before we begin our descent. Thank you."

Elena collected her meager belongings, amazed at how few things she had brought. Her old possessions were now abandoned either at college or at her home, and most of her new possessions were in her pack, stowed below.

The plane landed and taxied over to the terminal. As Alec climbed out of his seat, the flight attendant opened the outer door. Elena could see the pilot had also made his way from the cockpit to greet his passengers.

"I hope you had a pleasant flight, folks."

Alec shook the captain's hand. "We did," he told the man. "I will be sure to recommend your airline to all of my friends," Alec continued, grinning. "We fly a lot."

The captain returned Alec's smile. "Thank you."

Elena stifled a laugh, shook the pilot's hand, and then followed behind Alec out the hatch. It took everything she had to suppress a chuckle as she did.

The hatch led to a mobile stairway, which deposited them down onto the tarmac. There were few planes near them. And aside from the few passengers on the half-empty plane, the place was desolate. A handful of workers were carting luggage from the bellies of the nearby planes or performing what Elena figured were routine safety inspections.

The plane has landed, she heard a voice say in her mind. *I think she might be here.*

Despite having eavesdropped on the conversation, she knew the voice's owner searched for her.

It took all of her self-control for Elena to fight the urge to stop dead in her tracks. She didn't recognize the female voice and fought hard to resist the urge to find the voice's source. She knew somebody had to be nearby. A Daimon somebody.

With a Herculean effort of will, she managed to keep her legs stepping in perfect rhythm with Alec. If they were being watched, she knew she couldn't afford to draw attention to herself by craning her neck searching. She trotted after Alec and caught up in a few short strides.

She leaned close to him, as if to give him a kiss on the cheek. "We are being watched," she whispered in his ear.

Alec smiled and planted a peck on her cheek. Her skin tingled where his lips touched her. He whispered back, "They've probably broadcast your ability to hear Daimon telepathy to scouts all over. I believe this is a fishing expedition. They'll pounce on the first person to search the skies for them. As long as we ignore it, then to them we are white noise. A lead needing to be run to ground."

Hoping they'd appear to anyone watching like a couple in love, Elena laughed and hugged him. She hoped the real fear growing inside of her did not show through. "So, where do you think they would be hiding?" she asked. "I can't help but want to search for our tail."

"Whatever you do," he told her, "don't do it. They will be watching every move we make. We need to match our cover—we are a couple taking a backpacking holiday through Europe."

"Okay," she said. "I understand." Elena stopped, put her arms around his neck, and leaped into his arms, squealing with excitement. She took advantage of the situation and hammed it up for their audience. But she also had to admit she enjoyed having him this close to her. His lean, but powerful arms wrapped around her.

She gazed into his alluring eyes and warmth spread through her. He squeezed her tight against his chest. Leaning in, she brushed her lips against his, electricity passing between them. She could feel the heat of his breath on her neck as she cocked her head to one side. Her lips sought his neck, laying kisses with a feather-like touch. She could feel his groin press against her as he leaned back, holding her off the ground. Her face burned, her heart pounded. She wished they could be alone. Grabbing his face between her hands, she pushed hers closer to him.

Still leaning back, the shifting of her weight caught Alec off balance and he stumbled backward. The interruption snapped her from the moment. The heat of embarrassment colored her cheeks and she turned away from him, walking for the terminal.

I don't think these two are the ones we want, Mistress, Elena heard the voice say. *I think they may be another pair of backpackers.* The conversation paused. *Yes, Mistress,* the voice said again. *I will follow them to be sure. I understand completely.*

Elena leaned in to Alec. "We are going to be followed. Her Mistress has told her to follow us." After a brief pause, she asked, "What's our plan? What do we do now?"

Alec replied without bothering to whisper. "We're in London. Let's go sightseeing."

After picking up their luggage, they made their way through the passport and security checks, talking all the while for the benefit of their tail.

"I hope you feel plenty rested after your plane and car rides," Alec said at one point. "We have about a twenty-mile hike to get to the hostel we're staying at in Hendon Park."

Elena sighed. "Hon," she replied, taking his hand and pouting at him, "don't you think it would be safer to take a cab?" She batted her eyelids at him and smiled.

He stared at her, either not buying her plea, or impervious to her attempted charms.

She sighed again and resigned herself to the fact she would be walking. "Do we at least get to pass any neat landmarks on our way?"

"Actually, we are about to leave one now," he explained to her. "Heathrow Airport was formerly a military airstrip converted into a commercial airline terminal. Once we get to the hostel, we can spend the night there and then take the Underground into London proper tomorrow. We could visit Big Ben, Parliament, and Buckingham Palace. All the typical touristy crap."

"How about Notting Hill?" she asked with sudden interest.

"What's so special about Notting Hill?" Alec asked with genuine curiosity.

"What?" Elena poured it on pretty thick and acted surprised at his ignorance, adding some pouting for effect. "Haven't you ever seen the movie with Hugh Grant and Julia Roberts? I figured it would be great to visit, is all." Her tone became very sullen.

Alec kept step. "Well, okay. Sure," he said. "Why not? We have time to kill. This is a backpacking trip."

He hefted his pack and buckled it about his torso. "Now, strap your pack on," he told her. "We have some ground to cover before we can get to sleep tonight." Alec pulled out a cell phone and began dialing a number. "I hope we have a room at the hostel by the time we get there. I am going to try and call ahead."

He kept the conversation short, and as he hung up, he said to Elena, "They'll hold a room for us."

Having a definite place to sleep for the night brightened her mood. They spent the rest of the day keeping up their pretense of being tourists while making their way toward the hostel.

They reached the hostel, checked-in quick and were soon carrying their packs to their room. Alec waited while Elena soaked up a long, hot shower down the hall. Then he showered himself. Once dressed again, they decided to venture out to a small kebab stand, where they grabbed a quick meal. Afterward, they explored Hendon, finding a small Irish pub on Vivian Avenue in which to while away a few hours before heading back to the hostel for the night. Elena had not overheard any further communications from their pursuers.

The dark, smoky pub's half-timbered walls were hung with typical banners reflecting Celtic pride. On her sticky leather seat,

Elena nursed a very dark, heavy beer while listening to a rowdy crowd as they screamed and yelled at a soccer match playing overhead on a small television screen. After sharing a couple rounds of shots with the other patrons, Alec slugged down a couple of beers and watched the crowd closely. Elena noticed he studied people a lot, as if he were trying to read them like characters in a book.

He seemed to have read her mind. To herself she wondered, *Did he hear me while he was watching those people?* He turned to her, smiling. "No," he replied, apparently hearing her this time. "But I have to admit I am a people watcher. Humans have such a full range of personalities and such great potential when they overcome their personal differences. It amazes me time and again they fall into the same mundane traps. They have such short lives, and yet they spend so much time fighting with each other over foolish things." His voice a little less of a whisper than she would have liked it to be.

He chuckled kind of gaily and his speech seemed to be getting slurred.

He began again. This time, however, he did his best to simulate a whisper—one neither quiet nor discreet. "And here we are surrounded by this raucous band, fueled by alcohol, testosterone, and too many bad decisions, watching a sporting event which in the great scheme of things will not mean much of anything but still escalates their furor."

As he spoke, his voice kept rising in volume until it finally surmounted even the riotous din of the crowd behind them. "I mean, how many of these guys do you think are fathers? How many should be spending the precious few years of their lives at home with their wives and children instead of at a watering hole, crawling ever closer to the brink of alcohol dependence? How many do you think will go home and take out whatever disappointment or disdain for the game on their families?"

Elena kept her eyes on the patrons as he talked. She was sure his diatribe would at some point attract the wrong attention. To Elena's relief, the volume of his voice finally dropped. Too many of the nearby patrons eyed him warily.

"Humans have such great potential for love and compassion," he said through a drunken slur. "I have seen it. But instead, they tend to fall victim to stupid vices. They arrange their priorities so objects hold more fascination than the intangible moments of value between them, which they miss because they are not paying attention. They live for things instead of memories, experiences, and moments."

Another round of shots came their way. She didn't remember having ordered it. Neither did she remember Alec purchasing them. But as the liquid fire passed through her lips and down the hatch, it made a bee line for her bladder. Elena excused herself and made her way to the ladies' room in the back of the pub.

The bathroom walls were painted all black with a single row of mirrors hanging above the white-on-white sinks and counters. The stalls were all stainless steel. A few drinks had made the industrial simplicity of the décor fascinating. After flushing, she walked to the bank of sinks, ran the water as cold as it could go, and splashed her face in an attempt to sober up.

"One hell of a guy you've got there," a voice said. She glanced up into the mirror and saw a young petite brunette with short curly hair standing by the stalls, staring at her. If not one of the local bar flies, then she probably escorted one of the rowdy gents out front. Yet, there seemed something familiar about her. Elena couldn't quite put her finger on what.

"Yeah," Elena replied, "he's a one of a kind." She bent down to splash more water on her face. She really didn't want to be chatting it up with some seedy bar patron.

"It seems like he can't hold his liquor, though. He's pretty pissed." The woman continued, chuckling.

Elena noticed her standing next to her at the sinks touching up her lipstick.

"And what the hell was he rambling on about?" she asked.

Elena splashed water to her face again. Oh great! She had heard. She didn't want to try to explain Alec's strange behavior to some complete stranger.

"Trust me," Elena said to the woman, "I have no idea. He gets into these strange moods when he drinks." She had been talking to this woman for a few brief moments, but grew tired of her incessant questioning.

The woman continued, "Your man sure is cute—even if a little strange. He seems so young. In fact, I wouldn't guess him to be a day over two-thousand years old."

Elena's face felt cold as the blood drained from it. She had not seen the woman's mouth move while she spoke. She sobered almost instantly, the hackles on her neck rising as she stared at the woman's cold smile. She recognized the voice in a moment of lucidity as the one she had heard at the airport, their tail, their stalker—one of the Opposition.

My mistress was right, the woman's voice continued. *She told me it would be a matter of time before one of you two slipped up. The amazing thing is you both slipped up at the same time.* The woman turned to Elena.

The woman stood nearly a whole foot shorter than Elena and appeared much more fragile. Elena tried to gauge whether or not she would be able to handle this woman on her own. She knew from experience Daimon men were quite powerful, but never expected such strength from females.

Let me clue you in on some secrets. First, Daimon men cannot handle their liquor. In fact, all Daimones are very quickly undone by alcohol. The woman eyed Elena up and down before saying, *Second, you could never take me on.* To illustrate her point, the small woman gripped the countertop and crushed a small section of it into powder.

"What do you want from me?" Elena asked.

The choice is simple, the woman replied mentally. *Either come with me to see my mistress. Or...*

"Or?" Elena asked, realizing she would regret this decision.

Or you and your companion die, the woman replied. A placid and sickly happy smile spread across her face as she said it.

The woman's evident pleasure at making such a dire threat sent a chill down Elena's spine. She conjured up the most severe feeling of pain she could imagine and directed it right at the Daimon woman as she had done to the other Daimon in Canada. However, instead of the anticipated effect of crippling pain she had seen in the Daimon man, the woman's eyes flashed, and then she laughed.

Silly girl, the woman said to her mentally. *I am no mere weakling. Your foolish mind games have no effect on me.*

Alec...I need your help! Elena cried out, hoping beyond hope he would hear and come to her aid.

The woman started laughing even louder. A terrifying grin crossed her face. *He can't hear you. Alcohol impairs Daimon abilities. And Alec has had a few too many. I guess I shouldn't have bought him so many rounds!*

Elena didn't wait for the woman to move. Filled with blind rage over being trapped by this woman, she pressed her attack. If her death was on the menu, then she would take this woman with her as dessert.

Elena bowled into the small Daimon woman, throwing all of her weight into the attack. To her surprise, the woman fell backward with her arm clutching at the sink.

She didn't stay down for long, though and responded by pushing back at Elena with startling speed, shoving her back a few paces.

Elena responded as fast. She threw her hands up in anticipation of the Daimon woman's attack. However, she couldn't fathom what kind of attack to expect coming at her.

The small woman was lithe. She maneuvered herself underneath Elena's arms and thrust upward with both arms like lofting a volleyball lifting Elena off of her feet and throwing her into the far wall. Elena managed to turn herself sideways in order to absorb her impact with the wall and push herself off into a counterattack.

Elena rushed across the room. The woman crouched at her approach. Instead of missing her target, however, Elena lowered her center of gravity and leapt, flying over the woman's back. While sailing over her opponent's body, Elena stretched out and grasped the woman around the waist.

Elena's momentum carried her forward, and she tucked her head and rolled, pulling the Daimon woman off her feet and flipping her onto her head with startling force. The Daimon's legs flailed and slammed into the large wall mirror, shattering it.

But she did not stay down for long. Before Elena could right herself, the woman leapt up and moved back across the room. Elena stood and whirled to face the woman but was caught off guard as a fist struck her across the face. Surprisingly, it did not carry much force. Elena brushed the blow off and delivered her own to the woman's chest, forcing the woman back several feet.

The Daimon crumpled, winded by the force of Elena's attack. When the Daimon stood again, she clutched a large shard of the broken mirror, which she wielded like a knife.

The woman's glare spit hellfire at Elena. *You're going to die, child.*

The Daimon leaped, but Elena had already anticipated the move. She stepped to the side, and twisted her body away from the blow. As she turned, she grabbed at the woman's back and shoved as hard as she could. The woman's momentum, along with Elena's shove, carried her smashing right through the counter, crushing it into the concrete block wall behind. Elena wasted no time trying to decide if the Daimon would stop her attack. She moved in and grabbed one of the woman's arms from behind. The mirror shard came slashing at her face in the woman's other hand as she twisted out of Elena's grasp. With speed she had never realized possible, she grasped the wrist of the hand clutching the shard and squeezed it with all of the strength she could muster. Beneath her fingers, she could feel the woman's bones snap. Elena twisted her hand and could see the arm bend at a right angle. Filled with rage, she threw her fist at the woman's face. The woman's scream sent chills down her spine. Elena stepped in shock, her blow had dislodged the woman's jaw and it hung loose from torn flesh.

How is this possible? the woman's voice screamed into her mind. Sudden understanding dawned on the woman's face as she stared at Elena. *It's you!* she said pointing to Elena, *You are the Source!* Elena heard the woman's voice again, but much more faint. *Mistress! The girl is the Source!*

Yes, Mistress. The Daimon woman sprung to action. She swung the balled fist of her unbroken arm, but Elena caught her hand mid-swing. Again, she felt the woman's bones collapse in her grasp, as a scream of pain chilled her. It sickened her knowing she'd caused someone so much pain. But what alternative did she have? The woman was thirsty for her blood and had so far been unrelenting in her attack.

Elena released the woman's hand and pushed her away.

Fists pounded on the bathroom door. "Oi. What's going on in there?" The voice belonged to a Cockney. "You beach not be busting up me loo', 'ear? Or I'll bust some 'ads!"

Exactly what, wondered Elena, *is Irish about this pub?*

She then directed her thoughts to the woman's head. *Who are you?* she asked the woman mentally. *What do you want with me?*

I was going to bring you to my Mistress, the woman replied, *but now I am going to kill you. My Mistress wants to speak with you, but you will never live to see her. Nor will you see the damn Elder.* The woman groaned in pain.

Why won't I see the Elder? Elena asked. *Apparently, he's the one who has any answers about what is happening to me and why you people want to kill me.*

Do not call us people, the woman hissed in her head. *Do not dare to lower us to the same level of human scum!* The Daimon stood and lurched forward again with a tremendous effort. The whole conversation had taken place in a fraction of a second, in between the beats of the fist pounding on the bathroom door.

Elena raised her foot and kicked the woman square in the chest, sending her again sprawling against the broken remains of the counter. The blow had knocked the woman unconscious.

The fists against the door fell silent, but were followed by a louder, hollow thudding sound. A bald and rather burly unshaven man burst through the door on the third hit.

The man's eyes grew wide with shock as he surveyed the damage done to his bathroom. The walls to the stalls were broken, his countertop and sinks were destroyed, and a small brunette woman lay crumpled on the floor unconscious with blood dripping from the torn flesh of her lower face.

Elena raised her hands up halfway in surrender as she stepped toward the exit door. The man took a step back, and from behind his back he brought a well-used black wooden baseball bat with more than its share of dents and scars.

"Now, you be'ah keep your 'ands up dere, luv. I got the bobbies comin'ere." He turned his head to the bar. "Oi. Any of you boyos wanna lend a'and until the pigs show? We got a cat fight in me loo."

Elena narrowed her eyes at the man. "This woman tried to kill me," she explained. "All I did was defend myself."

The man studied Elena, then the unconscious woman lying on the floor. "Listen, luv. I don' care'oo done'oo wrong."

The woman on the floor groaned and twitched. "Listen, she is going to wake up soon," Elena said pointing to the woman." And when she does, she will be angry. Don't be fooled by her. She is very dangerous."

"I think I could handle this li'ul girl'ere," the bar owner replied.

Elena took a furtive step forward. "This is not any little girl."

"Stay right where you are," the man roared at Elena with obvious fear in his voice. He shouldered the bat as if he were ready to knock one out of the park. "Take anovah step and I'll smash your'ead in."

Elena took another step.

"I mean it," he said, his voice raising a few octaves. "You be' ah stop where you are."

She could see the fear in his eyes and knew it could make him attack.

"Do what you will," she said to him. "I'm not stopping. I'm leaving. So, you can either get out of my way, or, I'll go through you." She tried her best to be firm and convincing.

Another step forward and the man tensed his arm muscles. She could tell he meant business. Still, she took yet another step.

The man's powerful torso spun and his arms released their coiled tension. The baseball bat flew at Elena's head with remarkable speed but stopped dead in her grasp. The shock on his face told it all. She pulled on the bat and yanked the man off balance. He stumbled forward and fell sprawling onto the bathroom floor.

Elena stepped over him. "If I were you, I would stay down." Once past the owner, she raced to Alec's side. He leaned against the bar, nearly passed out.

"C'mon," she said to him. "We have to go." She yanked him off his stool, surprised by his low body weight.

Alec laughed without provocation as if he had heard the most fantastic joke. A hint of recognition leapt to his face. "Hey... It's you!" He chuckled again like he'd heard the greatest joke, "Did everything come out all right in the loo?" She could hear him draw out the word "loo."

Elena reached out to Alec's mind. *Sober up*, she told him. *We need to leave now! I was attacked by another Daimon.* His leaden eyelids told her the problem, he'd overdone it drinking and couldn't understand the urgency of the situation.

However, after a few moments of her pushing and prodding him into motion, he looked very serious. Through rum-soaked lips, he replied, "What do you mean attacked?" His breath stank of alcohol.

Elena pulled him from the stool. *The Opposition found us. There are police coming. We have to leave. Now!*

Alec's first attempt at standing resulted in him sliding off the chair and slumping down to the floor. Elena didn't wait for a second attempt. She picked him up in a fireman's carry, slung him over her shoulder, and made for the front door. None of the pub's other patrons seemed to want to challenge her. Seeing her catch the owner's baseball bat had been enough to convince them not to mess with her. They all watched her as she carried Alec out over her shoulder.

She headed right out of the door and diagonally crossed the broad street to the nearby tube station. Elena propped Alec up and purchased a couple of Oyster Cards for the Underground. They wasted little time and made their way to the first train available—a southbound line heading to Golders Green. Her nerves stayed tense during the entire trip to the station. She'd left the Daimon woman lying on the floor of the pub's bathroom without ensuring she could not follow. She feared each and every stop would be another opportunity for other Opposition agents to come find them. Luckily, during the ride Alec sobered enough to be able to walk and to scan his own card when they transferred to the Charing Cross line.

From Golders Green, they rode to Charing Cross in Westminster. Elena remembered from a geography class she had taken last year they were real close to the famous Trafalgar Square. It would have been nice to pay it a visit. After all, she wasn't sure if there would be another opportunity.

Alec had finally regained his wits by the time they reached the station. "We should get out of London as quick as we can," he said. And then, glancing around he asked, "Where are we?"

"We're at Charing Cross Station," Elena replied, a little thankful to have the Alec she needed back.

"Okay, good," he replied, "We're a couple of miles from the St. Pancras Station. Let's go for a quick walk."

The sun had sunk in the sky and the streets were lit with sodium-vapor lamps. They had left all of their belongings back at the hostel near Hendon Park. The only personal items between them consisted of Alec's cell phone, some leftover cash, their passports, and the clothes they had worn.

In the cold October air, Elena shivered. In the excitement of leaving the pub, she had left her jacket hanging on her stool. She shivered and huddled close to Alec.

He put an arm around her shoulder and pulled her closer to him. "Sorry," he said to her. "I keep forgetting you are more susceptible to the cold than I am. Perhaps we should take a cab."

She smiled with excitement at the prospect of getting out of the bitter night air. "Yeah," she replied through chattering teeth, "let's."

She had to admit the idea of wandering around this part of London as evening became night did not really appeal to her. She scanned the street. Nearby Trafalgar Square attracted tourists, which meant it would also be frequented by a wide variety of bums, pickpockets, and hoodlums. Nighttime would be worse since there'd likely be a good supply of drunken tourists ripe for the picking.

Alec raised his hand to hail a passing cab. As it pulled to the curb, he opened the door and ushered Elena in. The inside smelled bad, like hot sick, but she didn't much care—it was a ride. As Alec slipped into the car beside her and handed the driver a thick wad of cash. "Can you take us to Pancras Road?"

"Are you going to the rail station?" the cabbie asked.

"No," Alec replied. "I'm meeting a friend. You can let us out anywhere on the road, thank you."

The man thumbed through the wad. "My pleasure," the cabbie said from beneath his bowler cap.

The cab lurched away from the curb and back onto the road. While they drove, Alec tapped away at the screen on his cell phone.

The trip took a few minutes. After they stepped from the cab and onto the curb, the cab sped off. "Okay, so where are we headed?" she asked him with a yawn. The alcohol and adrenaline were working their way out of her system, replaced by exhaustion.

"Paris," he replied with a yawn himself. "And don't do that," he said pointing his finger at her open jaw. "It's contagious."

She glared at him. "What's contagious?"

Stretching his torso, he answered, "Yawning."

He stifled another yawn. "I reserved some tickets for us while we were in the cab. Ori has arranged for an associate of ours to meet us with some new IDs, so we should be able to get into France without any issue. All of the necessary paperwork for our trip has been taken care of. From Paris we can chart our course to the Elder. We'll need to stop somewhere to rest. I have some friends there who can accommodate us while we rest up and re-equip."

The walk from their drop-off point to the train station took a few minutes. On the way, Alec accidentally bumped into a rather tall, thin man with short-cropped black hair, but continued. As they reached the front entry to the train station, he pulled two new sets of documents from his pocket. Elena realized Alec's accidental bump was actually a transfer as smooth as something staged in a spy movie.

The train station was massive and its brick Victorian architecture intimidating. It conjured images of a time when aristocrats and industrialists planned the fate of the world's most powerful nations. She wished she could have seen more of it in the daytime. As she walked inside the building, it was apparent the exterior masked its engineering genius.

The lofty interior rose nearly five stories, with little obstruction from the ground level. She marveled at the massive blue steel-lattice archways, which contrasted with the red brick of the St. Pancras Midland Grand Hotel.

After studying the train schedules, Alec led Elena to one of the ticket machines. They picked up their two business-class tickets for a train leaving for Paris in about fifteen minutes. They didn't have much time to reach the platform, and no time to stop and grab a snack or even a magazine to keep occupied for the next few hours.

Elena knew she could trust Alec to watch over her. She decided to try to get some sleep on the train. But the noises from other passengers made it impossible. They headed off in search of peace. They managed to find an empty car to inhabit for the trip. Staring out the window into the moving blackness of the tunnel outside the train, Elena pondered what new twist lay around the next corner.

chapter 12

For the first time in a few days, Elena dreamed. It didn't last long, but in it she climbed a sheer ice-covered mountain face. She struggled to make her way up the escarpment alone, with Alec nowhere to be seen. Her outstretched hands felt the top of a wide flat ledge projecting from the rock. She climbed up onto the narrow platform. It was wide enough to hold her. She fastened a crampon into the frozen rock face, tested its strength, and satisfied, hooked her safety line through it.

The narrow ledge formed a right angle break in the mountain. A small oval entrance had been carved in the solid rock face, surrounded by a group of odd sigils and glyphs appearing to be a mish-mash of random Egyptian, Mayan, Aztec, and Sumerian symbols. However, she knew these symbols were anything but random. They marked the entrance to the Elder's tomb.

Without warning, the entire scene began to shake, though not as fast as she would expect of an earthquake. And no rumbling accompanied the movement. It felt like the whole world shook in a slow rhythm. Somewhere, from the far distances of the emptiness surrounding the mountain, she could hear whispering.

The whisper called her name, but she could not make out the two words following it. *Elena, aay, kaah. Aay, kaah.*

Grappling with the voice carried upon the wind, her mind began to finally make out the final two words of the chant. *Elena, wake up!* The voice belonged to Alec.

Elena's eyes popped open. The train sat still in complete darkness—the hackles on her neck stood on end. They were alone in the car, the seats around them were vacant.

"What's happening?" she asked, not able help the tremor in her voice.

It would appear we have stopped. Alec replied with his mind. *Do not speak out loud. There is something very much amiss here. Can you hear anyone speaking in your mind?*

Elena searched the darkness. Apart from Alec, she could not hear anyone's mental voice.

I hear no one, she said, becoming more concerned. *Where are we? Why is it so dark?*

The power is off, and it is night, he replied. His response confirmed what she already knew; he focused on something else. *I think we may be stopped in the channel tunnel,* he told her. *I am not sure, though.*

Why aren't you sure? she replied. *I thought Daimones almost never slept.*

She could hear some movement in the car behind them—slow, slight movement.

Did you hear something? she asked with a tremble.

Yes. Stay very still, he replied.

She stayed as still as she could, even holding her breath and clamping her hand over her mouth. For an extra measure of security, she shut her eyes as she had done as a little girl hiding from whatever monsters might lurk in the dark.

The handle for the door connecting adjacent cars moved. After a pause, she could hear the door opening.

Somehow, they've found us, Alec said.

It seemed odd she still could not hear any Daimon voices in her head. If not Daimones, then who would be able to...

And then it came to her. The Daimon woman from the pub knew about Elena being Daimones, and she had left her alive. Had she anticipated their next move?

She reached out to the woman's mind. *Are you there?* Elena asked the woman. *Is this you?*

A faint voice returned, nearly a whisper. *Where are you?* the woman's voice asked. *Are you moving? Your voice is far—you have left London.* She could hear the anger rising in the woman's voice.

To Alec Elena said: *It's not her. She's too far away.*

Then who is it? he asked with genuine curiosity.

She turned and poked her head above the seatback to watch the door continue to open as if in slow motion.

Red light from an emergency exit sign trickled down the aisle. As she continued to watch, she could see a figure stalking down the aisle. The black-clad figure had a strange set of goggles on its head. She had seen enough of her college friends playing first-person shooter video games to recognize them as night vision goggles.

Two bursts of light flashed through the darkness, blinding her. The flashes were accompanied by whispered gun pops. Alec's body jerked forward in his seat as the spate of automatic fire stuck him square in the side of his turned chest and then his head. Elena could feel her face spattered with something warm and wet. Darkness claimed the car again.

Another burst of light erupted before her and she felt the strong sensation of flying backward against another seat. Her chest felt as if somebody had struck her full force with a sledgehammer. Warmth spread outward from her chest. She landed against the far wall and fell over onto Alec's crumpled form.

She coughed, her breathing becoming labored.

Turn on the lights, a different voice said. *It is done.*

The lights came on, and her eyes were awash with white pain. The black figure walked closer, but she could not make out any features. In fact, her vision kept getting blurrier. She coughed again, and her throat burned as something thick and wet came up into her mouth. It had a metallic taste.

The target is dead...or will be soon, the new voice said.

The figure raised the submachine gun again, and she could see the barrel swing toward her. She tried to raise her hand to block the inevitable, but it wouldn't move. In her last moment, she wondered how much the projectile about to erupt from the barrel would hurt.

The muzzle flashed again.

chapter 13

Elena woke with a start. Below her, she could feel the train still speed through the darkness. But she was unsure if they were on the English side or the French side of the Channel.

Where are we? She asked, half expecting to see the barrel of the submachine gun still pointed at her face. The lights were on, and they were cuddled up with each other. She had apparently fallen asleep on Alec's chest. She had to admit she liked the feeling of waking up beside him. Wishing it could always be this way, she couldn't see herself in any other arms than his. As she adjusted her position to sit up, Alec tried his best to remove the Cheshire grin from his face.

The half-empty train car's other passengers appeared to consist of businessmen focused on either their laptops, smart phones, or some kind of paperwork. Alec turned to her. *I figured you would have asked out loud.* She could hear his mental laugh. *We made it through the tunnel. We are in France. Paris should not be too far from here.*

I had the absolute weirdest dream, she said to him. *You would never believe what happened.*

Oh yeah? he replied. *Try me.*

You and I were both murdered in the channel tunnel, she told him, *by a commando dressed in black with night-vision goggles.*

Strange. His mental voice sounded a little different. It seemed as if he knew something more, but chose not to tell her.

What do you mean?

He raised his eyebrows high, and then attempted to disarm her with a wide, calm smile. *Only that it's strange.*

Elena didn't buy his response for a moment. *You're holding something back,* she said. *Tell me what you meant. You had a tone when you said it. What did you mean?*

Alec sighed. *I think the stress of our present endeavor,* he said with the same tone, *is beginning to get to you.*

His reply agitated her more. *What? Stress? What stress?* she flared back at him. *Why would I be stressed? My whole world has been turned to crap, my college career is officially over, and now I am dreaming about militant commandos murdering me in my sleep. What makes you think I could possibly be stressed?*

Alec laughed and smiled at her. *Don't worry,* Alec told her. *My colleagues in Paris will be able to help us on our way. You won't have to worry much longer.*

Then aloud he said, "So, did you enjoy your little cat nap?"

Elena didn't let him waylay the conversation. She intended to get to the bottom of his tone. *Don't try and change the subject,* she barked at him. *You had a very distinct tone. What is it?*

Alec's smile dimmed and he sighed. *The fact you are dreaming of humans doing the Daimones' dirty work to reach you worries me,* he said. *They actually have done such things in the past. After the thrashing you gave the Daimon at the pub, you have proven yourself a formidable opponent. You may have developed some kind of precognitive powers, which can sometimes manifest in the form of dreams. So, if you are dreaming of being murdered by commandos, it's rather troubling to me.* He paused staring into her eyes. *I don't want to take any chances.*

Elena hung her head. She hadn't wanted to consider the last part. *Great,* she said to herself, but openly enough so Alec could read. *As if fighting Daimones wasn't enough. Now I have to take on their human minions as well?*

As I mentioned before, he said, *don't worry. We have our own minions and associates in Paris. And the Opposition will need to find us first. So, let's focus on getting to the Elder. And let the dreams of murderous commandos go the way of the dodo.*

Elena chuckled at the way he delivered the last line. *The Elder. Right. Let's focus on getting to the Elder.* She gave him a big smile and snuggled herself back in against him. She heard a low moan deep in his chest, and her heart beat a little faster.

His arms wrapped her in comfort, and she cursed this train ride needed to end. She wished it could last forever as her heart continued to melt from his electric touch.

"It's about midnight," he said, "and we have a little bit of time to kill. Are you ready for some food?" He rubbed his stomach. "There is a great little patisserie in Paris with the most wonderful pastries. They should still be open. We're about a half-hour away, at most."

"Sounds great! Let's go." Her stomach grumbled; neither of them had eaten in quite a while.

Minutes after the train had stopped they were making their way through the departing passengers, scanning them for suspicious characters. They chose not to linger too long, however for fear of raising suspicions themselves.

After grabbing some cash from an ATM, they stepped out of the west station entrance and hailed a cab. They were in luck. There were several taxis sitting and waiting with no fares. They climbed into the first one.

Alec gave the taxi driver an address, and the man swerved into traffic, speeding through Paris' streets. Elena's rear-passenger-seat tour of Paris was not as glamorous as she had imagined. Granted, they drove past the Eiffel Tower, but sitting in the back of a compact taxi cab at this time of night did not provide the optimal viewing position. Similarly, the Arc de Triomphe whipped past, a shadow of grayish stone against a blurry, dark, urban backdrop as they passed by at breakneck speed.

Their cab ride took about ten minutes before they finally arrived in front of a small bakery. But it had taken them too long to get there and the place had closed. They instead managed to find a secluded table at a nearby bar to while away the next few hours. Another hour or two exploring the streets of Paris in the wee morning hours brought them full circle to the small bakery.

Finally open, the earliest batches of pastries were still fresh from the oven. Instead of seating themselves at one of the little café tables in the corner, the pair took their treats to go. As they walked down the street, Elena following Alec's lead, she fell in love with authentic French food. Or at least authentic French pastries.

"Oh my God!" she exclaimed. "These are so good. I never knew a pastry could taste so good. Seriously, this is like a little buttery piece of heaven!" Alec laughed while she enjoyed the pastry and led her deep into the back streets and alleys of Paris.

About ten minutes later, they were standing outside of a small set of flats off some Rue de something or other. Elena's inability to read or speak French left her out of her element, a veritable fish out of water. From everything she had ever heard, Paris was about as dangerous a city as you could find as a tourist. Of course right now, anywhere she headed would be dangerous. After all, she had angels, and probably humans alike, trying to kill her right now. Fortune smiled on her, though as her nearly indestructible escort Alec could handle any petty thieves or con men with ease.

"So, what do you say to a hot shower?" Alec asked with a wide grin.

The prospect excited her. "Yes, please!" she said with gusto. She needed one. The smell of stale alcohol surrounded her, and a warm shower seemed like a step into Elysian Fields. Goose-bumps emerged on her flesh.

Alec pressed the buzzer for one of the building's flats. It took more than a minute for an answer. The tinny static-filled speaker made the deep baritone voice nearly impossible to make out. Apparently, though, Alec had very little problem understanding the confusing mixture of white noise and garbled speech.

The buzzer sounded, and she could hear the electronic door locks move inside the door with a click. With the building's ancient elevator out of service, the seventh-floor flat was solely accessible by a long hike up the stairs. Even for New York City standards, the walk to the stairwell made it apparent how seamy and filthy living conditions were here. Unnamable substances had stained the hallway carpeting, including, judging from the lingering stench, alcohol and urine. She walked past a puddle of vomit on the floor and kept hearing the distinct skittering and chittering of rats within the walls.

When they arrived at the mid-hallway flat, they found the front door left unlocked for them. Elena followed Alec inside.

The word small overwhelmed the flat's diminutive nature. Even compared to what she remembered of the studio apartment her parents had once rented in Brooklyn. The single room had one interior door leading to a combined shower stall, sink, and toilet. The idea someone could collect rent for such a confined space seemed ridiculous, but she had to respect the efficient use of every inch.

The quintessence of neatness, there was not a single item out of place. But it made sense, as even one misplaced item would have cluttered the space.

A solitary window provided ample light, which revealed a lone man seated on a folded futon resting against the wall beneath the window. He glanced up at Alec and his face brightened.

It has been many years, my dear friend, the man said to Alec mentally. *How long? Do you remember?*

Elena could hear the entire conversation passing between the two men. She found it a bit odd she could understand them. They were in France. She knew next to nothing of the French language, but yet as these two mentalists conversed, she could understand every word spoken. Perhaps there are no language barriers when speaking telepathically.

Yes, René, Alec replied with equal warmth as they shook hands, *I do remember. It has been more than two hundred years now since I was in Paris last. But it has been a mere thirty since we last spoke.* The expression on his face took on a more serious countenance. *How are things?*

They are not going so well, the new man, René, replied, his face turning sour. *The battles rage on, and the Opposition has been gaining much strength here in Paris. I have spoken with our leaders, and they refuse to offer me the additional resources I need. It would seem Paris is largely under the influence of the enemy.*

Elena would have described his expression as if he sucked on a lemon.

You will have to be careful in this city, my friend, René said, *for you can trust no one anymore.*

Alec nodded in understanding. *I was worried this would be the case. Your words of caution are well heeded, René.*

He paused for a moment. *You received my mother's advance notice?*

René nodded. *Yes, I did.*

He stood and walked over to the kitchen portion of the flat. She noticed in spite of his great height, he had gone to pot. His doughy body, sunken eyes, and sallow skin betrayed the lack of care he took in himself and the overabundance of cheap cologne, which smelled as if he'd bathed in it, could not sufficiently mask his strong body odor.

"May I interest either of you in a drink or something to eat?" René asked aloud. It surprised Elena his mental voice matched his physical voice so well.

Before they could even answer, René turned his back on his guests and fished in his cabinets for a few teacups.

Elena shook her head, about to open her mouth when Alec spoke up, "Sure," he replied. "We would love something to drink."

"Good!" René responded." How does tea sound?"

Alec stared at Elena and tipped his head toward René, indicating she should be the next to respond to the kindness extended by their host. After a mouthed protest, she replied, "Tea sounds wonderful."

René set himself to the task of preparing the tea.

Yes, they are both here with me, René's mental voice announced to nobody.

The voice entering her head startled her. It belonged to René, but she had heard no question for him to answer. She decided not to say anything and instead eavesdropped.

What are your instructions? René's voice continued.

Elena spun her head to Alec and flashed her eyes wide to attract his attention. Again while René's attention focused elsewhere, she shook her head and mouthed a single word to Alec, "Danger." Alec cocked his head sideways and furrowed his eyebrows.

She could tell Alec seemed conflicted. René was an old friend and he needed to confirm whether he'd actually become a threat.

"René, how have you been faring in the battles? You said our leaders have not been supplying aid."

René didn't respond immediately. His attention instead seemed to be focused elsewhere. Elena continued to eavesdrop.

I understand, René told his inaudible conversant. *We shall speak of conditions later. They will be here when you arrive. Is it true you were hurt by the girl? Is she really the Source?*

René responded to Alec, "Excuse me, dear friend, I missed what you asked."

However, Elena heard something quite different. René again spoke with someone else. This time, with a little bit of effort, she had managed to hear the voice. The female voice she did not immediately recognize but somehow sounded familiar. Unfortunately, she could not make out the words it spoke.

"Ah," Alec responded to René. "I was wondering, René, how you have been surviving through the battles. After all, if the Opposition is gaining so much momentum, and our leaders refuse to provide any additional support, I can imagine things are tough." Alec's voice took on an accusatory tone. "Such times could drive someone to extreme measures."

René responded gracefully, but Elena noticed he avoided eye contact. He peered over their shoulders as though he expected something to come crashing through the window behind them.

"I have managed to hold my own," the overweight Daimon replied. "My network of informants in Paris is quite extensive, and my accounts hold more than enough gold to purchase human support when it is needed."

Alec paused and studied at René with an obvious question burning in his eyes. "Is there anything we can do to help you while we are here in Paris?" Elena knew he itched to ask another question.

René's face remained expressionless and paled. "No, my friend," he replied with a slight, humorless laugh. "I cannot ask anything of you. After all, you are already on a tremendous quest of your own. And what kind of help could I expect from you and a—human?" René ended his response with a mirthful smirk and another forced light laugh.

Alec, responded, "Very good. Then, I don't have to explain why I am here."

"As I said before," René replied. "I received advance word of your arrival. Your mother's message arrived yesterday."

Alec probed, "So then, will you be able to help us?"

René stared out the window over their shoulders again. He was restless, and seemed to be in perpetual motion.

"To find the Elder? How could I help you find the Elder? He is hidden. There are rumors he is in South America, and other rumors he is in Africa. Personally, I like the stories of him being buried among China's famous clay army." Another humorless laugh. "It's my favorite. But no, I do not have his location."

"René," Alec began, "you have been a great friend to my family for nearly four millennia. You are one of the last third-generation Daimones who has ever met and spoken with the Elder." He added, "Surely you must have some idea?"

René shook his head excitedly. "No!" he yelped, as if he were being questioned under torture. "I don't." He had lost control of his voice. But before he continued speaking he managed to regain some composure. "As I said," he continued, "nobody does. But I may be able to give you some helpful information." He paused and glanced at his watch. "Unfortunately, it is not here and may take me some time to gather. Why not make yourselves at home? You can stay here until I can put everything together."

René was stalling. "No. We need to be going," Alec told him.

René gawked in a mix of confusion and fear. "What do you mean, no?" Elena could hear the rage permeate his voice. "It will take me some time to get all of the correct information together. There are legends and tales, which may have clues as to the Elder's resting place. It's a complicated puzzle." The man's voice kept cracking under stress. "Please, stay a little while. I can make you something to eat."

"Again, my friend," Alec nearly spat this last word, "I said no. We have other errands to run and must be leaving. We can return later for your results."

Alec turned toward Elena and gestured toward the door. "Elena, let's go. We're leaving."

She nodded and stepped toward the door.

"No!" René shouted at Alec. "You can't leave. I have information for you." René's voice strained with fright.

Elena interrupted. *No, René,* she said to him mentally. *You don't have any information. Nor are you any longer Alec's friend. I can sense it in you. You're lying. You were lying when you said you had information. But you were not lying when you told the Opposition we would be here when they arrived. You have been stalling to keep us here.*

René's face paled. *You can hear my mind?*

Elena nodded. René hung his head in shame.

Without warning, René moved with amazing speed. He reached across the counter and wrapped his hands around Alec's throat in less than an eye blink. Elena, however, reacted as quickly. As she'd done with Israfil, she summoned tremendous pain and pushed it into his mind with all her strength.

René stopped dead in his tracks. She could see his grip on Alec loosen. His eyes grew expressionless. A gush of blood poured down through René's nose, eyes, and ears, coating his shirt. His body fell limp to the floor in front of Alec.

Alec's eyes were wide with shock. *What happened?* he asked Elena.

He attacked you, she replied, her hands shaking, *and I reacted.*

Alec kept pressing. *But what did you do to him?*

Elena turned to him. Her reflection in the stainless steel toaster on the counter spoke volumes; her face had gone completely stark white. Numbness spread from her lips and through her face. She wanted to run away. Had she really killed someone? With her mind?

I...I...I did the only thing I could think of, she said. *I filled his mind with pain like I did with the other Daimon back in Canada. Except, when I did it last time it crippled him. I was afraid it wouldn't work on René because it didn't work on the woman back in London.*

Alec walked over to her and gave her a hug. She barely felt his arms squeeze her. Gazing up at him, she could see the concern painted on his face. Involuntarily, she shivered.

Elena, this is an ability powerful Daimones possess. He rubbed her back. *Well, it would appear either your abilities have grown much in the last few hours, or you haven't found your full strength yet. I would say you somehow destroyed his brain with your mind.* Alec held her by the shoulders, and locked eyes with her. *Are you okay?*

His embrace took the edge off of what she had done. She knew Alec wouldn't judge her for what had happened. She pulled back slightly. *Me?* she replied with amazement. *Am I okay?*

Alec nodded, his eyes locked onto her eyes. *Yes, you,* he said. *It's not an easy thing to come to terms with, killing someone. But don't be hard on yourself,* Alec continued before she could say anything. *You did the right thing. I am proud of you!*

Elena didn't understand. *Proud of me? Why are you proud of me? I wasn't attacked. You were. I killed a man. Not in self-defense, but in cold blood.*

Alec's voice became firm. *No! What you did was not in cold blood. It was most definitely self-defense.* He paused and his voice softened. *What do you think he would have done once he had finished killing me? He would have been after you next. It was self-defense, but...* Another pause. *Don't you realize? You saved my life!*

Elena nodded, half listening to what he said. *But...* she began.

Don't dwell on this, he interrupted. *What's done is done. This was a powerful and terrible man who would not have had any qualms about snuffing your life or handing you over to the Opposition.*

Elena nodded again, finally accepting what he said. Then, she decided to change the topic. *Did he hurt you?* she asked.

Alec smiled and hugged her again. *I'm fine,* he replied. *He barely managed to get his hands around me before you killed him.* She hugged him again, running the whole exchange through her mind. The conversations, the attack, René's conversations with...

She gasped. It all made perfect sense. The mental voice René had been conversing with sounded so familiar because it belonged to the woman back in London. *Alec, René was talking to someone else. It's why he was so distracted. He was trying to keep us here. Stall us until they showed up. Oh no, it dawned on me who he was talking to... I recognized the voice. He was talking to the woman from the pub in London. She is coming for us.*

Alec paused for a moment and scanned the room. *We have to get out of here. If what you heard was correct, then there are others on their way.* He paused. *René was an ally for a very long time and I can't believe he betrayed us to the Opposition. He was probably our greatest asset here in Europe.* Following his cue, Elena also scanned the place. Out the window, something moved on the horizon.

Elena pushed away from Alec. She could hear the din of voices in her head. *I can hear them. They are still far off, but their voices are becoming clearer. They're coming,* she told him, her voice cracking. *We have to leave.*

Alec didn't hesitate. He released her and moved toward the exit. *Elena, please put your hands in your pockets, and don't touch anything as we leave.* They had not touched much in the place, and Elena's fingerprints would not be on anything.

He opened the door, leading the way out of the flat. She followed swiftly and quietly pulling the door closed behind them with her foot. Outside the building they stepped out onto the cement sidewalk and headed to the nearest street corner. At the intersection of Rue de la Maison Blanche with Avenue d'Italie, they turned south and walked to the first Metro stop they could find. Elena knew they needed to put as much distance between themselves and Paris as they could, and fast. But she also needed some answers. Since she'd left school a few short days ago, she had constantly been on the run, pursued by some unknown organization who apparently wanted her dead and also seemed to be ahead of them every step of the way. And now, she had killed someone.

As they approached the bus waiting at the Metro station, she stopped dead in her tracks.

"Alec," she said, "wait."

He did not appear to hear her and kept walking forward. A little louder, she repeated, "Alec, wait!"

Several hundred feet away, he finally stopped and turned around. *Elena, why are you stopping? We need to get going! Let's go! You said it yourself. They are coming!*

He reached his hand out to her. She could see the urgency in his eyes. However, neither had any effect on her.

No, Alec, she said. *I am not moving anywhere until I get some answers. Answers that make sense.*

chapter 14

Elena, we don't *have time for this,* Alec barked. *We have to keep moving. They'll be here any minute and the bus is about to leave!*

No, she told him. *I am not going until I have answers. I am tired of running and not knowing why.*

He started walking back toward her. *And don't even think of carrying me,* she snapped. *I will scream as loud as I can and make sure we are caught.*

Elena, why are you doing this?

Doing what? she asked.

Putting yourself in danger like this? he replied.

See, there's the problem, she retorted. *What is the danger? I was attacked at my school by some dead football player, have been running for days on end, and am doing all sorts of weird things with my mind while being involved in some strange war I don't know anything about. And now I am killing people with my mind. I need answers, Alec. And I need them now!*

Alec stared at her for a few moments then began walking toward her again. *Fine,* he said in exasperation. *You'll have your answers. But we have to get somewhere safe first. They're gonna be here...*

Elena cut him off midstride. *Then you better start talking.*

He threw his hands in the air. *We'll both be captured and it'll be your fault.*

She glared at him. *Fine. We get somewhere safe, and then you start answering my questions. Or, you can forget about going to see this Elder.* She stared hard into his eyes. *Deal?*

Yes, he conceded. *Deal.*

They boarded the bus and sat together in silence along its route. Alec watched the buildings and storefronts pass by and signaled Elena they were getting off at the next stop. Within a few short minutes, they were crossing the threshold to a quiet little café.

Okay, Alec said in exasperation, *we should be able to hide out here for a little while.*

"How about we get ourselves a nice private table so we can talk?" Elena whispered. Alec followed Elena's lead, and they made their way to a secluded table.

Sorry, she said, *I figured if we were up front and center not saying anything it would seem suspicious. We don't want to attract any unnecessary attention.*

Alec smiled at her. *No,* her replied. *Good thinking.* A waitress came over and took their orders.

After the woman had gone and brought back their coffees, Alec began, *All right, Elena, I'll tell you what I can. But please understand there are many things going on even I don't understand.*

She smirked at him. She never had a perfect dig to interject into a conversation, but this time she couldn't resist. *Wow, I think you killed any illusions I may have had of you as an omniscient archangel type.*

He smiled back, but she could see there was something behind his smile. Something maybe like shame? She couldn't tell.

What's the face about? she asked him.

What face?

When I mentioned the word omniscient, you made a face.

Ah, he murmured. *You saw it? What am I saying? Of course you did.*

What is it, Alec? You're keeping something from me. She studied his face. When she spoke again her voice had changed. It implored, almost begged. *Please don't keep things from me. You're about the only person I can trust right now.*

Alec's face flushed with color. *Um. That's part of the problem. You trust me. Which—don't get me wrong—you should, but I am afraid I have also not been entirely truthful with you.*

What are you talking about? What is it? She had a sinking feeling in her gut.

He studied his folded hands resting on the table. *Well, you see, the thing is I don't think I am what you think I am. I am not omniscient. In fact, right now I have no idea what to expect. Right now, I am not entirely sure what I am doing as your protector. Every Daimon has a different awakening, and through this process each one of us learns our powers. Your powers, however, are far more advanced than mine. You can hear others' thoughts at will, while I can hear those either directed at me, or those inadvertently let loose. Your strength keeps growing each day. And you also seem to be able to add new powers as you need them, almost as if you create them at will.*

Despite her confusion, she kept her face as stoic and unreadable as she could. *You may not believe me,* she said to him, *but I kind of suspected something was different. But what does this mean?* Her tone dropped slightly, tinged with a hint of sadness. *I mean, who are my parents?*

Unfortunately, nobody ever told me. But I think they both must have been very powerful Daimones.

She perked up a little. *Really?* she asked. *Why?*

Well, you see, he explained, *it's the things you're able to do.* He paused. *Most Daimones can read limited thoughts and speak to each other mentally, but you can do much more. You can inflict mental pain. Hell, you can actually inflict physical damage with your mind. Those are abilities a very few third generation or older Daimones possess.*

Elena nodded. She found something attractive about the idea of being from a strong Daimon line. *Well, okay, here's another thing. What do you mean by third generation?*

It's how we understand our kind, Alec explained. *The Elder is the progenitor of our kind. Kind of like the prime. His first offspring would then be the first generation of Daimones, and so on. To my knowledge, two first-generation Daimones survive to this day, but they both have been in hiding for thousands of years. It is believed with each successive generation, the abilities we possess diminish. Most of the Daimones remaining in this world are sixth generation. Myself, I am the lone seventh-generation Daimon in existence. I was the last one born before the great plague rendered us sterile.*

Elena nodded. *Why am I here?* she blurted. *I mean, how was I born a Daimon if the plague sterilized our entire kind?*

He said, *I think whoever created you was unaffected by the plague. It is possible some of the older generations may not have contracted the plague since so many were in hiding during the wars.*

You never did finish telling me about those wars, she prodded.

Alec waited a few moments before responding. *Well, the funny thing is you likely already know the story. Do you remember the Christian tales of how there were angels cast out of heaven?*

She nodded. *Yeah, Lucifer was cast from heaven for rebellion and banished from the light of God.*

According to our own legends, there was a Daimon early pre-Christian humans followed as their god. This Daimon was a very cruel, wrathful, and cunning ruler who expected tremendous amounts of tribute from her human subjects. The Daimon revolted against the Elder, who wished us to remain humanity's benefactors. But many Daimones came to the Elder's defense, and there erupted a great war between the two groups. We are still today fighting the same war. It is the war for humanity.

Alec continued. *Daimones loyal to this ruler, we call them the Opposition, have been seeking out the Elder's hiding spot to eliminate him. But so far, his location remains hidden. As I mentioned to René, older generation Daimones can identify his resting place. René was one of them. He was reportedly one of the last Daimones alive to have ever spoken with the Elder.*

If he actually did, then we'll never hear it from him now. But I suspect he was telling the truth. If he had actually known, then why not divulge the information to the Opposition instead of defecting to their side?

Elena paused for a few seconds. *Okay, so now what can you tell me about my abilities?*

Still early, the cafe had few patrons. While Alec sipped his coffee, Elena managed to polish off the remainder of hers and order a second. Alec finally replied to her question.

Unfortunately, he said, *I understand little about your abilities or what to expect of them. No young Daimon I've ever heard of has had any of the abilities you've been displaying. The legends of such powers, as I mentioned before, concern very old Daimones who were much closer to the Elder. And, as I said, these were legendary.*

But why did the Daimon woman in London say she could not be hurt by my parlor tricks when I tried to inflict pain upon her? Elena asked him. *She was, at first, unhurt by my attacks on her.*

Alec's brow furrowed. *Describe her,* he said.

Elena described the woman from London and Alec's eyes grew wide with amazement. *Can you show her to me in your mind?* Elena conjured a memory of the woman and projected it into Alec's mind.

No! Alec exclaimed. *It can't be! You fought with Mairya and lived to tell about it?* He paused. *This explains a lot,* he said, *especially about why your abilities didn't work against her.* He stiffened. *Mairya is very powerful. She is an assassin for the Opposition. She has been referred to in several human religions as the Angel of Death.* Alec paused for a second. *Remember I told you a Daimon was followed by pre-Christian humans as a god? Well, according to the legends, Mairya was the Daimon's right hand. She did all of the dirty work. She was the punisher, the executioner, and the bringer of death. She is also a third-generation Daimon and very powerful in her own right. She has powers many of us do not understand and very few of us can survive. It was through tales of her murders I learned of some of the powers you possess.*

Alec's tone changed, *Did she ever say anything to you about why she was there?*

Yes. Elena replied. *She told me her "Mistress" wanted to speak with me, but once I resisted, she decided she had to kill me.*

So, he said thoughtfully, *you have drawn the attention of some very powerful enemies. Mairya's Mistress has walked this earth for many thousands of years. She has seen the rise of human civilization from small hunting and gathering tribes and clans to mega-farming, nuclear-powered democracies. And still she desires to place all of humanity under her thumb and demand tribute for not destroying it all. From what I hear of her abilities, she possesses such powers.* He paused. *Or at least she would if it weren't for those of us who constantly attempt to thwart her efforts.*

Elena sighed and said, *Well, then she shouldn't be much of a problem.* She hung her head in exasperation. After a few quiet seconds she added, *Why me?*

Alec took a few seconds and a few sips of his drink to get around to answering. *Well, the most obvious answer is you are the source of the Daimones DNA code your father found,* he said. *Aside from that, the best answer I can come up with is you are valuable. You obviously have tremendous power. I mean, I could never have survived an attack from Mairya, let alone get away from her.*

I think I escaped because I broke her arm, Elena interrupted.

Alec coughed, choking on his coffee. *Wait. What?* Alec's eyebrows arched high. *Did you say you broke Mairya's arm?*

I actually broke both of them. Crushed them in my bare hands. She paused. *I felt bad about doing it, but she seemed intent on killing me. I had to defend myself.* Elena paused for a moment, and then added, *And I nearly tore her jaw off.*

Alec choked on his coffee and spat it out across the table. Elena, surprised by this reaction, reached across the table and started slapping him on the back, lifting his arms up.

"Ow, stop...stop! Stop!" Alec had to shout to get Elena to stop pounding on his back. Several sets of eyes in the room were fixed on them. After several minutes, the eyes turned away.

Goddamn, that hurt! Alec complained.

Elena laughed. *Very funny, Alec!* Dripping with sarcasm, she continued, *Ha! Ha!*

No. Seriously, that really hurt! Alec pulled his shirt away from his shoulder quickly, and Elena gasped. His back, red as a beet, had several bruises already forming.

Oh my God! Did I do that? How? I mean, how could I hurt you? I saw you take a bullet and shrug it off.

First off, Alec replied, *don't worry about it. You didn't break any bones. It hurt like hell, though. Second, it's what I said before: your strength keeps growing. It'll be a lot of fun to see what other abilities of yours develop over the next few years. Finally, simply because it takes a lot to hurt us, doesn't mean we cannot be hurt.*

Alec glanced across the room at a flat screen television hanging on the wall. Elena could see his jaw drop open and his face turn pale.

Elena, he said, *we have to leave. Now.*

Why? She asked. *I don't hear any voices. You said we were safe here.*

Alec shook his head subtly, his eyes glued to the television screen. *We were safe.* He placed a distinct emphasis on the word were. *Slowly turn around and check out the television.*

As she did, Elena felt her face flush. There were artist-rendered drawings of her and Alec plastered on the screen with footage running in the background of the pub they had visited yesterday. She turned pale as soon as she realized a fire consumed the bar.

Alec translated the French news program, *there was a massive terrorist explosion at the bar we were at in London last night. And it appears we are the two key suspects in the investigation.* He paused as he listened. *Ah, and I guess we are to be considered armed and dangerous. Apparently, Mairya did not like getting beaten up by you last night. Unfortunately, this little twist of fate will make things a bit more complicated as we try to get across Europe.* His voice took on a note of caution. *All of Europe's police authorities now think we are armed terrorists.*

Alec stood and fished into his pocket for some cash. *Remember: Play it cool.* Alec slapped the Euros necessary to pay for their drinks and a reasonable tip down on the table, then stood casually and waited for Elena to join him. Together they walked together from the café back out into the morning light.

chapter 15

Despite having their faces plastered all over the news channels, Elena and Alec managed to leave the bar without attracting any attention. Luckily, the recent news broadcast would not have been seen by most of the on-shift drivers. They took a cab to the Parc de la Mairie in Choisy-le-Roi. From there, they made their way to the train tracks nearby and climbed aboard a slow-moving freight car.

They rode for several hours, keeping the doors closed, and saying very little. The car rolled west across much of France and to places they knew not where. As the sun began to set, the train slowed to a crawl. Elena peered out through the crack in the doors. "Alec, we need some food and something to drink. And honestly, I really need to pee."

"Agreed," he replied. "But I think we need to give it another hour until it's dark. We may be able to cover some distance if I am able to fly at night." He paused. "And if you really need to go, you can be discreet behind some boxes over there."

Elena rolled her eyes. Given the pressing urgency of her need, she knew she could not hold it any longer. But as long as she addressed one source of discomfort, she decided to bring up another.

Alec, I have to say these past few days have been absolute hell for me.

Do you really want to talk about this while you are doing that? She could hear the discomfort in his voice. *Or, can this conversation wait a few minutes?*

Elena grumbled. Did it really matter at this point? *I dunno. I guess it can wait,* she conceded. And then, she asked, *Why does it even matter?*

No response came until she zipped her pants. *It matters to me,* he said. *Even though I cannot see you, I think it more polite not to be talking to a pretty girl while she's doing what you are doing.*

In her corner, Elena blushed. He thought she was pretty. She remembered his strong arms wrapped around her, his sapphire eyes staring into hers. It aroused a desire within her. Despite the large set of wings springing from his back, she really didn't mind seeing him without his shirt, either. She allowed herself the indulgence of imagining their intertwined bodies in a moment of passion, enjoying the fantasy. As the train hit an odd patch of track it threw her off balance and rudely reminded her of the situation at hand.

Getting her mind under control, she slowly made her way out from behind the stack of boxes. She drifted back to his earlier comment about her being pretty. Her take away from the interchange had nothing to do with his chivalry and everything to do with him thinking she was pretty. She tried to suppress a smile.

I have a strange question. She paused. *I'm not sure how to ask, but are we related? I mean, are we family, or something?*

He seemed to consider this for a few moments. *Not in a traditional sense, no.*

Elena huffed. *How come you can never give me a simple answer?*

She really wanted to ask something else, but couldn't muster the courage. What were his feelings for her? Did he have butterflies around her, too? Did he feel for her the way she did for him?

Alec touched her arm softly and smiled, electricity passing between them as it had been when she'd fallen on campus. *Because, nothing is ever simple. Other than the fact we are both Daimones, we have no shared blood lineage. So, no, we are not related. However, it has been my responsibility to take care of you and watch over you since you were a baby. I have been your guardian and benefactor your whole life. Perhaps this is why I feel so protective of you.*

She wondered even as he said it if he spoke the whole truth. Could his interest in her be purely professional, merely a reflection of his duty to care for her? His job to love her? Was his the love of a parent for a child, or a guardian for his charge? She wanted it to be something more, needed it to be.

I have always cared for and loved you, he added.

His voice sounded a bit choked and her heart fluttered a little at his words. Her face felt flushed.

Yet, even as she watched him, he tensed, his face turning pale. Her heart sank. He spent too long choosing his words, otherwise he would have spoken instead of acting like a fish sucking air. She wondered what passed through his mind —what he wanted to say.

Aggravation tainted his voice as he blurted, *Elena, I don't have time for this nonsense. My job is to take you to the Elder. Nothing can get in the way of that happening. Do you understand me? Nothing.*

The words stung her like a slap across the face. Her heart sank. Nonsense? Job? She wanted to throw up. Her stomach turned sour. He was her companion, the one person she knew who actually understood something about who, or what, she was—something which she herself knew very little about. She hung her head and nodded.

She sulked back behind the stack of boxes where she had relieved herself fighting the urge to cry with every ounce of strength she had. It took several minutes, but after getting her disappointment under control, she responded to him.

Okay.

A barely audible sigh drifted across the car from where he sat. The sigh said it all to her. He knew he'd made a terrible mistake in the way he responded. At least, it's what she hoped the sigh meant. She wished he'd been developing feelings for her as much as she had for him; even though she'd been his ward—his charge for protecting, he'd fallen in love with her. But it was fantasy, her dream. This is real life. And despite the fact she flitted about

Europe with a bona-fide Angel, the rational part of her mind couldn't accept his sigh had any deeper meaning than being a sigh. She shook her head, attempted to get control of herself, and took a deep, cleansing breath.

When Elena finally stepped back out from behind the boxes, she asked, *I still do not see how I fit in?* As she approached he stared off at nothing.

We continue to be at war, and for the last several thousand years, there have been numerous omens and premonitions foretelling a young female with very strong powers would be the one to end the war. So, when your birth came to our attention, it was decided it would be in our best interests to keep your existence a secret. You were hidden away in the safest place we could imagine—with a human family. We all knew one day your abilities would emerge, as they had with us all, and you would eventually need to be brought into the Daimon fold.

However, once the Opposition learned of your existence, they moved quickly. They were diligent but unsuccessful in their attempts to find you. They tried stealing your father's research in hopes of finding you. But I got the jump on them. You see, they wish to have you for themselves because, as the prophecies forecast, you will be the one to end the war. But if they cannot have you to themselves, then you must be destroyed. That's the reason they're trying to kill you. Alec finished.

Okay, but how did they find me at college? She stopped pacing and sat on a crate across from him.

I'm not quite sure. My best guess is they probably suspected something and were watching you. Once they saw me on campus, they must have concluded they had their target. When they reanimated the football player and attempted to kill you, they knew they were right. I had to protect you. I couldn't let you be killed.

Elena interrupted him once again. *Daimones can reanimate the dead?*

Yes. Some can reanimate dead human tissue and control it. A number of the higher generation Daimones developed strange abilities when they were infected with the plague. It warped their mental skills, took their latent powers, and changed them. All of the myths about zombies, necromancy, vampires, and ghouls actually have some stray strand of truth to them. But we really don't have time to get into it now. Suffice it to say there are some really dangerous Daimones out there who would stop at nothing to see you dead.

Alec gently poked his head out of the cargo doors. Elena had been so wrapped up in the conversation she hadn't even noticed the train rolled to a stop. The sudden squeal of the brakes and the jerking of the train cars hitting their bumpers nailed the point home.

Alec spun around quickly and slammed the cargo doors shut. *Dammit!* he exclaimed. *There are six Daimones flying around out there.*

Elena stopped dead in her tracks, spun, and gawked at him. *Wait. Are you sure?* she asked fearfully. *How come I couldn't hear them?*

Yeah, I'm sure, he seemed perturbed by her first question. *I can see them flying around. Maybe you can't hear them because they're not speaking with each other telepathically.*

Elena scanned the interior of the freight car. The large sliding door in the roof of the car could be slid aside if necessary. From there they could fly out of the car and try to evade their stalkers. The problem was Alec would have to carry her.

Elena locked eyes with Alec. *I think we may have to split up,* she told him. *You cannot carry me and still move fast enough to outrun so many pursuers. I may be able to run and hide for a little while if you can provide a distraction. Then...*

Alec shook his head before she finished mouthing the suggestion. *No!* He began sliding the skylight open, inching it along very slowly. *They are smarter than you give them credit. They won't follow me for long if they don't see you with me.*

He paused and walked over to her. As he reached out to place a hand on her shoulder, she pulled away. *We'll have to make a break for it. Considering how much your strength has grown, I think we may be able to hold our own if it came down to a fight.*

Elena didn't say anything, but walked over to the sliding double-doors. As she watched through the small crack between them, all of the Daimones circling the freight car flew either higher up into the night sky or farther away from their location. Something did not feel quite right about it. The Opposition had her and Alec right where they wanted them. Why weren't they swooping in for the kill?

A series of spotlights painted the side of the freight car in blinding white light as the night sky lit up with flashing red and blue strobes. The blare of sirens echoed through the freight car. It all made sense to her. The Opposition backed away so the human authorities could do the dirty work.

Alec, we have to go.

Elena reached out, grabbed his hand, and before she could say more, they launched upward through the closed skylight, sending a rain of splinters into the night sky. She couldn't believe how fast they were moving. Alec carried them far faster than when they were on the run in Canada.

She peered below them briefly as they moved. The freight car in which they had been riding was surrounded by police and military vehicles perched and ready for an assault. It did not appear they were willing to take prisoners, either. They ascended even faster, tearing upward through the night sky.

Elena! Stop! he yelled. *You've gone far enough!*

What do you mean?

He hung from her hand like a child's teddy bear. His shirt was still on; his wings had not opened. But then, how were they flying upward? She searched to her left and to her right, but did not see any wings behind her.

Alec, you're kidding me, right? she asked. *I don't have any wings. I can't fly.* When he didn't answer, she barked at him, *How are you doing this?*

I'm not! he cried in exasperation. *You're doing this. Now, please let me go!*

How can I be flying? She asked him, her voice filling with panic. *You're doing this, aren't you? Please tell me you're doing this.*

He tried fruitlessly to pry himself from her grasp grunting, *Elena. Let. Me. Go.*

She let go of his wrist and he fell a few feet before his shirt tore away from his body as his great wings spread behind him. In the few moments it took for him to fly back up to meet her, the realization came upon her she floated in the air high above the railroad car. *Alec?!* she yelped with panic. *How am I doing this?* And then, she fell.

She plummeted at least a couple of hundred feet before Alec finally caught her and stopped her fall.

I'm not sure how you did it, he said to her, *but you've got to figure out how to do it again real quick.* He pointed ahead of them. *Here they come.*

All of the Daimones who had flown out of the area were now converging on them. In a matter of seconds, they were surrounded. There were far more than the six they had seen earlier, and she still could not hear their telepathic communication. She could usually hear any mental voices talking nearby her, but could not hear these Daimones. As one of them approached, she figured out why.

The Daimon man had a strange contraption attached to his throat. She had seen enough action movies to realize it was a microphone, which sat right above his vocal cords. They knew she could hear their minds when they were close, so they were not using telepathic communication. They were using walkie-talkies.

She gasped, and her baser instincts took control. She sped through the air, flying blindly away.

Elena, wait. Too fast. Alec's voice trailed off and disappeared from her mind very quickly.

She scanned the skies, unable to see Alec anywhere.

Oh, crap. Her heart raced as panic washed over her.

She began to fall.

She had to admit she did not like the feeling of uncontrolled freefall. Her stomach sat in her throat, her heart on the verge of stopping, while the earth rushed toward her. She tried to calm herself down, but found the freefall too distracting. Instead, she decided to focus her mind with internal monologue.

Okay, I have done this on two occasions, now. But how? she asked. *I didn't do it consciously. No! I merely did it. It is not a conscious thing.*

She focused her mind and focused on floating in air. Her freefall halted in an instant and she hovered hundreds of feet above the ground. Willing her body to move forward, it slid through space. Experimenting, she willed herself to move with astonishing speed and her body responded to the demand. In an instant, she moved so fast the entire earth rushed by.

Elena, she heard Alec's voice in her head, faint but present. *Where are you?* he asked.

She stopped instantly. And her sudden stop did not have the effect of inertia—like a car coming to a dead halt. Her body simply ceased movement. Surveying her surroundings, she realized she was lost, unsure from which direction she came.

I don't know. She replied. *Where are you?*

Alec responded, *I am about three miles east of where we were. The other Daimones are behind me, and I am beginning to wear out.* Oddly, she could hear the exhaustion in his mental voice. *I can't keep this pace much longer. They are nearly as fast as I am.*

Elena thought for a few seconds. She needed to find Alec. Her heart started to race and her palms were sweaty. She began to panic. The idea of leaving him alone to have to fight all of those Daimones was unbearable. She needed him. She had to find him!

She scanned the skies, but then realized she had moved so fast he could literally be miles away from her. *Damn! How do I find him?* she asked herself. *What other things can I do?*

An idea occurred to her. She knew she could always find his mental voice no matter how far he may be. After all, she'd proven it. They were speaking. So, why couldn't she use the same mental connection to find him? After all, if she knew his voice, then she should be able to trace it back to him. Right?

She focused on him and searched the skies but did not see much of anything. *Alec,* she called out to him mentally, *where are you?*

I am almost four miles from the train now. She could hear the panic in his voice. The Opposition must be right on top of him.

Barely visible against the sky, a translucent silvery thread floated in the air. As she focused her attention on the iridescent filament, it became increasingly clear to her from where it originated. It belonged to Alec and connected them mentally—a conduit along which their thoughts could pass between one another. And if it carried his thoughts to her, then it could lead her back to him.

Okay, Alec, she said, *I've got you. I'm coming.*

She focused on being by his side and moved through the air faster than even before, appearing in an instant right next to him.

Alec jumped in his skin. *How did you get here?* he asked.

I flew here, she replied. She could see both their mental threads as they wound between them. The threads were similar, but clearly distinct. Whereas his appeared about a finger's width in thickness and had an iridescent sheen, hers was as thick as her thigh and shone almost pure silver in color, casting a bright glowing halo.

Whoa.

Whoa what? Alec asked a little timidly, his wings beating the air forcefully.

She glanced over his shoulder and saw the other Daimones closing in on them fast. A few hundred yards separated them from Alec. She could see the expressions of sheer malice painted on their faces. They were going to hurt him! She couldn't let it happen.

We have to get out of here, she urged, *fast. We can talk later. Where do we need to go?*

Alec pointed in a direction. Elena grabbed him around the waist and moved with tremendous speed in one direction. After about five minutes, she stopped flying.

"Can you tell where we are?" She asked him. As she did, she could see no mental thread pass between them. She understood how they were found so quickly. They had spent their entire train ride speaking to each other with their mental voices. If Mairya possessed as much power as Alec had suggested, then she could likely do as much, if not more, than Elena could do with her abilities. Either Mairya or one of her compatriots had tracked them by their telepathic connections. She didn't bother contemplating for long, and decided this was the way it happened. Something inside told her she had the right answer.

"Before you answer, speak out loud. She can follow my mental thread."

"Your what?" Alec asked.

"I call it a mental thread," Elena replied. "It's how I found you. I can see your telepathic link as you mentally speak with me. I followed it back to its source...you. If Mairya or one of the others with her has abilities like mine, then it is likely they did the same to us while we were having our conversation on the train. I saw my own mental thread. It was so bright it would be very hard for anyone to miss. We have to remember to use our actual voices to communicate with each other. Otherwise, I fear we may leave ourselves open to detection again."

Alec seemed confused, an unasked question on his face. He opened his mouth to ask her something, but then stopped, scanning their surroundings. "I don't recognize this place," he said at last. "Perhaps, we should set ourselves down some place where we'll be hidden so we can find out."

She studied the ground below them. Nestled in a narrow east-west valley between two mountains, the place exhibited a densely populated grid arrangement. A river wound its way through the town like a snake, and an airport could be seen to the west, while a huge train yard occupied the center of the city, and farm fields lay to the east.

From her vantage point above the small city, she dropped like a stone into a tight alley situated within a cluster of buildings in a small plaza surrounded by a square city block, hoping she had not caught anyone's attention. On their way down, Alec grabbed a flannel shirt to put on from a clothesline strung between two buildings. They stepped out onto the fairly deserted main street and were greeted by the sight of a large Roman-style stone gate with three arched openings.

"We are in Innsbruck, Austria," Alec said as he stepped onto the main street.

"How can you be sure?" she asked him.

Alec pointed at the gate, "The Innsbruck Gate was constructed in 1765 by Empress Maria Theresa to commemorate the marriage of her son, Leopold II, Duke of Tuscany, and to mourn the death of Emperor Franz I, who died at the wedding." He turned and locked eyes, shock painted on his face. "Elena," he said, "we're in the Tyrolean Alps. We traveled more than five hundred miles in a few minutes. We have to get to Budapest. There is a third generation Daimon there I have known for quite some time. He should be able to help us."

Elena couldn't help but be skeptical of yet another of his trusted contacts. "Are you sure he will know where we need to go?" She paused, then added a little more firmly, "Are you sure we can trust him?"

Alec replied with a laugh in his voice, "Yes, he should be able to help. And yes we can trust him. His family has served as the Elder's protectors for quite a long time."

Her body ached with exhaustion. "I think we should find a place to rest for a few."

"Dawn will be approaching fast," he said in agreement. "We will find a place to rest for the day." He added, "I think we should try to stick to traveling at night. Tomorrow night, if you don't mind, you can fly us to Budapest."

Elena nodded weakly. "Don't we have to worry about being spotted?" she asked, barely able to get the question out. "I mean half of Europe's police agencies are searching for us, right?"

Alec stopped for a second. "We'll have to stick to doing the tourist thing," he resolved. "I have some Euros handy still. It should get us a change of clothes. As far as the local police are concerned, I doubt anyone would have figured we could have traveled so far so fast. We have outrun the Daimones. It will take all night for them to catch up."

"Okay," she agreed. "But the first inkling of trouble, and we are out of here. I don't care if it's midnight or broad daylight. We will be flashing through the skies before you can say buh-bye." Elena forced a smile. "Also, we have to remember not to use our telepathy. If Mairya is as powerful as I think she is, then she will be able to find us with little effort. If that happens, then we're really screwed."

chapter 16

"Good morning," he whispered into her ear. His breath on the side of her neck made her heart skip. "Did you sleep well?"

She couldn't speak with the memory of her dreams too fresh in her mind. The feeling of his bare skin pressed against hers, the caress of his lips on her flesh, the scent of his sweat, and the taste of his tongue in her mouth all lingered into her consciousness. The dreams had seemed so real, so life-like. Absorbing her surroundings, it was apparent she'd spent the whole night wrapped in his arms. Standing, she clapped her arms around herself as the brisk morning air stung her exposed skin. Her coat had been left at the pub in London. She would have curled back up to him for warmth, but due to the persistent memory of her dreams decided she needed to put distance between their bodies.

"Ahem," Alec cleared his throat loudly and repeated his question. "Did you sleep well?"

Elena nodded as she paced around the small alleyway. "Yeah," she replied, avoiding his gaze.

Alec's brow furrowed. "What's wrong?" he asked.

"Nothing," Elena sniped. She glanced at him for an instant, avoiding eye contact, and then stepped out onto the main street. "Let's go find some food and warm clothing."

Turning back, the sight of him burned into her mind. He stood alone, and seemed sad. Was it because he no longer held her body so close to his? But then the memory of her dream returned. It took all she could muster to put the dream aside. She needed to focus on the here and now. By "here" she meant cold, and by "now," hungry.

They found breakfast at a small café a few blocks away, and cold-weather clothing at a shop down the road. Hoping to remain unnoticed by the authorities, Elena kept her clothing choices practical and unremarkable in style and color.

After their purchases, they spent the rest of the day visiting the town. From time to time she caught him stealing the occasional glance when he believed she looked the other way. She couldn't help but think maybe there could be more to their relationship than its formality. At least she hoped as much. In spite of how much his words had hurt her she still couldn't help her attraction to and growing feelings for him.

As they made their way through the city they saw no evidence they'd been recognized from their mug shots and she'd been thankful to see their photos were not plastered all over the news here yet. Even so, the European law enforcement agencies would soon enough cast their nets wider in their effort to find the fugitives wanted for the London terrorist attack.

By evening, they had a satisfying dinner of roast duck and venison before the sun settled over the mountains. Having learned the effect of alcohol on Daimones, Elena made sure they steered clear of wine or schnapps. They needed to remain sharp.

Around midnight they managed to find a secluded alleyway and were aloft again. Elena couldn't help but chuckle at the one piece of irony in the past week's happenings. She had begun believing she was a mere human under the protection of her own personal guardian angel, and now found herself dragging the same guardian angel around the skies because he simply couldn't keep up with her.

"Okay," Alec said, "what are you laughing at?"

Elena glanced down at him and admired the most beautiful man she'd ever met. "Nothing," she said with certainty. Then, under her breath she muttered, "Slowpoke."

"I heard that," came his muffled reply.

She laughed louder.

They had flown northeast and followed the Danube. Within ten minutes, they were floating above Budapest. Alec pointed out a location on the east side of the river, above a once heavily industrial zone. They floated down amidst the rusting hulks and iron ghosts of an abandoned factory yard.

"He is here," Alec said as their feet touched the hard earth. "This has been his land for many centuries. Aden lived here before the proto-Celtic tribes first settled this area to extract and refine its nearby ores." He sighed, scanning the buildings, "I need to find him."

Friend. The deep baritone timbre of an unfamiliar mental voice weighed heavy on Elena. *Why have you not called out to me? I sense you are near. It has been so long.*

She scanned the air and found the mental thread. The fairly thin strand appeared deeply colored with mottled blues and greens. Tapping Alec on the shoulder, she followed it with her eyes to its source. "Follow me," she said to him, "I see where he is."

"Elena," Alec replied, "I don't think we should be wandering around here." She could feel him shiver slightly. His eyes narrowed and muscles rippled as his body tensed. "Something doesn't feel right."

She scanned her surroundings. He was right. She could see there were seven different mental threads passing around the grounds. The hackles rose on her neck as warning bells went off in the back of her mind. There shouldn't be so many people here. There were Daimones surrounding them on all sides. And then it became clear, they had fallen into a trap. She could not understand why she could see the mental threads but not hear their conversations.

Perhaps they used another special Daimon ability. She wondered what would happen if she tried to focus on one of the threads? Doing so she jumped, bombarded with a flood of telepathy.

He says he is your friend, the thread's owner said to his conversant, *but he does not reach out to you. You cannot trust him, Aden, if he is not willing to open himself to you. What if he has joined Her forces and works to destroy us?*

She listened to the conversation for a few moments longer. "Alec, they are skeptical of your loyalties, but I feel, based on their conversation, they are truly aligned with us in our mission. Let's simply introduce ourselves to him. We have come too far now to give up. Trap or not, we need to speak with him."

How do you know our doubts? Came the clear, deep timbre voice again.

"He is either reading my thoughts or yours," she said to Alec. "But either way, he is able to hear us when we speak." As she spoke her last phrase, it dawned on her one of the other mental threads sat close by, close enough to hear them. Their words were being broadcast to Aden through one of his companions.

"Alec," she said softly, "one of his companions is conveying our words to him." She nodded her head toward the source of the thread she had seen.

Alec spoke. "Aden, it has been a long time, dear friend," he said. "I am here to ask for your assistance. We cannot speak with our minds because Mairya is on our trail. She has been able to locate us through our telepathy. She has the ability to see our telepathic connections as we speak and follow them to our location. We must use speech in order to confound her. I would advise we all do the same in order to keep the purpose and direction of our quest a secret. Can we meet with you?"

A large form floated down from the top of the highest smokestack. Elena knew at once it belonged to Aden. The rest of the Daimones emerged from the darkness where they hid.

Aden's massive form stood nearly seven feet tall with a wiry frame. He wore no shirt and his physique appeared chiseled from stone. Like most of the Daimones she had met, he had a youthful appearance. He had shoulder-length hair as black as oil, and his silver eyes reflected the moonlight. The wings extending from his back were much different from Alec's. Whereas Alec had feathery white wings like those of a dove, Aden's were leathery and very similar to those of a bat. She also noted he had a wingspan nearly twice Alec's. She could imagine such a Daimon as this gave rise to the legends of vampires like Dracula.

His physical voice mimicked his mental one. "Alec," the massive Daimon asked, "what is this quest you speak of?"

"I would prefer we speak of these things in a more discreet place," Alec replied. "Would this be possible?"

He nodded. "Of course," Aden responded. "You may join me at my manse in Domos."

Aden launched himself skyward with great power, his wings beating the air with strong strokes. The other six Daimones, with a mix of dove-like and bat-like wings followed behind. Alec wrapped his arms around Elena and launched himself skyward. "Let's not reveal the full extent of your powers yet," he said softly into her ear as they brought up the back of the pack.

A short flight later, they had flown northwest from Budapest to a small mountainside overlooking the Danube. A small ruined temple appearing to date back many centuries sat at the crest. Most of its remaining architecture seemed a mix of Byzantine and Roman influences, with some earlier provincial elements visible in the design.

Aden and his troupe walked through the ruins and into a small Romanesque chapel built into the native hillside. Inside, they walked to the back of the structure, moved aside the altar, and descended a narrow stairway, which would lead them to the catacombs.

However, to Elena's surprise, the stairs led to a narrow hallway eventually opening into a well-lit chamber. The massive chamber spanned almost the length of a football field. Stairways leading both upward and down were situated on the right and left extents of the room, and a grand staircase occupied the far end.

"Alec, may I bid you welcome to my humble home?" Aden bowed with courtly grace. "Please, make yourselves comfortable while my companions and I don more appropriate attire for entertaining guests."

The large Daimon left the room up the grand staircase followed by his companions.

The others took a few minutes to dress and compose themselves. When they returned, Aden more fully matched her impression of a real Count Dracula. Dressed all in black his oily black hair and sharp widow's peak increased the intensity of his silvery eyes and the eeriness of his appearance. He wore a suit of fine silk, which seemed to have been hand tailored. His companions were also dressed in black but had at least added a modicum of color in the form of a handkerchief or shawl.

Alec walked over to his host with open arms and gave him a powerful embrace. Elena took a few moments to examine the companions. They were all much shorter than Aden, of average human height, but all of them shared his same silvery eyes and oily black hair. Given their similarity in appearance to Aden, she figured they were all his offspring.

"I trust, my friend, you will be staying for dinner and for the night?" Aden directed the question to Alec. They had eaten a little while earlier.

Alec bowed back to Aden. "Yes," he said with the manners of a courtier, "we will."

"Ah...wonderful," Aden said, raising his hands and gently clapping them together. "And now to the most important matter at hand." He bowed to Elena, "I apologize for my rudeness, but I am Adnachiel."

He stood before her and offered his hand. She placed hers in his and marveled at the size difference.

Aden led them into the dining hall. "As you are my guest and a companion to my dear old friend Alec, you may call me Aden. In literature, I am referred to as the Angel of Independence. I am not, however without my loyalties." He seemed deliberately to keep the nature of his loyalties unspoken.

Aden guided her gently to her seat at a massive dining table appearing to be carved from a section of a massive tree. A full forty people of his size could have comfortably sat around the table without once rubbing elbows. But with their host, Elena, Alec, and the other six seated, it seemed to Elena to be a rather superfluous show of power and wealth. As she sat, Aden asked, "And you are, my dear?"

Alec spoke up next. "I am also sorry for my rudeness, Aden," he said gracefully, "This is my ward, Elena. I am her protector."

Aden's eyes flashed briefly. "You are not human, Elena."

She liked Aden's direct approach, but still wondered how he knew.

"Yes, Aden," she replied. "I am aware I'm not human, even though until recently I thought I was."

"So then," Aden responded, appearing quite pleased with himself, "you are the newborn." He turned to Alec, who had taken a seat next to Elena at the massive table. "And it was you, Alec. You were chosen to be her protector. I can understand why. You and your family have been the most tactically adept of all Daimon warriors in this great war." Aden sat down, propped his elbows on the table, and leaned forward as the remainder of his companions followed and took their seats. "I take it then," he said to Alec with a sly grin, "you are seeking the Elder, are you not?"

Alec nodded. "Yes," he said, "we are."

Aden nodded his understanding, "And you need my help to find him."

Again, Alec nodded.

"Has the girl exhibited any powers, yet?" Aden asked almost as a side note.

Elena watched Alec, but when she could not see him give her any indication as to which way to answer, she replied, "Yes, I have."

"Ah," Aden clapped his hands softly, "so you are awakening. This is wonderful news. It would appear the war will soon be coming to a close." Elena noted his clapping soon turned to wringing. "If the prophecies are correct."

Elena could see a small mental thread reach out to Aden from another room to the right. "I believe our dinner is nearly ready," Aden said. "So come, my guests, and dine with us today. Surely, you must be famished after your long travels."

Elena saw another thread lead from Aden to someone outside the room. He raised his hands as a dozen people dressed in tuxedos came walking into the dining hall carrying silver platters filled with food.

The word dinner could not capture the sheer magnitude of food covering the massive oak slab before them. Spit-roasted pigs and lambs were served with all manner of breads, fruits, and vegetables. There were quite a number of dishes Elena did not even recognize and figured were local traditions. She noted a wide variety of juices available, and a distinct lack of wine at the table.

A half-hour into the meal, Aden finally broached the topic of Mairya. "So, you say Mairya is following you?" Elena could hear the note of curiosity in his voice. "Personally?"

"Yes," Alec replied with disappointment. "She is."

Aden smiled. "What have you done to draw her ire?" He laughed a dark, wicked laugh. Elena felt a little ill at ease.

She answered before Alec had the opportunity. "She is after me."

"Why yes, dear, of course she is," Aden replied with a laugh. "With a mandate directly from Her, I suppose. However, this type of task is usually delegated to her very capable and murderous underlings and not Mairya personally."

Elena blushed a little and studied the table. "She is also very upset with me."

"Oh ho." Aden chuckled. "And how so? What could you have done to make her so angry?" Aden sipped his drink.

"I broke both her arms and nearly tore her jaw off."

"Excuse me," he said, "you did what?"

Elena repeated her statement for him.

"It's preposterous," he finally blurted. "It is not possible. She is a very powerful third generation Daimon. Far more powerful than I. And, if you pardon the expression, a nasty bitch." He laughed, waving his hand dismissively. "There is no way you could have hurt her so bad. I couldn't even do it."

Alec spoke up, "Aden, it is true."

Aden took another gulp of his drink, studying Elena over the top of the goblet. "Then," he said as he put in back on the table, "you really are the one prophesied."

Several mental threads wound in multiple directions from Aden's head. They were all his, for she recognized their appearance from the one she'd observed earlier. She wondered if he could really be trusted and debated whether or not she should eavesdrop on his mental conversation.

She could see an onslaught of mental threads return. At least ten of them were from very close quarters on the outskirts of the room, and the remaining several dozen appeared to have originated from far away. From these she picked up a handful of comments: *Be careful. She will be very powerful... If this is true, then her powers would be very useful to us and our cause... She is too dangerous, and she cannot be allowed to live...*

She locked eyes with Alec, a little fear in her eyes. Aden must have seen this, and all of the mental threads were severed. To Elena, he said, "My dear, is something troubling you?"

She paused, debating whether confronting him or not would be placing them in danger. If Aden were truly an enemy and if this were a trap, then it would be prudent to refrain from revealing too much of her own abilities and maintain the element of surprise should it be necessary to fight their way out.

She considered for a few minutes and then realized all eyes in the room were upon her.

"Aden," she said, "I apologize for sounding too forward, or abrupt, especially as you have provided this magnificent feast for us and have been such a gracious host. I do not want to be rude. But I am a little concerned. You see, I fear things are not as they appear with you." Alec shifted nervously in his chair as she spoke.

Aden laughed, and almost as if on cue, so did his six companions. "Oh. And what is not as it appears?"

She contemplated the best way to say what she wanted to say. Stalling, she said, "Well, you have not yet introduced us to your relations here. And it seems to me there are more beings here within your manse than appear at this table."

Aden laughed some more. "You are very right. I do apologize. These 'relations' of mine, as you put it, are my children: Melachin, Sammal, Irhael, Ba'eral, Felicia, and Sophia." In turn, as he progressed down the line, each child nodded at the mention of their name.

"Now," he continued, "as to the other beings in this manse, of course there are. I have quite a few human servants I pay to tend the house."

"And are all of these servants telepathic like yourself?" she accused.

Aden's expression did not change. "My dear, what are you talking about?"

"You have been speaking with many individuals telepathically throughout dinner," she said to him. Alec shot her a glare, but she ignored his warning. "In fact," she continued, "some of your conversants are located right outside the walls of this room." As Elena spoke, her voice became more excited, trembling with anger.

Aden's face became a mask of rage. "Child," he bellowed at her, "you dare to insult me in my own home?" He stood quickly and pushed back against his chair with such force it smashed to pieces against the far wall. His leathery wings tore through his silk suit and spread out to their fullest extent as he roared back.

She could see mental threads shoot out from him in all directions and she gasped. Had he contacted the Opposition? She had to do something. Her heart pounding, she focused her mind on all the mental threads, seizing them with her own in hopes of finding out the messages they carried. But instead of divulging their secrets, they merely stopped in mid air.

He glared at her with fire burning in his eyes. "How dare you hold my thoughts! Not only do you insult me, but you attack me as well!"

She could feel his mental threads push against her mind, but she simply pushed back against them. Slowly, the threads retreated backward under the force of her mental push. She pushed gently, however, afraid she would hurt him otherwise.

Aden bellowed with a bestial rage. His massive fists slammed down on the table, sending millions of cracks and fractures spidering through the centuries-old oak.

"Who has sent you?" Aden bellowed with rage, "Who?" Turning to Alec, he screamed, "Alec, this is no mere child. She is far more powerful than any Daimon I have fought in the many millennia I have walked this earth. She is dangerous, and she does not understand."

Alec stood. "Aden, my friend. All you say is true. I was there when she injured Mairya. I was there when she crushed René's mind with her own, and I have seen many more things of which she is capable but does not yet understand. We are here to seek the Elder. She needs his guidance—his tutelage, for she is far too powerful to learn her abilities on her own."

Aden studied them both, his silvery eyes moving from one to the other and back again. As though someone had flipped some kind of switch, the storm of rage passed and Aden appeared as calm and collected as he had been before the confrontation.

"Child," he said to her in a gentle voice, "do not fear me. I am not your enemy. The enemy is out there. They are the Opposition. If it were up to them, then we would all be captive under their yoke. Release your grasp on my mind, and we may again talk as civilized beings."

Elena relaxed a little pulling her mind back as his mental threads shot outward briefly and then retracted. Aden retracted his wings, and walked to one of the walls to retrieve another chair for his place. He removed the torn silk jacket and shook his head, "Such a shame. This suit cost me thirty-thousand Euros."

He brought his chair over, placed it at the head of the table, and sat down. He knit his fingers together as he placed his hands on the fractured surface. "Thank you," he said. "I apologize for my outburst, but, you see, it was necessary. I needed to provoke you in order to see for myself what abilities you had. I see now you have developed some rather interesting abilities, and I can do away with my unfortunate pretense. Now, may I ask you some questions?"

Elena nodded. "Yes, if you answer some of mine first." She had a cool edge to her voice. She understood now he may seem intimidating, but she would probably be able to handle him if a fight ever arose.

"Yes, yes, of course. What can I tell you?" his deep voice had softened considerably.

"So," she asked abruptly, "who was it you were talking to?"

His warm smile returned. "I was talking to a great many of my colleagues at the same time. You were correct when you assumed several were outside of these walls. There are ten, in fact, of my compatriots located in the rooms adjoining this. They all have very special talents. Some were trying to ascertain what powers you possess, and others were simply eavesdropping on any conversation you were having with Alec."

"Well," Elena retorted, "I am sorry to say Alec and I have not been having any conversations. I believe she, or one of her team, can see my mental threads and follow them. Because of this, our telepathy led us into a trap."

"Yes," he said, "I understand you have not been conversing telepathically. I have also heard of some of the older generations having the ability to see others' thoughts. Some could even hear them if they wanted. I have one such specialist in the next room. Other Daimones had the ability to block minds, as you did to me now. You see there are a wide variety of abilities for powerful Daimones. But not all of them have been discovered; in fact, some have been long forgotten. Unfortunately, many of our younglings have never manifested these skills, and it is believed as the bloodline stretches farther from the source, from the Elder, and becomes more diluted with each generation, increasingly fewer abilities are passed on to the young. This is likely why Alec, here, has so few abilities himself. Elena, your progenitor must have been a very powerful Daimon indeed for you to possess the abilities you do."

He continued, "Now, how did you know I was conversing with others?"

Elena hesitated. "I could see your mental threads—the telepathic connections between you and your compatriots." She blushed a little bit. "I also didn't like what I was hearing. Somebody told you I was dangerous, and I should not live."

Aden began laughing. "You see, this is the problem with eavesdropping. You sometimes get one part of the conversation, not the other. The part you missed was my correspondent was referring to Mairya, not to you. I, myself, and all of my allies are sympathetic to your goals. We wish to help you reach the Elder, and we will gladly give our lives to end the stranglehold of the Opposition."

"Alec was right in coming to me," he continued. "I believe I will be able to help you. My hope is we can provide enough interference to confound Mairya's lackeys in their pursuit of you."

"I do, though, have one last question of you and Alec." Aden glanced from one to the other as he paused. "Alec mentioned René is dead. Would you two care to explain? He was a close and dear friend of mine."

Alec hung his head. "Aden, it is with great regret I bring such terrible news. Elena and I went to Paris to seek René's assistance. However, he was not himself. Elena caught parts of a conversation between him and Mairya. She instructed him to detain us until she could arrive. I am afraid he was persuaded to join the Opposition."

Elena watched Aden's reaction as Alec told him the story. She noticed despite his previous outburst, he remained impassive.

"When Elena confronted him," Alec continued, "he attacked me. However, the fight was over in seconds. Elena somehow managed to destroy his mind with her own."

She felt like a new Christmas toy being ogled by a spoiled, rich child.

"And that is what I am most interested in," Aden said. "I have heard of Daimones being able to cause mental pain. But there were two I heard of who could destroy another with their mind. The Elder, of course, is the first I had heard of. After all, without him, we never would have been. There are no limits to his powers."

"The second Daimon who could kill with their mind was Mairya."

Elena started as he revealed her name.

"And to think," he continued, "you have actually fought her and survived! It is simply astounding! It makes me wonder who your maker actually is."

Elena paused. "Aden, you and Alec both mentioned Mairya is a third generation Daimon, correct?"

"Yes," he replied.

"And it is very hard for lesser generations to harm higher ones, correct?" she asked.

"Yes," he responded. "With very few exceptions, the lower generations are physically and mentally weaker than the higher ones. So, it is very hard for a lower generation Daimon to truly harm a higher generation," he explained.

"But it is not impossible," Aden cautioned.

To which Alec added, "If you'll remember those Daimones I vanquished in Canada—they were actually a higher generation than I am. I happened to get lucky and best them in battle is all."

Elena nodded. "Okay, then how could I hurt Mairya so easily?"

Aden smiled. "Well," he began, "I speculate your progenitor must have been either first or second generation although I am not so sure any of them still survive. I believe there was one second generation Daimon, Nakir, hiding out in Romania, but I have not heard much of him in the past few centuries. Not, at least, since the Huns invaded the region in the fifth century.

Aden sounded giddy as he continued, "Nakir was actually famous for his cruelty in the battles against the Huns. His penchant for impaling his victims and his knack of swooping down upon his enemies gave him the moniker of dragon—*dracul*. Ten centuries later, Vlad III emulated his strategy and became the inspiration for the popular story, Dracula."

As the night wore on, Aden finally stood from his seat and asked, "How long has it been since you had a decent night's sleep?"

Alec laughed in reply, but Elena's head drooped as she said, "I don't think I can remember the last good night of sleep. It's been nothing but catnaps since I left school. It feels like forever."

"Good," Aden said to her. "You will be sleeping here for as long as it takes to rest your body. Do not be concerned about Mairya. You will be safe here. Not only have you eluded her, but even if she found you, she would be foolish to try and attack me. I may be younger than she is, but she has yet to win a battle against me." Aden exhibited a broad, toothy grin uncharacteristic to the polished courtly persona he presented.

"Please follow my daughter, Felicia, to the room we have prepared for you, and get yourself to bed," Aden said, gesturing toward the doorway. "Rest as long as you need. There will be food for you when you wake."

Elena followed Felicia up the grand stairway and down a long hallway to a large sleeping chamber. The chamber had its own bathroom and a large custom bed. It didn't matter, though, what amenities the room had because she cared solely about crawling into the bed.

Felicia turned to her. "There are pajamas you can use in the chest over there," she said pointing to a cedar chest on the far side of the room. "And there are linens in the bathroom in case you would like to freshen up."

Elena very much liked the idea of a pair of fresh pajamas, and once Felicia had left the room, she rifled through the chest. There were designer pajamas of many sizes and varieties. She picked out a set of silk Fendi pajamas in her size and put them on. She neatly folded her clothes, which were a few hours old, and placed them at the foot of the bed.

Slipping in between the satin sheets, she noticed the weight of the fur comforter, and it made her feel safe and warm. She curled up and brought the covers tight around herself, clasping them in her hands under her chin. However, sleep remained a ways off as she considered her host, deciding on whether or not she could actually trust him.

chapter 17

A thin trickle of light dribbled through a tiny window high in the chamber wall beyond the foot of the bed. The light splashed across her face, bathing her in its glow. She sat up, pushing the heavy fur comforter off with great effort. Despite its weight, the satin sheets and the silk pajamas, she had been quite comfortable through the night. Climbing from the bed, she found the floor to be pleasant and temperate as she made her way to the bathroom. On the sink she found a brand new toothbrush and a note saying, "Elena, Aden has given us a few essential supplies." She didn't recognize the handwriting, but guessed it came from Alec.

After a warm shower, brushing her teeth, and taking care of her other needs, she headed back into the bedroom. Laid out on the bed were clean lined jeans, a long-sleeved T-shirt, and a wool sweater and socks. Felicia must have laid them out for her. Had they been here last night when she fell asleep? She couldn't remember seeing them, but welcomed her host's hospitality.

She dressed quickly, pleased everything fit her exactly right—almost like the clothes had been tailored to fit her. A pair of comfortable leather hiking boots had been placed under the right side of the bed. They were probably the most warm, comfortable hikers she had ever worn.

The clothes had not been on her bed when she woke. In order for the clothes to be here, someone must have come into the room while she showered. Out of the corner of her eye, Felicia sat on a plump golden chair against the far wall.

"Hello, Felicia," Elena said, despite finding it odd the woman sat in silence, watching her.

The woman nodded. "Hello, Elena. Did you sleep well?"

"Yes." Elena paused for a second,

"It has been very nice of you and your family to show us such hospitality."

Felicia chuckled. "There is no need to thank us," she told Elena. "Be sure."

Felicia's tone made the hairs on Elena's arms stand on end. Something seemed not quite right about her manner.

"So, where is Alec? Is he up, yet?" Then, she added, "What time is it, anyway?"

Felicia read the expensive timepiece on her wrist. "It is late. You have been asleep for some time. Alec is with Aden. They have been detained by some pressing matters. If you would come with me, I can show you to your meal."

Elena nodded and followed Felicia out of the bedchamber, down the hallway, and to the great staircase.

"So what time is it?" Elena repeated her question as she followed.

"It is a little after noontime," Felicia replied. "Come, our servants have prepared a brunch for you. There are all sorts of Hungarian specialties."

As Elena began to descend the staircase, her senses were assailed by a variety of aromas. In the dining room, the table had been laid out with several meat dishes, deviled eggs, omelets, pancakes, fruits, and jams, bottles of champagne, juices, pots of coffee, and a wide variety of pastries and breads.

"Aden and Alec have both already eaten, so please enjoy." Felicia motioned to the food.

Perhaps Elena had gotten the wrong impression of her before. She watched as Felicia headed out one of the doorways and left her alone to the abundant breakfast feast.

She gathered a large plate of food and poured a hot cup of coffee, adding milk and two spoons of sugar. She sat down at the table and began shoveling in her breakfast, finding it to be delicious. She enjoyed as much as she could eat.

It took her about fifteen minutes to feel full. She stood and swallowed the last swig of her third cup of coffee as Felicia came back into the room.

"When do Aden and Alec expect to return?" Elena asked.

"When she has finished with them," Felicia replied with a smirk.

Panic stirred in her. She opened up her mind and scanned the room. There were mental threads flying about everywhere. And then Mairya's thread appeared in the air. She didn't understand how she knew it was Mairya's, but she knew. Elena lashed out at Felicia with her mind for conversing with Mairya.

Despite wanting to destroy Felicia for betraying her, Alec, and Aden, she couldn't bring harm to Aden's daughter. And to do so may destroy her chances of finding the Elder.

She reigned in her punishment of the woman and settled upon paralyzing her a little rather than destroying her mind. Spittle began to pour from Felicia's mouth, and her body slumped to the hard stone floor. Then, Elena focused her attention on her true target.

Very good, Newborn. Mairya invaded her mind. *You have learned much in the past few days. I am truly impressed. Yours truly is an "Awakening." However, you neglected to recognize my Mistress has allies in nearly every corner of this world. Now your beloved protector and his former mentor are about to endure some truly diabolic machinations of my own devising.* The woman's mental voice laughed coolly in her head.

No! Elena shouted at her. *I have beaten you once. I will do it again!*

Mairya's spoke with rage. *You will never again harm me. Your luck in resisting me will soon come to an end, child! Do not dare to think you can resist me forever!*

Elena's head twinged. The seeds of a dull ache grew over her eyes followed by a sensation akin to her brain boiling. Grabbing her head with both hands, she collapsed to her knees, tears rolling from her eyes.

See, child. I told you, you could not resist me forever. It's too bad I will have disappointed my Mistress by killing you.

Through the numbness now overtaking her senses, Elena turned her attention to Mairya. Following the woman's mental thread, she forced back at Mairya with all of her might. The pain in her head slowed, and then stopped, Elena watched as the mental thread receded back into Mairya. The connection attempted to snap off, but Elena couldn't let her get away. She wanted to end it and end it now.

Focusing her mind on the origin of the mental thread, Elena willed herself to be there. Her eyes blurred for a fraction of a second and she lost sight of the mental thread. As the room came back into focus, she found herself standing a few feet behind Mairya.

How did you do that?

Alec's voice intruded in her mind. Scanning the room, she found him in the corner of the room. Her mind scanned her surroundings. The lofty room contained all manner of torture devices and resembled a dungeon right out of some gothic horror film. And then it occurred to her she had seen Alec strapped to one of the devices in the corner. It resembled a pair of rollers with ropes at the head and foot positions connected to large hand cranks and gears. She knew from her history textbooks this particular device was called as the rack, its purpose to stretch and break a person's joints, causing them excruciating pain. And Mairya took sick pleasure in using it.

Alec, she said to him, *are you okay?* She couldn't keep her concern for him out of her voice.

I'll be fine, he replied. *We heal fast.* She could hear the pain in his voice and his tone didn't sound too convincing.

Where is Aden? she asked. She could see Alec's eyes move slightly. She followed his gaze and saw Aden strapped into another device. This one resembled a large cruciform frame with screws placed over the joints. Aden didn't move or scream. He lay there on the device as several Daimones kept turning the screws, increasing pressure on his joints.

Elena's conversations and observations happened within fractions of a second. Eavesdropping on the conversations flying through the room, Elena heard Mairya yell for several of her cohorts to grab her.

Three Daimon males rushed toward her with spectacular speed. But to Elena, they moved in slow motion. Watching them move, she stayed a few steps ahead.

Two of them stood to her right, with the closest to her left. He lunged with outstretched arms, but Elena had already anticipated his move. She flew up into the air and hovered as two of the attacking Daimones, the one on her left and the closest one on her right, crashed into each other. The third Daimon saw the collision and dodged, crashing into a stunned Mairya. Elena snatched a knife out of the hand of another Daimon across the room and landed next to Alec. She cut the ropes on the torture device then rushed over to free Aden. Instead of trying to unscrew Aden's device, she simply tore the device apart with her bare hands. She had avoided the attacks and freed both of her friends before Mairya had even stumbled backward from the force of the other Daimon crashing into her. She landed again to Mairya's right and waited for the falling Daimon woman to turn toward her.

Shock and astonishment covered Mairya's face. She lashed out at Elena with one of her fists. But she caught the blow in her hand, and crushed the fist, breaking several bones.

That, Elena spat at her, *is for torturing Alec.*

Elena followed her attack with another, breaking Mairya's elbow joint by forcing it in the wrong direction. To Elena, it was justice served cold to hear the satisfying crunch and her whimpers of pain and surprise. *And that is for Aden.*

Leave me alone, Elena barked at Mairya. *Stop hunting me. I do not want to hurt you. But I will if you make me.*

Mairya glared at her in a mix of fury and pain. *But I want to hurt you, don't you understand? I want to kill you.*

Why? Elena asked. *Why do you want to kill me?*

Because my Mistress told me to, Mairya yelled. *She can see now where your allegiances are. You have become a traitor to your species and therefore have become our enemy.*

Elena flew quickly, grabbed Alec and Aden, and left the room through an opening in the carved stone ceiling. She could hear Mairya's mental scream of rage and frustration. Both Alec and Aden clapped their hands to their heads, but as Elena flew faster, they quickly reached the limit of Mairya's mental range. Elena could see the woman's mental thread had stretched thin to the point of transparency.

"Elena," Aden began, "I swear it was not I who told Mairya where you were."

Elena nodded. "It was Felicia."

"My Felicia? No, impossible! She would never betray me. She's my best aide. I trust her with my most sensitive plans. She could not have done such a thing. I don't believe it."

His mental thread shot through space, likely in an attempt to contact his daughter. But given Felicia's recent betrayal, she decided to block his mental thread before it could reach her.

"Aden," she said to him, "we cannot afford to give away our location to Mairya. She will not be far behind us."

Aden laughed. "That is what you think. Do you recognize where you are?"

She didn't.

"These are familiar skies," he told her, "and for the life of me cannot understand how we are here. This is at best a five hour's journey for a winged Daimon, and you have made it here in a matter of seconds. Mairya will not be catching up with us any time soon."

Elena finally released both Aden and Alec so they could fly of their own volition. "Aden, wasn't it you who told me last night nobody would dare to attack you in your own manse?" she asked. "And even if they dared, no attack would be successful?"

Aden turned away, obviously embarrassed.

"And didn't Mairya carry off a successful coup?" she continued her questioning. "Didn't I rescue you from your very own dungeon?" Aden seemed a little cowed by her questions. Elena paused. "Aden I don't want to underestimate what Mairya is capable of. She's been resourceful enough to stay hot on our heels since she and I brawled in the London pub."

Aden tilted his head. "Pub? Wait a moment. Are you referring to the terror attack in London?" Then his face lit with recognition, "It is you two the human authorities are looking for?"

Elena nodded. "I hope you can see your old friend and I are not terrorists."

Aden shook his head. "She will want vengeance. If she decides to kill you, then she will make your death slow and painful."

His head dropped. "I am worried about my other children," he said. "I fear Mairya will use them to get to me. And in turn, to get to you."

She couldn't let Mairya use the blood of innocents against her. "Aden," she said, "do you wish to go back and save your family?"

He inhaled deeply, caught her eye, and shook his head. "No," he said firmly. "You are far too important to be lost on some fool's errand. Mairya will likely exact her vengeance on you by killing my family. It would be no use to try and save them. To try would be a trap."

"Do you not think Felicia will be able to protect them?" Alec asked. "After all, they are her siblings, and I did not see any of them being tortured."

"She may," Aden said hopefully, "but I can't be sure. I have to be honest I did not anticipate her betraying me to Mairya."

"Well, I am sorry to say this," Alec responded, "but we cannot worry about them right now. We have to complete our..."

A voice cut Alec off mid-sentence.

I see you, Mairya's voice hissed with acid. *You will not escape me.* And then, there they were, three Daimones approaching at fantastic speed. She could see from the appearance of the mental thread one of them was Mairya.

She is here. Elena spoke to both Alec and Aden who spun around and followed her line of sight.

How? Both Aden and Alec asked, almost in unison.

Aden responded. *No! Camael is with them.*

Who? Elena asked.

Camael is known by humans as "He who sees God," Aden explained. *He is a third-generation Daimon who has the most developed powers known. He is even more powerful than Mariya. He is also the Mistress's mate.*

Yes I am, came an unfamiliar voice.

Elena scanned the skies and saw it came from a large Daimon male who carried both of the others. She recognized Mairya immediately but could not see the other so clearly. And then she heard Aden's voice in her head. *No,* he said. *It cannot be.*

Camael let go of the other two Daimones and Elena could see the source of Aden's reaction. The other was Felicia. Aden bellowed with rage.

Felicia, he howled, *how could you betray me! How dare you side against me with my enemies.*

Father, it is you who is the traitor, she retorted. *You are a traitor to your own kind! We are gods among the mortals! It is we who should be ruling them. We should not be warring amongst ourselves and living in secret. We should be revered and take our rightful place as gods!*

Felicia, you are very mistaken. Your mind has been corrupted by them, he said pointing to Mairya and Camael.

No! his daughter fired back at him. *You are an idiot! And you have chosen the wrong side.*

Aden flew at his daughter with rage painted across his face. *I trusted you,* he growled as he cut the air.

Alec followed to restrain Aden.

You've made many bad decisions, his daughter taunted. *Trusting me was another.*

As Aden and Alec were scuffling with Felicia, Camael flew toward Elena like a bullet. *You will not survive,* he howled at her as he approached. *My Mistress's will shall be done. Mairya has failed too many times.* His voice took on a cold, evil tone. *I will not.*

Elena wasn't positive she could handle Camael, but knew it would be an uphill battle to fight them both. Without warning, and with all the might she could muster, Elena forced her will against Mairya's mind and pushed as hard as she could.

The Daimon woman arched her back at an acute angle, her wings falling limp. As Elena watched, Mairya fell from the sky with blood flowing from her eyes, ears, and nose. In a single attack of her mind, she had vanquished the powerful executioner.

Camael's eyes followed the dead form of Mairya as it fell from the sky. *Good,* he said with a wicked sneer. *You have saved me the trouble of having to kill her myself.*

Camael's mental thread emerged and broadened until it had enveloped his entire body. Watching it, she understood what he did—he'd created a mental shield around himself. Following suit, she focused on shielding herself, mimicking his actions. She noticed his mental thread glowed as if alive with electricity, but it was eclipsed by the glow of her own, which shone like a supernova.

So, you have learned how to shield yourself, he said. *Now, let's see how strong your shield is.* Camael smiled.

She watched as his mental thread splintered and shot off a small dart to deliver his message to her. This Daimon had tremendous control over his telepathic arsenal. She watched his attack so she could figure out how he did things.

A thick, spiraled cord of mental thread emerged from his shield, tightly wound and as thick as Camael's thigh. Watching it, Elena knew it would hurt when it struck. The cord crashed into her shield with tremendous force. She could feel the pressure of the blow in her mind, but noticed no other effects from his attack.

She summoned a similar attack, conjuring a thick cord of pain and terror, making it as thick and dense as she could. To her, it resembled the base of a pine tree from back home. She pushed it at Camael with all of the strength she could muster, wound it back, and then struck him again.

The effect of her attack shocked her—the first blow physically pushed him back, and then the second blow pierced his mental shield briefly and struck him in the chest. His body twitched and jolt with the strike.

The expression on Camael's face terrified her. She first believed his appearance was a reflection of his pain, but as it changed to something more akin to perverse pleasure, a chill crept up her spine.

Child, he chided, *you will pay. You got lucky once. You will not get lucky again.*

Camael started a barrage of attacks against her. Another, larger twisted cord struck at her, followed by a series of mental darts. The first blow jarred her, shoving her back several feet, while the darts sent microscopic cracks spidering through her shield. Elena redirected more of her focus on maintaining her shield. When she failed to launch a counter-attack, Camael pressed his advantage and unleashed another bout of strikes.

But this time she could not feel anything penetrate her shield. With a wicked grin, he stared her down, lowered his head, and advanced on her at a full rush. His physical blow against her body sent her reeling. She forgot about flying and began to fall toward the ground below. The effect wore off in short order, and she regained her composure, reset her shield, and took a defensive posture like she had seen in martial arts movies.

Camael did not give her a second to relax as he drove forward again with almost instantaneous speed. She sidestepped his advance, and swung a double-fisted chop downward across one of his wings as he passed. Camael began falling in a tremendous spin. Elena took the opportunity to press her attack and pounced. Flying downward at incredible speed, she grabbed his other wing and wrenched it in two different directions with each hand, snapping it. Camael screamed in pain and put as much distance between them as he could.

Elena's jaw dropped open. She had expected him to fall with a broken wing. Camael, though, righted himself and hovered in front of her, a wicked sneer on his face. *Foolish girl,* he reprimanded, *I do not need my wings to fly. Your weak attacks do not bother me.*

His words could lie, but she could see the pain in his eyes. His taunts were hollow bravado.

He responded with another attack. He bowled into her again, knocking her so hard her neck snapped forward quickly. Stars exploded in front of her eyes and fog overtook her brain. Her shield dropped and she could feel wind tickling her skin as she fell from the sky.

As she fell, he threw several mental attacks against her. One of the darts struck her and her mind filled with terrible visions of Alec and Aden being flayed alive by some bizarre creature with long razor-like nails tipping its fingertips.

She shook the vision from her head and focused on regaining both her flight and shield operational. The shield surrounded her as another round of attacks flew her way. Her freefall stopped a few hundred feet from the ground and she willed herself back into flight, heading right for him with all her might.

He attempted to dodge, but she corrected her course and hit him with both of her fists held straight out in front of her. The blow struck him right in the midriff. He doubled over, and she continued flying straight with him wrapped over her hands. His fists pounded on her back. For such a large Daimon, the blows were not very powerful. She ignored his attacks and wrapped her arms around him. Given the disproportion in their size, Elena's arms reached part way around his massive bulk. Squeezing with all her might, she could hear several bones break inside him.

He cried out both mentally and vocally, writhing to get away from her grasp. Elena pushed him away and drove a fist right at his throat. Reflexively, he dodged the blow, but in his haste had missed her second blow, which struck the small of his back. The blow carried all her force, and it made him double over sideways. As she watched, his shield fell.

Almost instinctively, she summoned another tree-sized mental strike and thrust it not into, but through him. The effect of the attack shocked her. It actually tore a physical hole the size of the mental thread she had summoned straight through his chest. His heart, lungs, ribs, and spine were all gone. She could see through the hole she had punched through him with her mind. His lifeless body plummeted to the earth far below.

Elena sought out Alec and Aden with her mind. Both Daimones were still fighting with Felicia. She seemed to be a formidable opponent for them both.

Flying toward them, she could see by the tendrils of mental thread weaving about they fought a purely mental battle. She shielded herself and interjected in between the two warring parties. At once, the mental threads were broken and all of the combatants were stunned, turning to her.

Elena, she is a very powerful mentalist, a voice cautioned her. *Do not be fooled by Felicia.* Aden spoke behind her. Out of the corner of her eye, she could see he shook off the effects of his own battle with his daughter.

Elena. You had best not interfere, Felicia said to her cordially. *This fight does not concern you. This is between me and my father.* Felicia's mental voice sounded sweet as molasses.

Felicia, Elena retorted, *you involved me when you decided to betray your father and hand me to the enemy. Mairya is dead. I crushed her mind. Camael is dead. I tore his body apart. And if you continue to fight, you, too, will die. I do not want to kill you. But I will if I have to.*

Elena could see the shock on Felicia's face. Felicia's mental threads scanned the skies behind her, presumably expecting to find Mairya and Camael. They never found their mark since both targets were dead.

How could you? she howled at Elena, fury marring her otherwise pretty face. *They are two of the most powerful Daimones who ever existed!*

Correction, Elena jibed. *They were two of the most powerful—before I killed them.* Elena's blood flowed as cold as ice, she'd lost her patience with Felicia.

Felicia, she continued, *you have chosen the wrong side in this battle. If I were you, I would reconsider. Your father loves you, and it would cause him great pain for me to kill you.*

I do not care what will cause him pain, Felicia blurted in a furious rage. *For it is pain I want him to have. I have listened to his endless prattling about living in harmony with humans for centuries. I have fought my own kind, my friends, my lovers, at his side for centuries. And here we are, trapped in some mountain manse secluded from our own kind as well as from the very humans we should be living with harmoniously. And why? Because humans could never accept the simple fact of our existence.*

Elena laughed. *You and your friends have called me foolish. But you're the fool. Humans never need to know what we are. Our kind could blend in easily. The inconvenience would be moving around on foot in order to avoid suspicion. The problem your kind has is you don't want to blend in.*

Felicia became more excited. *We should be gods!* she shouted back at Elena. *Think of what we are, what we can do! We are the superior beings!*

Elena could see on the horizon there were several shimmers of mental thread coming, seeking Felicia. Understanding struck her. Elena knew if she engaged with these mental threads, then their owners would suspect something amiss. So instead, she diverted the threads in different directions and covered Felicia with her shield. She needed to stall the threads from reaching her.

You crafty minx! Elena shouted at her. *You were stalling so the reinforcements could catch up. You three were the scouting party. The rest of the militia is on its way.*

Felicia smiled coyly. *I guess you caught me. As my father said before, I was his left-hand. I commanded his strategy. And you, child, have fallen prey to a simple distraction. They will be here in a few minutes. Then you will be dead. You may be able to win against opponents one on one, but you cannot defeat as many Daimones as are coming for you.*

They needed to leave before the cavalry arrived. What to do?

A mental thread sprang from Felicia's head and shot back toward the approaching crowd. Elena's shield stopped it. Then she extended her shield to encompass Alec and Aden.

You are blocking my thoughts? How can you do this? You are a child! You should not have such powers. Who is your sire? From what bloodline do you hail? Tell me!

Elena knew she could interact with the mental threads. She could stop, redirect, and even shield herself against them. What would happen if she pulled on one? With a snap-decision, she grabbed hold of Felicia's mental thread with her mind and pulled it as hard as she could. She knew she couldn't kill Felicia, Aden's own flesh and blood, but hoped the move would somehow inhibit or damage the woman's mental abilities.

What? The woman shouted. *What are you doing?* She pulled back on her thread, but it stayed under Elena's control.

Elena pulled at the thread again, harder than she ever imagined she could. Felicia cried out in pain. With a final great pull from Elena's mind, Felicia's mental voice fell silent, leaving her physical voice shrieking in agony. The thread did not tear. Instead, it pulled cleanly out of Felicia, a silvery shining ball dangling from the end. She gasped as understanding flooded through her. The ball hanging from the thread contained the source of Felicia's telepathic powers. Even though the woman still flew, because her wings were a physical appendage, she no longer tried to communicate with her telepathically. As Elena examined the object, it pulled against her, resisting her will, trying to return to Felicia.

Elena knew she could not let Felicia recover her mental powers. It would mean she would be able to find them more easily because of her connection to her father.

Elena contacted Alec. *I need you to hold her. I do not want her to get away.*

Elena reached out to Aden. *Aden,* Elena said, *I have removed the source of her mental abilities. She will not be able to find us or to communicate with the others.*

How? Aden asked, stunned. *Is it even possible?*

I guess so, she replied. *I did it. But now what do I do with it? She is too dangerous for us to let her regain her abilities. What now?*

Not sure what to tell you, Alec said. *You are doing things I have heard of in legends. I have never met a living Daimon who could snatch abilities away from others.*

So what would they do in these legends? Elena asked.

In the legends, Alec explained, *many of the Daimones who did these things were very bad. They were often tyrannical rulers who sought to punish their underlings by devouring their powers. I am guessing many of these were first or second generation Daimones.*

How would they devour another Daimon's abilities? Elena asked. *Did it harm them?*

Not that I ever heard, Alec told her, *but it essentially meant the devouring Daimon permanently held parts of the weaker Daimon within them. They forever had a strong mental connection nobody could ever break. The devourer could always find the devouree no matter where they were located.*

Okay, Elena asked, *but how did they do it in the legends?*

Alec shrugged. *The legends never told how it was done, merely that it was done. It was always described as absorbing the light or swallowing their shimmer of thoughts. But it was never explained how it was done. I never understood it because I lack the ability to see thoughts.*

But Alec, she said as a realization came upon her, *right there, I think you told me how it is done.* Elena focused her mental energies upon the shimmering sphere of Felicia's thoughts, willing it to be a part of her. She could feel the sphere follow her own mental thread and meld with her.

In an instant, she could see herself through Felicia's eyes, staring back at her own body floating in midair. The sight of it startled her. Aden hovered there, and she could feel Alec's arms wrapped around her. Through the melding of the ball to Elena's mind she had a unique connection with Felicia.

Felicia screamed at her in a language Elena could not understand. Though she could not understand the words, she understood their meanings: anger, confusion, frustration, rage, and fear. All of these emotions intermingled in the tirade.

Elena responded with perfect control on her emotions. "I have stripped you of your powers."

Felicia gawked at her in confusion.

"Felicia, I have taken your mental powers away from you. As I told you before, you have chosen the wrong side. We cannot allow you to provide information to our enemies."

Felicia's face contorted in a mask of rage. "Bitch!"

Elena ignored the impotent insult. "Sorry, but we have to leave," she said to her. "If you attempt to follow us, I will break your wings." Elena started to fly away, and then added, tapping her head. "Oh, and I don't need to be here to break them. I can do it from anywhere."

Alec released Felicia and began to follow Elena. Aden said a quick goodbye, and then followed behind.

Elena drew in her shield so it no longer contained Felicia. *Aden, can you please take us to the Elder?*

I thought you didn't want to use telepathy for speaking, Aden said to her. *You mentioned Mairya and the Opposition could follow them.*

First, she said, *Mairya is dead. So is Camael. Second, I have learned how to shield them from my thoughts.*

Yes, Aden replied, *but they can still be seen.*

True, but only within a visible distance, Elena explained. *I am hoping to be out of range rather fast.* She turned back and saw the mental threads from the crowd of Daimones were approaching. *Come,* she said to them. *Hold on to me.* Both Aden and Alec gripped each of her shoulders. *Now, Aden,* she asked him, *which way do we need to go?*

Aden pointed off to the east. *About five hundred miles that way—to Rakhiv, Ukraine.*

chapter 18

They hurtled through the air at unimaginable speed. They had been moving for about five seconds when Aden told her to slow down. In two more seconds, they were hovering above Rakhiv.

Nestled in a narrow valley divided into unequal portions by the Tysa River sat the town of Rakhiv. The river bisected the valley from the northeast to the southwest, and the majority of the area's settlement lay on the western bank.

As they hovered together, Elena released her grip on both men. Aden turned to her in stunned amazement. "Your speed," he said to her with awe, "is astonishing. I have only ever seen one other Daimon move so fast." Elena smiled at the compliment, noting her powers had grown even in the past few hours since they left Aden's manse.

"We should land over there." Aden indicated, pointing to a small tributary south of the town flowing into the river. The valley surrounding the tributary was fairly secluded save for a small development of homes near its confluence. "We need to make sure we blend in with the humans while we are here. Some of our kind live nearby and frequent this town. We need to be cautious of spies. We must keep our abilities hidden. We will be walking to the Elder's lair from here."

They fell from the sky to within mere feet of the ground, and then slowed before touching down. The fast descent should have kept them from being spotted, Elena hoped. She scanned her surroundings. They were in a small clearing at the confluence of two small tributaries as they merged into a larger feeder stream to the Tysa. Elena enjoyed listening to the bubbling of the stream as it coursed past them. Because of its steep descent from the mountains, the stream had not frozen over much despite the unseasonably cold weather.

Elena glanced at her two half-naked companions. "You two need some clothing," she said to them both.

Aden nodded in agreement. Alec replied, "Yeah. Except where can we go?"

Aden spoke up. "You will have to go into Rakhiv," he said to her, "and bring us back some clothes. There should be some shops in town."

"But I have no money," Elena said.

Aden reached into his pants pocket and removed a thick wad of bills. "I always keep some on me." He smiled. "You can never tell when you are going to need it."

Elena made her way into town, found the first shop she could, and bought them some heavy sweaters, coats, and hiking boots. She managed to return in a little less than an hour, pleased she guessed their sizes fairly accurately. They would be able to blend in with the townspeople and tourists milling about—even Aden with his near seven-foot height.

Aden smiled slyly. "I speak the regional dialects, but be aware, English is not completely unknown here." His gaze bounced between Alec and Elena. "I think we should all use English," he said. "If I underplay my knowledge of the local languages, we could use it as an advantage in scouting for people speaking to others about us. There are several small hotels in town which could accommodate us very well," Aden said to Elena. "And I am sure they will be able to take whatever cash you have left. With luck, there will be no one alive who could remember me by sight. It has been nearly a century since my last visit here."

"From here on out," he continued, "I suggest we act as humans. We have to be sure not to arouse suspicion in case of any Daimones who may be nearby could be sympathetic to the Opposition. We will also need to make some preparations for our visit to the Elder. There are some outfitters here where we can buy supplies. I suggest you two take the day to rest up while I make the preparations," Aden offered. "I have some untraceable accounts here in Rakhiv even my dear daughter, Felicia, knew nothing about. It would appear at least in some small way, I did not trust her entirely after all."

"Aden, I have to ask you something," Alec said, his voice sounding grave. "Have you ever taken Felicia to see the Elder? Has she ever been here? Does she have any idea, however small, where he may be?"

Aden did not even hesitate. "No," Aden replied, "none of my offspring know where the Elder is. As a child, my parents brought me there, but I never brought any of my own offspring here. It would have put the Elder at risk, and I would not ever risk his being discovered by the Opposition."

Alec nodded. "Okay. I wanted to be sure. I would hate to have such a small head start on the Opposition. It would be nice to think we have put them behind us for a while."

Elena nodded. "I agree. I will keep an eye out on the skies to try to figure out if there is a lot of mental traffic flying about. It could indicate we were noticed, or we are being spied on."

They had reached the highway and walked a mile along its two lanes. Not a single car passed them the entire way. Once inside the town limits, Aden excused himself so he could make the arrangements for their trip. Alec and Elena kept walking.

For the most part, Rakhiv was drab. The one- to two-story homes and business buildings were dressed in stucco ranging humbly from shades of white to shades of tan and beige.

Apartments and newer buildings on the north side harkened back to the architecture of the region's Soviet occupation. These were also plainly painted, but expressed more of the regional feel through occasional bright pastel colored buildings.

An early but deep snow covered the entire landscape around them. The main roads were fairly clear, but the side roads were covered in packed snow and barely wide enough to fit a single car at a time. Parking lots on the outskirts of town and the banks of the river were piled high with snow from the roads. The white-blanketed mountainsides were stunning with their mix of greens and browns standing in stark contrast to the snow. At least Elena could say one good thing about this whole adventure: it gave her the opportunity to see so much more of the world than she ever believed she would.

Alec and Elena chose one of the hotel restaurants in town for lunch. Elena ordered a classic Ukrainian meal consisting of a bowl of borscht followed by a plate of cheese dumplings called *varenyky*. The dishes more than satisfied her hunger and were delicious. Alec had ordered *hybivka*, a mushroom soup, and *kotljetys*—meat fritters. Elena enjoyed the samples he offered her from his plate also.

During their lunch together, she allowed herself a few minutes to study him, exploring her feelings for her attractive and mysterious stranger. Despite the emotional rollercoaster he had put her on over the past few days her feelings for him continued to grow. She could feel herself getting lost, staring into his eyes.

But then, his feelings for her were a mystery. Sure, he cared for her—he had been assigned to protect her. Though, she couldn't tell if his feelings had ever grown into something more. She'd thought they shared some intimate moments, but then he dismissed her when she tried to ask. She cringed at the memory; it still stung.

Since then, they had shared new moments.

"Alec, I need to understand something," she said. "Do our kind fall in love and marry?" She couldn't believe she asked the question. She could feel her cheeks flush, and turned away from his gaze.

He reached his hand out and covered hers. She knew he wanted to either grab her attention or comfort her, but she still felt the electric tingle where they touched. She caught her breath and shivered.

She turned back to him and gazed into his eyes.

"Yes, Elena, we do fall in love and marry. However, our love is beyond human comprehension. A more appropriate way to explain it is we bond. There is an almost primal connection once we have come in contact with our mate. It's as if our biology chooses the mate who will be our best match. We become electric to each other. It's almost like we're two poles of a magnet—constantly drawn together. When we mate, we are empathically bound to one another and share an attraction no other living being outside of our bond can ever fathom.

"Remember the old saying about how old married couples can usually complete each other's sentences?" Alec asked.

Elena nodded.

"Well, bonded mates can each share what the other is thinking. They remain their own individuals, but at the same time, it's like sharing a single mind."

She sank deep into his eyes. "Has this ever happened to you? Have you bonded with someone?"

Alec's face flushed. She watched as he turned quickly away from her and studied his watch. By his reaction, she knew he had, and wondered who he had bonded with. Clearly the memory caused him pain, or shame. Otherwise he wouldn't have turned away from her. She wanted to pry, to learn more about this beautiful creature and what made him tick, but feared what she would learn. Deep down, she wished—he had bonded with her, but knew given his lifespan he had likely bonded long ago to a mate who had died at the hands of the Opposition.

"It's getting late," he said. "We really need to see if we can find Aden. We should get going." He dropped some money on the table, and began to put on the coat he'd bought during the day.

"I'm sorry. I was trying to..."

"No worries," he interrupted, avoiding her gaze. "We need to get going." She could hear something bothered him from the sound of his voice. But in his reluctance to discuss it, he left the room without another word. She scrambled to put on her coat and run after him.

Once outside, Elena scanned the skies for any threads flying about, but found nothing.

It took them about a half hour to track down Aden. They found him walking out of a corner food market with his arms full of grocery bags. He greeted each of them with a kiss on the cheek. "Hello, my friends. The preparations are coming along nicely. We will be ready to leave by about ten o'clock this evening." Aden dangled a wire ring with three keys hanging off it. "The hotel rooms in this area, I found, were rather pricey. For our purposes, it made better sense to sublet a flat not far from here. Nobody would ask questions if we didn't show up for a few days. We should go there now so we can talk."

"Good idea," said Elena, "Lead the way."

Aden's flat sat across the main road a few doors down from the grocery shop on the top floor of a three-story house converted to rentals. The flat's walls were plain, painted a bland shade of off-white, while its oak floors were so freshly coated with polyurethane the smell still permeated the air. Upon entering, Elena became a little light-headed from the fumes.

She glanced around the living room. An old Zenith television, complete with an aerial antenna, occupied a central place on the carpeted floor. The room also contained a 1960s-style couch and love-seat combination, and a couple of plush chairs. There were dozens of shopping bags strewn all about the furniture and floor. Some held food for their planned trek. Elena picked up a couple of the other bags. They were heavy. She moved them off one of the stuffed chairs and put them on the floor.

"Please be careful with those, my dear," Aden said. "There is some delicate merchandise in those bags." He opened one up, and removed a pair of handguns. "These aren't too bad. I haven't had the chance to load them yet."

Aden and Alec began pulling a wide assortment of weapons and equipment from the bags. They laid everything out on the living room floor.

"Are we planning on confronting the Ukrainian army or something?" Elena joked.

Aden looked at her gravely. There was no humor in his eyes, or his voice. "Worse," he paused for a few moments. "There is something you both need to understand, I am sure you have heard about how the Elder and older generation Daimones went into hiding. Well, they didn't do so without making sure they were very well protected. I have protected him for millennia. But the simple truth is we must be prepared for anything once we reach his den."

Elena cocked her head, "What do you mean?"

"The gentleman from whom I purchased these very pieces of hardware," he said as he gestured across the firearms, "informed me there are some criminal types camping outside town, some of whom have found work acting as security for a wealthy benefactor living up in the mountains to the west. There is a chance this could be the Elder or one of the other older generation Daimones."

"Great," Alec said, "hired thugs."

Aden nodded and then continued, "We will need to be sure we are very much prepared for any eventuality which may arise. Especially since we will have to be human when we are in sight of others."

Elena examined the gear spread out over the floor. There was a lot of warm climbing clothing. There were coils of rope, grappling hooks, knives, frame packs, sleeping bags, and tents. The armaments included six handguns with four clips of ammunition each, boxes upon boxes of extra ammunition, three bull pup assault rifles, and a pistol-grip shotgun. There were also three long cylinders beside the assault rifles Elena recognized from movies to be suppressors.

"Assault rifles? Handguns?" she asked in disbelief. "You both realize the most experience I have with using anything like this is playing video games, right? I mean, until last week, I was a college student hoping to get a job in a genetic research department somewhere, not a commando."

Alec spoke. "You are not the same person any longer. I had hoped you would be able to continue on your chosen course and become a genetic researcher. But the game has changed. You were exposed, and now you are in danger, even though you have developed some tremendous abilities." He walked over to her, and embraced her. "None of us ever wanted to walk the road now lying before us."

Aden cut in. "It is truly my hope Ori was correct in sending you to find the Elder because it would be a terrible mistake to bother the Elder unnecessarily."

She remembered what she had heard from Ori's conversation. The Elder wanted to meet Elena. He had requested this meeting. She wondered why Ori had neglected to tell Aden, but also decided to follow her example. She must have had her reasons, otherwise he would have had the full story.

"So, this is all one great big gamble?" she asked, feigning agitation.

Alec and Aden turned to each other. She knew they did not communicate telepathically, but at the same time, she also knew they were both thinking the same thing. They nodded to each other, but Alec spoke. "Yes. This is all a gamble, and it may cost us all our lives. But with the Opposition hunting you, this is your best chance for survival."

Elena walked over to the row of guns and picked up one of the handguns. She pulled the slide back and let it slip forward again. "Okay," she said, "then somebody will need to show me how to use these things."

Aden smiled. "It would be my pleasure. Once we get up into the mountains, we should be able to have some target practice without arousing too much attention. I will need to make sure we have plenty of extra ammunition."

It didn't take them long to load their field packs. There were two to three changes of clothing for each of them. Because of their strength, it didn't really matter to any of them how much they loaded into each pack. But if they were stopped by authorities, their packs might be searched. The extra boxes of ammunition were either well hidden in the packs, or rolled up into their bedding.

All three of them were dressed in warm climber's outfits. Under their parkas, they wore a shoulder holster for a handgun, and a holster for a second handgun, hidden at the smalls of their backs. The cargo pockets on their pants contained extra clips of ammunition, and their knives were tucked into their boots. Thanks to the compact design of their assault rifles, these were concealed in their bedding rolls along with extra ammunition.

Each had enough food to last a week. There were granola bars, dried meats, cheeses, and crackers. They each had canteens, thermoses, and small water purifying kits they could use to refill their water supply from streams or even from the abundant snow.

As they were walking out the door of the flat and locking it behind them, Elena turned to Alec, "I feel stupid."

"Why?" Alec asked.

"We're leaving at night to hike through the mountains in search of what may be certain death. Not my proudest moment."

Alec smiled at her, "Hey, at least you're not sitting in some biochemistry class listening to a boring professor drone on about how his book revolutionized the field of genetic research."

She put her hand on his arm. "No, it was a couple of days ago. And I completely wanted to ditch class in order to spend some time in the library with this mysterious guy I ran into on campus." She stiffened, unable to believe she flirted with him. After all they had been through, she flirted with him again. And at a time like this.

Dammit. What's wrong with me? Elena wondered.

She stopped talking, turned away from Alec, and followed Aden.

"So, are we going to at least get a ride up the hill?" she asked him. "Find a cab?"

Aden laughed. "No," he said over his shoulder. "We will start walking from here. We should be able to disappear into the mountains pretty quickly. If we get a ride, then there will be a cab driver or a motorist who could reveal the location where we were dropped off. I do not want us to be traceable. No matter what happens to us, we cannot let the location of the Elder ever be discovered."

Outside on the street, the small city slept. The majority of people teeming about seemed to be focused around the outsides of several pubs situated not too far from the flat. Elena scanned the loafers milling about in the street, none of them attempted any form of telepathic communication. Nor were any of them interested in a couple of hikers wandering out of their flat.

She followed Aden as he led the way northwest out of town on a small side road. Situated alongside a tributary to the Tysa, the road wound its way up between two mountains on the west side of Rakhiv. As they followed the road westward, there were fewer and fewer houses. Sheer rock faces on the mountains to the north and south of the valley overhung the road, and the weight of the snow hanging from the rock shelves threatened avalanche.

A little more than a mile outside of Rakhiv, they were in relative isolation. Any houses they saw, mostly consisting of the vestiges of small farms, were spread far apart from one another. To the north stood a broad expanse of woods rising up the mountainside, and beyond it to the west, a small tree-lined seasonal stream formed from winter melt water cutting its way down the mountain to meet with the tributary they had been following.

They followed the small stream northward up the mountainside until a break in the trees signaled the presence of a roadway diverging from the stream's path. They stayed in the forest adjacent to the roadway in order to hide their tracks in the snow. As they ascended higher up the mountainside, the snow became deeper. In fact, it nearly reached her hip and their progress slowed.

"Hey, Aden?" she called out. "I take it you neglected to purchase any snowshoes, or cross-country skis, or anything, huh?"

Aden ignored her question and simply kept pushing his way through the snow. With his greater height, he moved much faster. Her muscles ached from lifting her knees almost to her chest with each step. On the verge of calling it quits, some dark shapes appeared in the distance. She decided to soldier on, and as they approached, it became apparent the dark shapes were actually a small group of shacks nestled in the snow.

Despite Daimones being much stronger and faster than humans, they were not completely tireless. And the effort she had been putting out so far had really exhausted her. She surged forward in order to catch up to Aden. Alec remained at the back, keeping an eye out to either side of them to ensure they were not being followed.

"Aden!" She spoke his name loud enough to get his attention, but in the quiet desolation of the woods, she might as well have bellowed it through a megaphone. The snowy corridor between the trees amplified her voice.

Aden raised his right hand with a closed fist and stopped dead in his tracks. Elena did not understand the signal and nearly plowed right into him. He turned and scowled.

In a hushed tone bordering on nonexistent, he whispered to her. "Elena. When I raise my fist, it means to stop right where you are."

Embarrassment overcame her. "Sorry," she replied in a tone almost as hushed as his own.

Aden scanned the small cluster of crude buildings. "I don't think there is anybody in this little camp. There are no visible tracks or paths in the snow. I think this is probably a camp used by migrant loggers."

"Good," Elena replied. "Do you think we can stop here and rest for a little bit?"

Aden nodded. "I don't know. Logging around here usually doesn't resume for a few more weeks. There is always the chance, though, a supervisor or someone will come back early to get the camp ready for the loggers to arrive. However, I don't think anyone will come tonight."

"Speaking of tonight, what time is it?"

Aden glanced down at his wrist. He had taken the opportunity to purchase a watch while out on his errands in the morning. "It's about three-thirty in the morning. We can stop to rest once we find somewhere safe up in the woods. These types of camps are never vacant for long. Wait here until we see if it is safe. We'll come back for you in a few moments."

Aden shrugged off his pack and laid it on the ground next to Elena. He removed the assault rifle from his bedroll and attached the silencer. "In case there is any trouble."

The moonlight reflecting off the snow created a ghostly glow. It amazed Elena at how well she could see. She watched as Alec followed back along his own footsteps and then cut off into the woods. She couldn't help but admire his form in the moonlight. He had a great body. *Dammit! Stop!* she scolded herself.

"Watch for my hand signals," Aden said to her before he set off to follow the tree line along the other side of the clearing.

Elena crouched in the snow and watched for any evidence of either Alec or Aden. Nothing. Not even the crunch of snow underfoot. She waited for what seemed to be an hour, until she heard a whistle from across the open field. Two figures stood side-by-side at the far end of the camp. Both of them waved her forward.

It may have been paranoia given the whole situation, but warning sirens were going off in her head. Hadn't Aden told her to watch for hand signals? He said nothing about whistling. They were trying to confirm the camp had been abandoned, so why would they be whistling to her? She could see the assault rifles both men carried, and from the distance they looked a lot like Aden and Alec. But she didn't trust it. It seemed too much like some kind of odd setup. Her fear may have been unfounded, but it could have also had something to do with their track record so far, where every person they believed they could trust had betrayed them.

She grabbed Aden's pack in one hand and removed her handgun from her lower back with the other. She slung the pack over her shoulder and started slowly across the wide-open field. Instead of making a beeline across the clearing, though, she headed straight for the closest building. When she reached the back corner, she stopped and listened, staring at the two men across the field.

She wanted to reach out to them telepathically, but knew she couldn't. If her mental thread were observed by any of the Opposition's agents, it could lead anyone right to her, and the Elder. She slid her back across the building, creeping slowly to the corner closest to both men.

Ducking low, she sprinted across the clearing to the corner of the next building. Unfortunately, it did not afford her an opportunity to confirm Aden and Alec stood across the field.

She heard low laughter as she rounded the corner. But the sound held no humor, it sounded sinister and wicked. Ducking behind the corner, she raised the pistol in front of her.

Quietly to herself she whispered, "Okay. Here we go."

She dropped Aden's pack and whipped herself around the corner with the pistol pointed straight out before her. But before she could pull the trigger, the gun jerked upward in her hand, and disappeared from her grasp.

"What the hell are you doing?" Alec asked. His voice betrayed both his confusion and his fear at nearly being shot at point-blank range.

Overcome with relief, she leapt up, throwing her arms around his neck. If her squeezing his neck bothered him at all, he didn't so much as give a hint.

"Oh, thank God!" she exclaimed. "I figured you guys were captured or something. Aden said to watch for hand signals. Then I hear this whistle, and I panicked."

"What did you expect us to do?" Alec asked. "We couldn't contact you telepathically. We have to act like humans. I would have to say, though, your reaction is probably the best human reaction I have ever seen," he laughed. "Very authentic."

"What do you mean?"

"Well, it was authentic on two counts. First, you were suspicious about us. And then, you were so excited it really was us." He smiled devilishly. "Good hug!"

She flushed and punched him in the shoulder. He winced a little but laughed nevertheless.

"Jerk," she mumbled under her breath as she turned away to retrieve Aden's pack, but couldn't help smiling to herself. Maybe there was hope for him after all.

When they reached Aden, she smiled, seeing he procured three pairs of snowshoes. "Our going should be a little bit easier now," he said as he tossed the shoes to the ground. "Alec and I found evidence someone has, in fact, been here recently. The tracks were filled in by snow, but they were still there. I think we should get going in case same somebody comes back."

After putting on the snowshoes they headed off into the woods, their progress much improved. Following the woods back to the creek, it wound its way farther up the mountain. Despite having acclimated better to the cold air since leaving Paris, Elena enjoyed the warmth her new clothes offered.

They came upon a small stone structure set into the mountain at the head of the small creek. A small trickle of water flowed out of the structure. It resembled a cave entrance in some old epic tale. Elena imagined a slew of elves, dwarves, and orcs inside.

chapter 19

Words were inscribed around the cave opening, and Aden translated them. "It says these are the Rakhiv Mineral Springs. I remember this cave. It goes deep into the mountain."

Inside, Aden told them about the cave. "For more than four centuries, both the cave and its spring have been revered as mystical by the locals. There are legends an angel lives in the spring and grants wishes. The doorway we stepped through was built about three hundred years ago by a local lord, and his peasants would come and leave offerings outside."

He paused thoughtfully. "I think this angel was either the Elder or one of his entourage. I remember coming here with my parents when I was very little but do not remember the way through the tunnels. The Elder lives beneath the mountain, and we must now find our way through its depths to his resting place." He stretched his massive arms out in wide, sweeping motions. "Welcome to the Elder's lair."

Elena couldn't help but be puzzled. "Aden, if this legend is so widely shared, then why hasn't the Opposition managed to find the Elder?"

Alec answered, "The answer is really a lot simpler than you think. As you may have observed, humans are very superstitious creatures, and because they are so superstitious, there are literally millions of legends about our kind. These legends are so common most of us tend to ignore them. Unless, of course, there is a Daimon living nearby, then there is a reason and source for the legends."

She studied the vast darkness of the tunnels beyond, the source of the trickling water, and then turned to Aden. "So, I take it you packed us some flashlights and extra batteries?"

"Yes, I did." He handed out two miner's type head lamps. "I believe I packed enough batteries for the trip. In the worst case, we can always improvise a torch."

Elena nodded. "Let's go, then."

As they made their way back into the tunnels, she examined the space, surprised the walls and ceiling were braced with ancient wooden frames. "How old is this place?" she asked out loud as she examined the worm-holed timbers.

"Old," Aden replied. "Older than you can imagine. It was abandoned long before my generation was even born."

"Surely someone must maintain the tunnels—make sure there are no cave-ins."

Aden shook his head. "Sadly, there is no one. These tunnels have been untouched for thousands of years."

The tunnel ended abruptly at a large cavern with a lofty ceiling and walls of undressed stone. A small trickle of water flowed through a narrow stone channel at the base of a foot-high tunnel at the far end. Scour marks upon the walls, though, suggested the stream could at times be very deep and fast flowing. She imagined this often happened during the spring, when melting snow would inundate the mountain's aquifer.

The cave extended deep into the mountain. They followed the perimeter, searching for a way through, but could not see another tunnel save for the small opening in the rear wall. The cavern appeared to be a dead end.

"So, where do we go now?" Elena asked Aden in frustration. Her voice echoed off the walls, and the question rebounded repeatedly.

He peered up, scanning the ceiling and upper portions of the rock walls. "I remember flying in here," he said softly.

"But I thought we were not supposed to use our powers," Alec noted.

Aden glanced to the left and to the right. "Do you see any humans? Or Daimones?" He paused for a moment, "Elena, can you see anything up there?"

She searched but did not see any mental threads flying through the air. A brief flash of something shining on the floor caught her eye, but she figured it a glint from their miner's lamps reflecting on a wet stone.

"There's no other choice." She began to levitate up off the ground, examining the walls of the cavern as she rose toward the ceiling. There were no breaks in the solid stone walls. The upper cavern walls were very smooth and appeared to be well worn, as if water had been flowing and circulating for ages, slowly scouring out this chamber.

A few drops of water struck her on her head, drawing her attention further upward. At the apex of the chamber, nearly fifty feet above the floor, she found a nearly perfectly circular opening in the ceiling.

"Hey guys!" she yelled down, "I think this is it."

Aden and Alec both removed their coats and shirts, and put on their packs. They allowed their wings to expand and stretch to full width, then rose slowly up in the air to join Elena.

Alec spoke first after examining the opening for a few seconds. "This can't be the way," he said. "The opening is too narrow. My wings won't fit through. How would a Daimon be expected to fly through there?"

"This has to be it," Aden persisted. "I distinctly remember flying in this very chamber." He pointed upward. "This is the way forward."

"Maybe," Alec retorted with frustration, "but our wings won't fit and neither will our packs." He glanced at Elena. She didn't like his expression. "Someone will have to go up first," he said, "and we'll have to hand the equipment up."

She knew this to be the sole way forward. The solid walls showed no sign of any other entrance, leaving them no other choice. "Let me go up," she said to them both. "I can scout ahead."

Alec seemed about to object but said nothing.

Aden spoke next, "Please be careful. We can always leave our packs here and then come back for them."

"Why don't we tie a rope to the packs and pull them up once we get up there?" Alec asked.

Elena gazed up into the passageway. "I like that idea. But I will still need to go up and see how we can get through. Since I don't rely on wings to fly, and I am the smallest, I am the logical one to go."

She floated up into the opening before either Daimon could respond. A light trickle of water flowed down along the edges of the rock, covering the interior with algae and scum. The opening belonged to a rather long, smooth vertical shaft abraded into the stone by the same flowing waters, which created the chamber below. It took her about a minute to float carefully through the tunnel. Though narrow at the mouth, the tunnel widened at the top. Both men would need to climb through instead of using their wings. Scanning the walls of the shaft, there were no visible handholds they could use in the perfectly smooth surface.

She could see the end of the tunnel above. It was pitch black inside, but the light from her headlamp pierced some of the darkness from the chamber above. It had to be a large chamber because all she could see above was more darkness. Elena floated slowly up to the top of the opening. Her head rose gradually above the edge to a wide, expansive stone floor covered with a shallow sheet of water.

She lowered herself back down the shaft a little faster than she had ascended. Alec and Aden were both still hovering where she had left them. They had attached a rope to all three of the packs.

"Well, boys," she said. "It's pretty narrow up there. You won't be able to use your wings at all. I'll have to bring the packs up first. Then we can use the rope for you to climb up. The shaft walls are slick with water and slime, and there are no handholds."

"Okay," Alec said, trying to see if Aden agreed.

He did. "It sounds like a good plan to me."

The whole process took about ten minutes. Once up top, they donned their packs and spread out a little bit. Inside the immense new chamber, each of them stood at least one hundred feet from the opening, the lights from their headlamps unable to locate a definitive edge to the cavernous expanse.

Alec broke the silence. "Hey!" he called out, "I think I found where the water is coming from." Elena turned around and followed his stare, though she could barely see him at the edge of her own lamp's beam. He must have been at least five hundred feet away from her.

She floated over to him in a split second and hovered. There, stretching far out of sight before them was a massive underground lake. But there was something strange, something different about the water. It seemed almost bright. She turned off her headlamp.

"Alec, turn off your lamp."

"What?" he asked in confusion, "Why?"

"Do it," she insisted, and he switched it off.

As her eyes adjusted, she noticed a definitive soft glow emanating from the water. Inside were thousands of small, bioluminescent fish swimming about.

"Aden!" she called. "Turn off your headlamp. There are fish glowing in the water. We can see fine without the lamps. The lamps are actually working against us."

"Right, I remember that part. We flew over the glowing pond to a massive doorway, and then we had to walk down a long tunnel. On the other side was..." His idea trailed off.

"Was what?" Elena asked.

"Hmm? Excuse me?" Aden replied.

"Aden," she asserted, "what was on the other side of the tunnel?"

"Oh." He chuckled a little and impishly said with a wink, "You'll see."

He surveyed his surroundings and pointed off toward the far side of the lake. "We have to go this way." He leapt off from the cavern floor and flew off across the lake.

Alec turned to Elena. "After you."

She flew off after Aden, followed by Alec.

The vast lake stretched for what seemed to be several thousand feet while the cavern's ceiling rose at least two hundred feet above their heads, carved by eons of flowing melt water.

Aden's massive wings beat the air and caused ripples on the surface of the otherwise mirror-like lake. The ripples sent flashes of bioluminescent light dancing across the walls and ceiling in a ballet of shimmering motion. The three flew in silence. At the far end of the lake, they could finally see a water-worn cavern wall emerge from the darkness ahead. Massive mineral columns rose up from the water and connected to the ceiling. Between the two most massive columns, she could see an opening.

Surrounded with ornate carvings of Daimones and humans interacting, the opening had been cut into the cavern wall. Above the opening were several unrecognizable symbols of a language Elena had never before seen. However, she somehow understood the writing.

"Beyond these gates lies the city of Sheol, from whence we came and to which we all must return." Elena spoke the words.

Aden gawked at her, stunned.

"Elena," he said with wonder and a slight chuckle, "yet again, you are keeping things from us."

"What are you talking about?" she asked him, completely perplexed by his reaction.

"You can read ancient Malachim?" he asked. "Simply amazing. I can read a few phrases or words here and there I learned from my parents," he told her. "There are very few of us beyond the second generation who have ever learned how to read the language."

Alec added, awestruck. "I don't know much. I don't think my parents ever knew any of it. And yet it appears you read it fluently."

Their responses to another of her awakening abilities shocked her. She didn't want to linger much on the subject and tried to change it by asking, "So, what do those words mean?"

Alec responded. "In human Hebrew belief," he explained, "Sheol was the underworld. It was the place where the souls of those who died would congregate."

Aden interrupted, "But humans corrupted the understanding from Daimon history. Sheol was the Daimon name for our home city. It was the place where our kind were once born, raised, and for those of us unfortunate enough to die, buried. It was the Elder's home before the Opposition revolted. Since then, the memory of this place has been lost to our kind except in legend. A few of the surviving older generations remember this place. I think I am probably the sole third-generation Daimon to ever have been here."

"So then how the hell did I know what it said?" Despite her best efforts to change the subject, she couldn't fight the question creeping into her head. "It wasn't like I was guessing, or like I think those letters look like English. Those symbols should be completely unintelligible to me. Yet, I can read them and understand their meaning." She looked to Alec and Aden imploringly and asked, "How is this possible?"

"I don't know," Aden replied. "It is beyond my understanding. I can't blame it on you absorbing Felicia's abilities because she didn't know Malachim either. Even for our own kind, this has been considered a dead language," Aden explained.

"Well, then maybe I am a reincarnated Daimon or something." She shook her head. "This whole thing keeps getting crazier and crazier. I really hope the Elder has some answers for me."

They crossed the threshold into a long hallway. All along the walls were images portraying Daimones working alongside humans to build all manner of things, helping build Egypt's pyramids and temples, erect statues in South America, teach humans written language, and even how to make fire. The story told by the pictograms detailed thousands of years of shared history and cooperation. It ended, though, during the rise of Egypt. The last image depicted the legend of Moses parting the Red Sea—the part of Moses taken by a Daimon.

"This is amazing," Elena said. "It's a full chronicle of your history!"

"Our combined history with humanity," replied Alec.

Aden continued, "Well, everything up to the war. It has not been added to since then. You see that section there?" He pointed to an area at the far end of the corridor.

"The empty section?" she asked

"Nobody has been around to update it. Neither this section, nor the Hall of Record." Aden sighed. "I remember it. My father brought me in there when I was here and told me some of the tales of our kind. It is one of my most cherished memories."

As the words left his mouth, two large stone doors came crashing down at either end of the corridor, sealing them off from the natural glow of the lake's bioluminescence and plunging them into perfect darkness. A new sound filled the room.

They all switched on their headlamps and could see the tunnel fill with water.

"Okay, Aden," Elena asked addressed him in a panic. "Do you remember how your parents made it through this?"

Aden shook his head. "No," he said shakily. "We were never trapped. We simply continued through to the other side."

Elena scanned the walls for any sign of some kind of a switch or button which could disable the trap. However, the walls seemed to be as smooth as the water-worn shaft. Giving up the fruitless task, she decided to study the murals painted on the walls for any clues. But the already waist deep water, began to flow a little faster into the space. *Dammit!* she shouted mentally.

Elena, that's it! Aden replied. *My telepathy had not yet developed when I came here. Maybe they had some kind of telepathic way to stop the trap.*

Elena scanned the walls again in search of clues but could not see anything useful depicted on them. Given the tunnel consisted of a complete arch down its entire length, she couldn't see anything useful there either. There were no indentations, no protrusions, nothing.

Oh, the hell with it! She wound her mental force into a thick, powerful cord the size of a mighty oak's trunk as she had when she had battled Camael earlier. She thrust it at the nearest stone door with all of her might. The door shattered instantaneously, and all three of them were washed through the tunnel by the force of the water.

They were inside Sheol.

Elena picked herself up off the floor. The water from the trap had mixed with the floor's dust and coated their clothing with thick, dark mud.

She took a few minutes to examine their surroundings. She didn't think it would be possible, but the ceiling here stood even loftier than in the lake cavern where they'd been moments before. It must have been at least a hundred feet higher. The floor had been carved into a cobblestone pattern. She flew up toward the ceiling in order to get a better perspective on the layout of the vast city, which lay before her, surprised natural light flooded into the cavern from high above.

In the dim light could be seen literally hundreds of buildings of many different sizes stretching throughout the city, separated by small streets and alleys. The streets on the outskirts of the city were laid out in a rough grid pattern. The heart of the city radiated outward from a stepped pyramid. She could see a small temple located at the top of the pyramid.

The surrounding cavern walls contained a veritable beehive of openings, each of which had been cut and surrounded with ornately carved motifs. A wide but shallow river, flowing to one side of the pyramid, bisected the city.

As she approached the ceiling, she could see dozens of openings cut in it through which dawn's dim light filtered to the city below. On closer inspection, the interiors of these openings bent and twisted and as she peered inside, she noticed the light reflecting along a series of mirrors.

She looked back, Aden and Alec had both followed her up above the city.

So, Aden, she asked, *where do we go now?*

I don't know for sure, he replied. *Why don't we look around a little?*

Alec and Elena glanced at each other, then at Aden, their collective curiosity piqued. They wanted to explore the amazing time capsule which had laid untouched by intelligent life, save for the Elder and whatever caretakers he had, for millennia. They all three floated down to the floor below.

The pyramid's great height obscured much of the city beyond it, but Elena took a few moments to study its architecture. The buildings were monumental in height, on a par with the skyscrapers of the world's most populous cities. She assumed there were no elevators, and there were no ladders visible on the exteriors. But then again, Elena rationalized, when the inhabitants were capable of independent flight, such implements were not necessary. The buildings were like tall multistory birdhouses.

There must have been thousands of residences within the city. Choosing at random, they entered one of the closer apartments and found it had been vacated on short notice. Must and spores permeated the air. Motes, kicked up by their feet, danced in the beams of light. Clay pots and bowls were still resting upon worm-ridden tables. Moth-eaten cloth hung near the windows and doors, and half-rotted baskets littered the floor. If people had moved out thoughtfully, she reasoned, then there would not have been such litter lying about. She could see, deeper into the residence, metal implements like knives and spoons, fasteners for disintegrated clothing, and even wash basins and water cans still lying about on the floor. Everything had been abandoned as though the trappings of life merely awaited their inhabitants to return and resume life as usual. It amazed her none of it had ever been touched in all this time. The mystery intrigued Elena, but it also disturbed her to consider what had made the thousands of Daimon inhabitants to up and leave.

"Aden," Elena called to him as they walked from one apartment to another, "what happened here? Why did everyone leave?" She couldn't keep the note of fascination from her voice.

The story my father told me, he explained to her mentally, *was there was a major uprising against the Elder. In his rage, the Elder cast all Daimones from the city and forbade them ever return.*

Wow, she replied. *It certainly explains why everything is so pristine.* To her, it seemed like stepping into a time machine and viewing the past. She could see Daimon men, women, and children sitting at the tables, eating from the bowls, and flying from apartment to apartment. The city captivated her, its array of abandoned belongings spoke of a rich, vibrant life within. However, the life had been long ago, and all its relics were the ghosts of times past.

I think we should check out the temple, Elena said, pointing to the stepped pyramid near the heart of the city. *I think it's a good candidate for where the Elder may be.*

Aden nodded in agreement.

Sounds good to me, Alec said. *I'm out of my element here and open to any suggestions.*

chapter 20

The journey to the pyramid seemed awkward and eerie. They could have flown, but Elena had insisted on walking in order to be able to search for any clues suggesting the location of the Elder's resting place. Not a footprint or the track of a scurrying rodent could be seen in the thick dust coating the cobblestones. Artifacts and relics left on the ground were coated in the same thick layer.

Despite the time elapsed since Sheol's abandonment, there had been no cave-ins or signs of structural damage to the cavern. None of the buildings had fallen into ruin. The pristine condition of the site stunned her.

The only sounds which broke the death-like silence of Sheol came from the soft tinkling of the gently flowing river as it coursed through the city and their footfalls. The sharp stench of must and mold permeated the cavern. The glinting sunlight cast strange shadows and patterns across the walls of the buildings as they passed. There were no other Daimones around. Alone, they could explore as they wished. But one building in particular drew their attention more than the others.

As they approached, it became evident the massive stepped pyramid measured more than a thousand feet on each of its sides, and stood nearly two-hundred feet in height. It consisted of four tiers, roughly fifty-feet tall each. The tiers were made of packed earth faced with expertly cut granite blocks adorned with images of Daimones and humans, similar to those they'd seen in the corridor before. A central staircase of 240 granite steps connected the ground below with all four tiers and the temple at the top.

As they walked up the steps, Elena examined the granite carvings, noting something strange about them. The humans portrayed were dramatically different from anatomically modern humans. They more closely resembled Neanderthals, or even earlier types of proto-human ancestors.

"My God!" Elena exclaimed. "These carvings are wonderful."

Aden responded, "Yes. But I don't understand what these human-like creatures depicted on them are."

"I do," Elena replied. "These depictions show early human ancestors." She began pointing out specific examples. "Over here," she said pointing to one, "this one is Australopithecus afarensis. And over here," she said pointing to another, "this one is Homo habilis."

"Fascinating," Aden said in a sarcastic tone while trying to stifle a yawn.

"Don't you understand what this means?" she continued. "Daimones have been around for millions of years. Australopithecus alone went extinct nearly three-million years ago. And here we have carvings depicting them co-existing with Daimones. This is astounding!"

Distracted by the carvings on the steps, she nearly slipped and fell twice on her way to the temple at the pyramid's zenith. At the top, they found this tier different from the others as it had been carved from blocks of what appeared to be obsidian, instead of the packed earth of the layers below. The blocks were massive, but fit together so well she could almost see no seams between them. It gave the appearance the entire structure was carved from a solid piece of black glass.

Something glinted brightly out of the corner of her eye, drawing her attention down to her right. Scanning the place, however, the light moved quickly away and she noticed a small puddle of water fed by drops of water falling from one of the light tunnels above. Probably the light reflecting off a water drop as it made its descent from high above, she couldn't help but think it moved oddly—almost like it moved with purpose.

Casting the distraction aside, her attention turned back to the temple. Aden and Alec were already searching the structure for evidence of where the Elder might rest.

"Elena," Aden called, "you need to come and see this." Elena trotted over to where they were standing.

As she approached, she could see the temple itself appeared to be made from obsidian. There were carvings all over the surface similar to those she'd seen on the steps. Awestruck, she knew if this place were ever discovered by humans, it would be an archaeological find to potentially rewrite much of human history. The carvings documented how angels had helped humans along in their development for millions of years. She shuddered considering what the world's religions would do with such information.

So, Alec asked, interrupting her, *how do we get in? I do not see any doors, openings, or indications this is anything more than a large, carved block of volcanic glass.* Elena could see his mental thread shimmer in the air. But she also noticed his voice sounded muffled, almost as though the obsidian somehow had an effect on his telepathic abilities.

"I don't know," she replied. Aden turned, the expression on his face conveying his agitation at not being included in the conversation.

Elena turned to Aden and explained, "Alec was asking if there was a way for us to enter the temple. It looks like solid obsidian."

Aden shrugged his shoulders, a minor note of frustration in his voice. "I am not sure," he replied. "I have no recollection of the temple. To borrow Alec's earlier comment, I am out of my element."

Elena examined the structure closely. It differed from pictures of Meso-American temples she'd seen in school as there were no openings to be found. The surface was smooth and flat, save for the images of Daimones and early hominids carved into it.

There must have been some way inside. Elena floated upward to the roof of the structure. From the temple roof, she commanded a tremendous view of the city below them. Back the way they came, she could see the vast city grid with its numerous residences. The same view greeted her to the left and the right. To the left the river interrupted the city's grid.

She turned her back toward the way they had entered Sheol, and gasped at the sight before her, previously obscured by the great pyramid on which she now stood.

Beyond the great pyramid, a vast avenue as broad as the pyramid stretched toward the far cavern wall. Occupying the center of the avenue was an immense reflecting pool of clear water emitting the same bioluminescent glow as the lake in the cavern where they had previously been. The pool was somehow fed by the nearby river, but within it Elena could not see so much as a single ripple upon its surface. It was almost as though the glowing fish swimming within were passing ghost-like through the pool's waters.

The pool's eerie glow illuminated the cavern before her with such efficiency she could make out a broad plaza, roughly the size of the temple's own base, at the far end of the reflecting pool. Within the plaza she could see all manner of statuary rising from the cobblestone floor. And beyond the plaza stood a gargantuan archway connecting to what appeared to be another chamber beyond.

Gazing out upon Sheol, she welled with emotion. This amazing discovery was part of her, part of her history—where she ultimately originated from. She belonged to the race who had built and once thrived in this vast and ancient subterranean city and who had been humanity's protectors and great benefactors for time immemorial. A tear rolled down her cheek as the light of Alec's headlamp crest the rooftop's edge.

She quickly put her emotional moment aside as he approached. "Are you okay?" he asked softly as he put an arm around her shoulders and pulled her close to his bare chest. She nodded as she felt the warmth of his body through her clothing.

"This is who you are, Elena," he said to her. "Who we are."

Had he sensed what ran through her mind? Despite her efforts to keep the emotion from spilling out, another tear rolled down her cheek. He captured it with one finger and threw his arms around her body, drawing her closer to him. She could feel his warmth and let out a gasp.

Reflexively, her own arms snaked themselves upward and wrapped around his neck. His head bowed slowly down toward hers. She could feel herself slipping away into his alluring eyes.

Their lips were touching and fire spread throughout her. She tingled in places she'd never imagined possible. Her heart hammered hard against her chest. Their tongues danced against one another and she had a yearning for more. She wanted him, needed him. Her desire had never been stronger.

"Ahem," came Aden's deep baritone. "I, uh, hate to interrupt, but we have more important things to be doing right now." Her face and ears burned with embarrassment. Aden's impeccable timing had smothered the whole moment. Elena focused on curtailing her passions, reminding herself they were here to meet the Elder.

Elena crushed herself against Alec, burying her face into his chest, happy with the confirmation Alec shared her own desires.

She pushed herself gently out of Alec's embrace and turned away from both men. After a brief moment to gather her thoughts, she focused her energies on ascertaining a means of entering the temple. The obsidian temple's roof appeared to be seamless and solid save for one piece of five-foot square granite near its center.

"What do you make of this?" she asked both men, indicating the granite block.

Alec responded, "It looks like either a plug or some kind of cap for an opening."

Elena examined the obsidian around the granite and could barely discern faint traces of what appeared to be a frame surrounding the block. "I think you're right," she replied. "This may be our way in."

Aden nodded in agreement. He stepped over to the block, knelt down, and tried to find some way to slip his fingers into the nearly imperceptible joint between the granite and obsidian. His efforts were fruitless as he could find no way in budging the heavy stone block.

"Dammit," he cursed under his breath.

Watching his attempts, Elena had a thought. "Aden," she said, waving him away from the block, "step back, please."

Aden laughed ruefully. "Very well. I bow to the lady."

She turned away from him and conjured her mental thread. With tremendous effort she directed the iridescent manifestation of thought to slip around the edges of the granite block and lift it from its resting place. The block lifted easily into the air, floated twenty feet away, and then settled gently onto the smooth black surface. She looked at Aden's face, now painted with a mask of stunned amazement, and merely grinned.

She swept her arm toward the opening and said, "After you. Age before beauty." Alec laughed at Aden's expense.

Elena looked inside the yawning black void of the opening, absent of any light.

Aden switched his miner's torch on again and, gave them a weak smile. "How is it possible I can see nothing?"

He began to descend an almost completely indiscernible obsidian stairway winding its way down into the temple. Elena and Alec also switched on their lights and quickly followed.

As they came to the base of the stairs, Aden blurt out in astonishment, "It's a sepulcher!"

Deceptively smaller than she had expected it to be, the chamber's walls were lined with niches containing desiccated and decomposed bodies. The stuffy air held no smell of rot or decay, as would be expected. Instead, the many bodies appeared to be mummified. At the edge of the light's beam could be seen another stairway descending deeper into the temple below.

As she moved to continue downward, however, she noticed an inscription written around the opening in the same language she'd seen in the corridor outside the city. It read: "Enter those who despair, for those who do not must beware." She said the words to her companions. "Aden, what does it mean?" she finally asked.

Aden shook his head. "I'm not quite sure," he said thoughtfully. "It sounds like some kind of warning. It could be something to warn against grave looting."

Elena chuckled a little, finding the warning ironic. "It's funny," she said in a low voice, "a race of beings capable of creating a place like this thousands of years before modern humans existed would have to worry about grave robbing."

"Is it really far-fetched?" he asked her. "Daimones are as jealous, greedy, and power hungry as any other race of beings. I mean, look at why you are here. One powerful Daimon tried to usurp control from the Elder, and the war has waged ever since. We may look like angels, but we are not perfect."

Aden chimed in, "Very true. There are lots of treacherous Daimones on both sides of this war. Humans are the real victims, usually because they wind up our pawns."

Elena paused for a second. "If there's a warning against grave robbing, then it would stand to reason there was something within the grave to rob or...someone?"

"It's entirely possible," Alec suggested, "but do you think someone as important as the Elder would be so easy to find? Right out in the open? In the first cemetery in the city?"

Elena considered it for a few moments. "Well then," she said, "how about this? We head down and scope it out. It doesn't hurt to look, right? I mean, what's the worst that could happen? If he's not down here, then we climb back out and keep looking."

"Sounds good to me," Alec replied. Aden simply nodded. But as they made their way over to the opening, he called over to Elena, "You go first."

"Sure," she pointed her headlamp down into the darkness below.

As they descended further into the pyramid, Elena noted the vastness of the space. The greater expanse, however, made for many more bodies, fewer of which were mummified, owing to increased moisture in the room. The walls around the chamber's perimeter were dressed in the same smooth, glassy obsidian.

Their search of the niches did not identify any evidence of the Elder. The burials were communal with no caskets or solitary tombs anywhere. After a quick discussion, they agreed to explore the next layer down.

By the third level down, Elena noticed the size of the chamber had not changed. The farther they were from the natural, although redirected, light in the upper layers, the more the darkness became oppressive. As they continued to the lowest of the pyramid's tiers, another warning much more dire than the first had been engraved around the entrance promising certain death for any who would disturb their ancestors' remains.

As Elena approached the stair to the lowest tier, Aden called out to them. "I will stay up here," he said to her. "You two go ahead without me." He pointed to remains in one of the niches and said, "This is my grandfather." Elena looked at him, wondering how exactly he knew whom the body belonged to. However, the burning curiosity of whether or not the Elder would be below them ate at her. She needed to head to the lower tier to find out.

The darkness below seemed almost alive, seeking to crush them. Shadows moved and danced across their vision as they descended to the pyramid's lowest level. The cramped room smelled of dampness. Elena scanned her surroundings and quickly slid out of the way so Alec could step inside the small chamber. Surveying the place as Alec approached the bottom she noticed unlike the upper tiers, which had bodies lying on the floor and in niches and shelves, there were no bodies located below chest-height.

As Alec stepped from the bottom stair and moved over toward her, his right wing brushed against one of the nearby shelves disrupting several bones. The disturbance, after thousands of years of stability, caused the remains to instantly disintegrate. They crumbled to piles of dust, wrappings, and bones. Elena could see the glint of gold and silver within the dust. Instinctively, she reached out to examine one of the gold pieces.

As her finger touched the precious metal a sound came from above which startled both her and Alec. Rumbling assaulted their ears from all around. Above, an obsidian panel slid across the entrance. The headlamp's glow caught movement. Water seeped and poured through the wall. The floor shook as more water erupted from below.

Aden, Elena screamed out, *help us, please. We triggered some kind of trap.* Her body shook as she looked around. Alec rose along the stairs pulling Elena close behind.

The water rose fast. In seconds, it covered the floor, and moments later reached their knees. *Dammit!* Elena screamed. But no one answered her cry, not even Alec.

"Alec, can you hear my thoughts?"

"I haven't heard anything."

"I've been reaching out to you and Aden," she said in exasperation, "but neither of you responded. What the hell?"

Alec remained quiet for a moment. She directed her beam at him but the headlamp could not dispel the stygian darkness of the obsidian chamber. He stared off into space and then turned his eyes upon her. "Didn't you hear me?" he asked her. Elena looked back at him, perplexed.

"What are you talking about?" she asked.

"I tried to contact you," he told her.

"I can't hear anything," she conceded. "There must be something blocking our abilities." Elena conjured a mental strike, but before she could even see it fully form, it absorbed into the surrounding obsidian. "It's the obsidian," she shouted at him. "It's absorbing our mental energy."

They both whipped their heads around as they heard something splash in the water. The dancing shadows caused by the light of their lamps refracting on the surface of the rising water made it hard to make out details of anything below. But soon something surfaced a few feet away from their location and then sank back into the water.

"What the hell?" Elena exclaimed, her voice shaking. She'd been more confident before when dealing with the Daimones. Without her powers, she was impotent, as if she'd never begun to awaken.

Alec craned his neck hard at the sound of another splash off to his right. Something swam in the water and given the warning, it would not be friendly.

"Elena," he called to her. "Climb up here. Get away from the water."

"Dammit," she screamed. "Something brushed my leg." They both trained their lights on the water. She screamed out as fire exploded through her right calf. She jerked it upwards. However, whatever had gotten hold of her had a strong grip and fought back.

Plumes of crimson blossomed in the water as the wound bled freely. He swung his headlamp toward the source and Elena's heart sank. She recognized the long, sleek body of the fish attacking her injured leg from one of her zoology texts. It belonged to a barracuda.

Alec reached down and pulled Elena up out of the water, cradling her in his arms. Her slick blood ran down his left arm. The barracuda attached to her leg had relinquished his grasp as she rose from the water. The water boiled with activity as the fish swam through the plume of her blood.

By the time Elena reached her hand down to explore the wound with her fingers, it had started healing. The pain had diminished, and the blood had coagulated. Alec placed her gingerly upon a step above his own location, carefully eyeing the rising water at his feet.

She wanted to shut down in despair. When things were bad back at home or at school, she could cope with the situation and find a solution. But here, trapped in a flooding fish tank filled with man-eating fish—frustration, anger, resentment, and fear overwhelmed her.

Her blood boiled as it all took its toll. Without thinking, she lashed out, striking at the massive obsidian block that had slid in place to block their escape from the fatal trap with a rage-filled scream. A split second after her fist flew into the air, she realized punching the solid surface with as much force as she'd directed could be a bad idea. At the very least it would hurt, but she figured it more likely the blow would crush the fragile bones in her hand and wrist. But by the time she realized it, she had already passed the point of no return.

Yet as flesh met volcanic glass, the effect startled her. She felt no pain as the obsidian cracked.

A web of cracks spidered out from the point of her fist's impact, spreading across the glossy black surface of the block. Astonished, Elena examined her fist. It appeared intact. She quickly flexed and contracted her fingers a few times until satisfied nothing had been broken in her foolish belligerence.

She threw her left fist, striking the same impact point. A third and final blow from her right hand succeeded in shattering the massive obsidian block into pieces, which began raining down around them into the water below. They worked to clear the debris from the opening. Within a matter of seconds, they were ascending the stairs back into the third tier.

"Aden," Elena yelled as she crested the stairs. "Aden, where are you?" Her cursory scan of the room did not reveal him anywhere she could see. And being they were still in obsidian-lined rooms, she couldn't try reaching out to him telepathically. She ran up the next few flights of stairs, ultimately bursting through the opening atop the temple and nearly bowling Aden over.

"You're out!" he shouted. She could hear the surprise in his voice. "What happened?" he asked. "You had climbed down when the floor suddenly closed up."

When Alec finally joined them on the roof, he and Elena related to Aden what had happened in the lower tier. After the few minutes it took to tell the story, Aden finally asked, "So, no luck with finding the Elder down there, then?"

Elena shook her head. "No, not so much. And, even if he was down there, he's barracuda food now, anyway."

Aden nodded. He eyed them both, and then asked, "So, do you want to hear something interesting?"

Elena looked at him blankly, not sure how to take his question. "Uh, sure," she replied. "I hope it's something good."

"Oh, it is," Aden responded. He pointed to the far wall of the cavern housing Sheol. "Do you see the gate over there?" he asked. "It is the entrance to the old city. It is where I think we will find the Elder's resting place. It's where my mother went when we were here."

She hadn't even considered the possibility there could be more to Sheol. Looking to Alec, then back to Aden, she nodded. "Then, what are we waiting around here for?"

They decided flying would be the most efficient way to continue. Their search of the new city had been fruitless, and they were certain they would not find any clues to the Elder's whereabouts there. Approaching the arched gateway on the far wall, beyond the reflecting pool and the vast plaza, Elena could see the massive portal with greater clarity. It must have been five-stories tall, surrounded with the images of all manner of creatures. There must have been hundreds of different animals depicted around the opening. Elena could even see some large reptiles. *Are those dinosaurs?* she asked her companions.

Alec answered. *Yes, I believe so,* he replied. *The Elder has been alive for a very long time. None of us actually know how old he is. So, yes, it may be possible those are drawings of dinosaurs.*

Impossible, Elena insisted. *The dinosaurs went extinct about sixty-five million years ago.* She had to admit despite it being a new skill it felt good to be using her telepathic abilities again. She would have to remember the effect obsidian had on Daimon abilities.

Well, Alec retorted, *then you can ask him when we reach him. You asked a question, and I was answering it.*

As they flew through the portal, Elena saw the river bisecting the city flowed through the gate as well. Beyond the portal, they followed the river along into another cavern much smaller than the last.

Aden guided them. *This is the old city. Our kind lived here for many millennia before the population grew large enough to necessitate our spreading out into the other chamber. Once some of the newer generations began moving into the new city, the old city was held in reserve as the center for our government and for the homes of our eldest and most powerful.*

Elena could see the buildings here were much older. The tremendous state of disrepair seemed sad, but what disturbed her far more littered the ground below.

Strewn across the cavern floor were the lifeless remains of literally thousands of Daimones. Intermingled with the bones were pieces of armor and different types of weapons. Considering they had flown from a sepulcher, she found it eerie so many dead lay unattended on the floor below.

Aden continued. *This is where the battle was fought. The leader of the Opposition tried to assassinate the Elder. She brought with her a massive entourage of her followers from the new city who were sympathetic to her cause. To kill the Elder would have been the ultimate symbolic gesture for her cause. It would have represented the casting off of the old traditions of human–Daimon cohabitation of the earth and a demonstration her will was mightier than his.*

Her attempted coup failed, though, Aden continued, *because the Elder has many who are faithful to him and to his mission. My parents were among those who fought to protect him. The Mistress was defeated and cast out of Sheol. But the Elder was angry at all of us and so cast out of Sheol all but a handful of Daimones. My parents were among some of those unfortunate enough to be cast out in his rage. Even so, they were called back to him in gratitude for the tremendous service they had done in protecting him.*

Below us you see the bodies of all those who died in protection of the Elder, he said reverently. *Their bodies still litter the streets because there has been nobody here to give them a proper burial.*

Elena scanned the city below and found it much smaller in scale. Compared to the numerous buildings she had seen in the new city, the old city had a few dozen. And these buildings were spread much farther apart on the landscape. It seemed to her these were the mansions of the wealthy, standing apart from the urban development of the new city.

The small river wound its way through the old city. Many of the larger buildings were located close to its banks. Several ponds were visible in the yards of these estates. As she followed the river with her eyes, she could see its source lay somewhere beyond one of the cavern walls at the far end of the chamber. Of course, the larger estates were located much closer to the source of the river.

Out of the corner of her eye, Elena saw something moving along the ground. She quickly moved downward to explore. As she approached, it looked like part of the floor had an iridescent, moving glow, similar to the glint she'd earlier seen. The shimmer reminded her of a mental thread. Not an accidental optical illusion, but something sentient.

There is something moving down there, she cautioned Alec and Aden. *It seems to be aware of us, but I don't know what it is.*

A deep voice erupted in her head like the rumbling of an earthquake. *You do not know what it is? Or you do not know who it is?*

No, she replied to the voice, *I know now both what and who you are. You are the Elder.*

The tendril of telepathic thought rose above the ground and solidified before her. She could see a massive tendril glowing with unimaginable power. It bore a striking similarity to her own tendril.

It moved toward her slowly, almost like it studied her, and she instinctively shielded herself. *Do not fear me, Elena. We have much to discuss. It is long since you have been home.*

Home? she asked. *What do you mean home?*

Come, he invited. *We will discuss it.* In an instant, his mental tendril latched itself onto her shield and retracted itself. As the tendril moved, so did Elena. In the blink of an eye, she no longer floated above the old city. Instead, she sat on a plain wooden chair at a finely crafted table. Before her, an ornate chessboard held a game already in progress. The small, brightly lit room seemed familiar, like something from a dream. On the walls were fine paintings with inscriptions in Malachim. She chuckled to herself when she noticed one of the inscriptions actually read, "Home, sweet home."

Where am I? she questioned.

This place, this room, is a projection of your mind. Your body is still within Sheol with your companions. But inside here, you are with me.

Across the table from her sat a middle-aged man with glacier-blue eyes and curly platinum-blonde hair. His high cheekbones were sharply defined, and he had a strong jaw and an aquiline nose. He reminded her of what Michelangelo's David would have looked like in real life. She couldn't help but feel they had met before.

I look exactly how you want me to look, the Elder replied. *I do not really look this way.* He paused. *And, yes, we have met before. In fact, you would not exist if it weren't for me. You were minutes old, but your memory is quite astounding.*

What are you talking about I wouldn't exist if not for you? What do you mean? she demanded.

Elena, isn't it evident? The Elder smiled widely with pride. *I created you.*

chapter 21

The words he had said echoed in her mind: "I created you." Those were his words. Numbness spread through her face. She had hoped for answers to the millions of questions burning in her mind since she left her college, her mother, and her life behind her. Instead, the Elder gave her a statement forming a million more.

The weight of it all took a toll on her. Without thinking, she blurted: *What do you mean, you created me?* She could not mask the mixed emotions boiling inside her. *I came here for answers. To find out what it is I am. Why strange things are happening to me. To find out why some woman is trying to have me killed! And you go ahead and unload something like that. You created me. Isn't it bad enough I'm adopted and belong to some ancient race of Angels? Now I'm some freakish test-tube baby, too?*

Shock overcame her followed by a mix of conflicting emotions. Her words were meant to be half scolding, but also half inquiring. She craved answers.

He chuckled softly in reply. *You know, you share a lot of similarities with Her. In fact, you are nearly Her genetic equal.*

What do you mean, Her genetic equal? Her who?

Don't be irrational, Elena. You already know the answer.

Elena laughed lightly and smiled back. *The Mistress. But how can I be her genetic equal?*

You and Lilith are both created from my genetic code. We three are nearly perfect matches. The difference is in you I joined my genetic code with a race of beings I greatly admired, humans.

What or who are we? she asked. *Where did we come from? Why did you make me? How come I can fly, but don't have wings? How can I do so many things with my mind? Are we good, are we evil? What other powers do I have?* The questions continued to pour forth.

The Elder raised his hand and stopped her abruptly. *Before answering, I think I should properly introduce myself. My true name is unpronounceable by any human tongue, but I have been known for many as Yehoshua, or Joshua. I suppose in a way I inspired the story of what many religions revere as God. In truth, I am actually a genetic scientist.*

Elena gasped. The correlation logically made sense, but she couldn't view this man as God. He sat here right before her, not some almighty sitting in the clouds.

Elders have existed for more than sixty-five million years. Though I share the Progenitor's DNA, I, myself, am the sixty-third in a series of Elders. I am a genetic copy of the Progenitor—a clone. I have been alive for nearly a million years. But the time of my body's demise is soon coming.

Elena sat up a little straighter at the mention of his age. To look at him, he did not appear to be so old. She would have believed him to be in his early thirties.

Regarding our origins, the Elder continued, *I am sorry, but I do not know where we came from. The Progenitor knew and this knowledge was never written.*

The Elder paused, and she sat there watching as he studied her. *I knew I was right to make you.* A touch of pride infiltrated his voice. *Whereas I was foolish to make Her. When I created Lilith, she was to be my companion and mate.*

Elena felt chills run up her spine. This powerful being had genetically created its own mate. It made her fear the answer of why she had been made.

You, on the other hand, he continued, *were created for another reason. You were created to be my replacement.*

The chills ceased, replaced instead by numbness. Her mouth felt dry. Replacement? So this was the purpose. She was to be the new Elder? But, how? Why? What did it even mean?

He must have read the questions on her face. *Elena, you were created to do what none other ever could. To be an Elder—the true Elder. You are destined to take my place, and to surpass me. The role of the Elder is to be a protector, a guardian—mankind's guardian. Elders have fostered the human race for millions of years. Sometimes we protect it from external threats, sometimes from us, and sometimes we even protect it from itself. Most importantly, we protect it from the cataclysm we know is approaching.*

Elena opened her mouth to ask a question, but the Elder raised his hand and continued speaking. *All great civilizations implode. This truth has been passed along from Elder to Elder. Many times the human species was about to implode on itself. But we Elders were there to stop it. When human populations prospered and began to grow at a rapid pace, I created the Daimon race to help in my task. Earlier Elders had also created helpers, but always with the same result. The helpers ultimately sought to enslave those they were created to protect. The other Elders always slaughtered their helpers. My answer, however, was to create you.*

Elena cocked her head questioningly. *When I created you, I combined my genes with human genes, and then redoubled them many times over, creating a genetic code with innumerable combination possibilities. Those combinations are what give you your powers. You asked what powers you have. Well, because of these combinations, your powers are limitless. And they are what will make you humanity's ultimate guardian. One day I am sure you will surpass me.*

The Elder stopped speaking and Elena sat silently, mulling it all over. In complete shock, she could not think. She had wanted answers. Answers about herself, her powers, and what happened to and around her. A ray of hope finally pierced the bleakness, fear, and despair she'd been feeling.

The ray began to dim, though, as the weight of his words settled in. Yes, he answered her questions. But at the same time he handed her tremendous responsibility, passing the mantle of "Guardian of Mankind" on to her. She wanted her life back, not to save the world. She wanted a life as a college student. A life living at home with her mother and hoping to follow in her father's footsteps as a genetic researcher. A life with a mysterious man with startling blue eyes. A life, which made sense.

The Elder instead told her she could no longer have life. It was a myth. A dream. Her life had been predestined through the simple act of her creation.

The weight of it all overwhelmed her. She wanted to crawl into bed and hide. She crossed her arms and stared blankly at the chessboard.

What if I don't want this? she asked.

Then there will be no other to take your place. We will all die under Lilith's iron fist. I am dying and can no longer fend her off. I promise, if you stay with me I will teach you things of which you can only dream. I can give you millions of years of knowledge, more than all human scientists have collected since the dark ages. You'll learn to cure illness, and to manipulate genes—all with your mind.

After a pregnant pause, he added, *Stay with me and I can teach you.*

What about my life? What I want? An angelic face with piercing blue eyes came to mind. Her stomach twisted into knots at the thought of leaving Alec behind. She wanted to throw up. Sadly, she asked, *How can I leave him?*

You don't have to, Elena. I don't want to take your life away. The Elder smiled warmly. *I want to teach you to reach your full potential.*

To become the Elder, she completed his thought.

Yes. To be the new Elder. Otherwise, the other life you want can never be. Don't you understand? Lilith will enslave all Daimones, she will enslave all humans, and she will kill you—the only being alive who could challenge her. But for you to survive, we must begin with your training. If you cannot control your powers, life as it is now known will end. He paused. *So, what do you say?*

She understood his meaning. She had no real choice. The most logical step for her to go was forward. Without the knowledge of how to control her abilities, there would be no way for her to keep the ones she loved safe. Or for her to be able to reclaim her life someday.

Elena stared hard at him. *Okay, when do we start?*

Scott Wieczorek is a professional archaeologist working in the American Middle-Atlantic region. He has written numerous short stories and several full-length novels ranging from science fiction, to paranormal mystery, to horror. In addition, he writes reviews of books by Independent authors. Samples of his work are available on his blog at wieczorekfictblog.blogspot.com.